THE
IN-BETWEEN
BOOKSTORE

Also by Edward Underhill

Always the Almost
This Day Changes Everything

THE
IN-BETWEEN
BOOKSTORE

A NOVEL

EDWARD UNDERHILL

AVON

An Imprint of HarperCollins*Publishers*

THE IN-BETWEEN BOOKSTORE. Copyright © 2025 by Edward Underhill. All rights reserved. Printed in the United States of America. No part of this book may be used or reproduced in any manner whatsoever without written permission except in the case of brief quotations embodied in critical articles and reviews. For information, address HarperCollins Publishers, 195 Broadway, New York, NY 10007.

HarperCollins books may be purchased for educational, business, or sales promotional use. For information, please email the Special Markets Department at SPsales@harpercollins.com.

FIRST EDITION

Interior text design by Diahann Sturge-Campbell

Black and white dissolve text background © Ayvengo/Stock.Adobe.com

Library of Congress Cataloging-in-Publication Data has been applied for.

ISBN 978-0-06-335763-1

24 25 26 27 28 LBC 5 4 3 2 1

TO LAURA, FOR EVERYTHING

THE
IN-BETWEEN
BOOKSTORE

CHAPTER ONE

AUGUST 12

The Lower East Side of Manhattan is not the sort of place where bars are guaranteed to have signs. If you can't find a bar without a sign (or, occasionally, any obvious entrance), chances are you aren't cool enough to be in that bar to begin with. You should probably go back to Midtown with the rest of the tourists.

I've lived in New York City for twelve years, but I'm still not cool enough to find the incognito bars. Maybe part of the problem is that the only time I go out is with my friends, and Olivia is always the one deciding where we go. I wouldn't have put it past Olivia to throw her birthday bash in a bar with no sign, which is why I'm relieved when I spot the neon letters in a window slightly below street level, spelling out SPEAK EASY.

Olivia insists on finding a new-to-us establishment for her birthday party every year, solely because Ian made some offhand remark, five years ago, about how eventually we'd all get old and settled, and start going to the same places over and over and over again . . . and Olivia can't back down from a challenge. Ever. Especially not on the night she turns thirty—which, I'm pretty sure, is what Ian-from-five-years-ago would have defined as "old."

Back when he made that remark, we all laughed. Why would you ever go to the same place over and over when you've got all of New York City right outside your door?

But here I am, about to turn thirty myself, and honestly, I'd take *old and settled*. Part of me would really rather be sitting on my bed watching a baking show on my laptop right now.

Although maybe that's because today was shit. Maybe if today hadn't been shit, I could summon a little more enthusiasm for Speak Easy.

I really need to stop dawdling on the sidewalk.

Deep breath. Run a hand through my short but stubbornly wavy hair, which is probably waving in all the wrong directions thanks to the sauna that is Manhattan in August. Push my glasses up on my nose, because I'm sweaty and sticky and they've been sliding down ever since I left the RoadNet office. For the last time.

I hoist my heavier-than-usual messenger bag up on my shoulder and head into the bar.

The air conditioner above the door is on full blast, and it sends a welcome shiver down my back . . . for all of five seconds until I'm out of its range and into the crowd. It's almost six thirty on a Friday, happy hour is in full swing, and everyone in the city is desperate for AC. The whole bar is a cacophony of talking and laughing and slightly distorted but lively jazz music filtering over the speakers. Speak Easy is clearly leaning hard into the Prohibition vibe. The fringed chandeliers are dimmed, the walls are panels of deep mahogany wood and red velvet, and the bartenders are all wearing waistcoats.

The patrons, by and large, are not, but there are a lot of black jeans, tattoos, and piercings that perfectly toe the line between cool and classy. Questionable but undeniably hip facial hair. More than one guy unironically wearing suspenders. It's peak Lower East Side. Half these people probably went to art school or at least want to dress like they did.

I am definitely not cool enough for this bar. I might have multiple degrees in Literature No One Cares About, but I don't have a single tattoo, the holes in my ears closed up about ten years ago, and I'm wearing a light-pink polo shirt.

"Darby!"

At the grand height of five-foot-four, I take a minute to spot Olivia through the crowd, waving from a booth set back in one corner. She's wearing a party-store tiara with the number 30 on it in plastic bling.

"Excuse me. Sorry . . ." I duck and weave through the crowd to the booth. "Hey, guys. Sorry I'm late."

"Yeah, we were starting to wonder . . ." Olivia waves her hands at Joan, who scoots out of the booth so Olivia can get out and wrap me in a hug.

From the other side of the table, Ian says, "Where have you been?"

Moping on a bench in Washington Square Park for twenty minutes, trying to get it out of my system. "Just . . . got held up." I manage a grin. "Happy birthday."

"Thanks, babe." Olivia scoots back into the booth while I hug Joan and then slide in next to Ian, stashing my messenger bag under the table.

"Okay, we've got Darby, so"—Ian gives Olivia a very intense look— "can we please order food? I'm about five seconds away from eating this." He picks up one of the single-page menus from the table and waves it. Ian is a freelance video game designer, only puts on pants when he leaves his apartment, and frequently gets so buried in whatever he's doing that he forgets to eat lunch. Practically every time we go out, he shows up hangry with no idea why.

Olivia rolls her eyes. "Yeah, yeah, let's order." She grabs the menu away from Ian.

Now I feel a little guilty. I should have texted. Invented some excuse about train delays if I couldn't fess up to moping. I'm usually chronically early. I have absolutely no chill. "You guys didn't have to wait for me."

Olivia just waves a hand. "We needed everybody to vote." She turns the menu around, face out. "Are we doing sexy fries or sexier fries?"

Ian blinks at her, like this is not getting through his hangry fog. "What?"

"It's the whole reason she picked this bar," Joan says, looking at her phone. I have a strong suspicion she's checking her email. Joan Chu joined our friend group when she started dating Olivia three years ago, and she has the most adult job of any of us—she's a lawyer. She works in housing law, on the good side, which means she doesn't get paid fancy money, but she does still go to court, in slacks and an actual blazer. She also checks her email constantly, even when she's solidly Queer Punk Joan, with her hair up in a bun to show off her shaved sides and wearing a genuine motorcycle jacket—because Joan genuinely rides a motorcycle.

She fits right in at this bar.

"No, I thought this sounded like a cool place," Olivia says defensively. She pauses. "But also, I looked up the menu online and was like, I *have* to find out what sexy fries are."

Ian squints at the menu. "Okay, well, *sexier* fries are the gay version of sexy fries, right? I mean, that's the only logical explanation . . ."

"I think the actual difference is cheese," Joan says, without looking up from her phone.

"So it's basically poutine." (Ian grew up in Toronto.) "Let's get both. Now. *Food.*"

"Okay, okay." Olivia sweeps her long braids over her shoulder. "Sexy fries, sexier fries, and a pitcher for the table?"

"We have cocktails," Ian says, pointing at his half-empty glass.

"And beer and fries are classic," Olivia says. "Anyway, if we let Darby have a cocktail, he'll get shit-faced. Remember Joan's birthday last year?"

Well, that's slightly unfair. "That was a cocktail and a half," I say. "And I didn't get *that* drunk."

"Fine," Ian says. "Beer and fries. Whatever. Just get me calories."

"On it." Joan scoots out of the booth, sticking her phone in her pocket and disappearing into the crowd, headed for the bar counter.

Olivia leans on her elbows, looking at me. "So did you get stuck at work again?"

Crap. I knew this was going to happen. *Train delays.* Why didn't I just say train delays?

But now it's too late, because if it had really been train delays, I would've shrugged and said it easily. Now I've waited too long, and Ian's eyebrows are disappearing into his strawberry blond hair because he knows something's up.

I rub my hands on my jeans. My palms are sweating. "I . . . kind of got fired."

Olivia stares at me. So does Ian. If this was a movie, there'd be dead silence right now. But it's a Manhattan bar IRL, so Louis Armstrong's gravelly voice keeps right on crooning, and someone lets out a loud peal of laughter nearby.

Which feels about right in its own way.

"You got *fired?*" Olivia's the first one to recover.

"Shit," Ian says. "What happened?"

"All right, order's placed." Joan reappears at the table. "Who got fired?"

"That was fast," I say. A desperate attempt at a subject change.

Joan doesn't fall for it. "Yeah, I get noticed. Did you get fired?"

I'm really starting to regret using the word *fired*. "Well, it was more like . . . I got laid off."

"Did they lay off anyone else?" Joan looks deadly serious. "I mean, if there's any chance it's because you're trans . . . I know I'm in housing but I got this friend who handles discrimination cases—"

"No, no, it had nothing to do with that." I'm handling this all wrong. "I don't think anybody at RoadNet even knows I'm trans. And it's not just me. The whole company's folding." I've got that feeling in my stomach again—the same one I had when Greg Lester, the CEO of RoadNet (although he preferred the title Lead Thinker), told me the news this afternoon. Like I'm suddenly plunging down a roller coaster. "So everybody's laid off. It's done."

Now they're all staring at me.

"They didn't give you a heads-up?" Olivia looks ready to hunt Greg Lester down and pop his head off like a Ken doll. "I mean, how does a whole company fold and nobody knows it's coming?"

I shrug. It's one of about a hundred depressing thoughts that crossed my mind while I tried to pull myself together in Washington Square Park before trekking over here.

Some other highlights:

Why did I think taking a job writing grant proposals for a company that's literally remapping streets for other companies designing self-driving cars was a stable employment option?

Why did anyone think RoadNet deserved start-up money when Google Maps . . . exists?

Why didn't I at least swipe some of the free granola bars on my way out?

"This is why start-ups are terrible," Ian says, rubbing his scruffy chin. Ian only remembers to shave about once a week. "I was reading this article that was all about how they don't know how to run themselves like real companies. They're just a bunch of straight bros who think they're geniuses and have a lot of money. Total grifters."

"But tell us, Ian," Joan says mildly, "how do you really feel?"

He glowers at her. "Yeah, yeah, but this is why I turned down that job at Rizzl, remember?"

Olivia leans her head back and groans. Ian reminds us about his offer from Rizzl more often than he remembers to shave. Rizzl was a video game start-up in Silicon Valley that tried to get Ian to come work for them several months back. He took great pleasure in turning them down and even greater pleasure when the whole company went belly-up a month later, after it turned out they'd poached a lot of ideas from independent game designers and then never paid them.

"What are you gonna do?" Joan asks.

"I could probably get you a job at my Starbucks," Olivia says. "We're pretty much always hiring."

It's a nice offer, but somehow it just makes me feel even lousier. "Um, thanks, but I have no idea how to make a latte."

She shrugs. "I could teach you. Or maybe you could be a dishwasher or something at one of the comedy clubs. I mean, I know it's not glamorous, but it would be something."

Olivia has been living the broke artist life in NYC since we finished grad school. She's a barista by day and a stand-up comedian by night. We've all been to a bunch of her shows, week after week, just to try to put a few more bodies in the audience. It's usually the same ten comics on rotation at every different venue—nine white guys and Olivia, the single Black woman.

She's good, though. She's actually really funny.

And I also have no idea how she isn't drowning in debt.

"I don't know." It feels cowardly as soon as it's out of my mouth. "With the new rent and everything, I should probably try to find something . . ."

But I can't bring myself to say *something better paid*. It's not like I was raking it in at RoadNet, either. Turns out even start-ups don't want to pay the people writing their grant proposals very well.

But I still took that job. Because it paid a little better than entry-level jobs in publishing, even though that's where I dreamed of going when I was in grad school. And it seemed less tenuous than putting my literature degrees to good use and trying to get an adjunct job.

I told myself that was enough. I told myself this job was here, and I got hired, so that meant I should do it.

Joan chews her lip. "And you're absolutely sure the management company gave you thirty days' notice, right?"

She's already asked me this at least three times since the management company for my building informed me they were raising the rent on my tiny studio two weeks ago. "Yeah. I'm sure."

"Damn." She glowers. "It's so annoying when they actually follow the rules."

"We got some sexy fries?" One of the bartenders—a burly guy with chambray shirt sleeves rolled to his elbows, revealing a patchwork of tattoos on both forearms—approaches our table with a tray. He sets down two big baskets of fries, a pitcher of beer, four plates, and four glasses. "Enjoy."

Ian dives in, grabbing a plate and pulling out a handful of what I think must be the sexy fries, based on the lack of cheese. "Holy shit," he says, stuffing fries in his mouth. "These are amazing."

And that's all the permission any of us need, because we're suddenly diving into fries and pouring glasses of beer and ignoring everything I just said. The next few minutes are all of us eating and drinking and comparing the sexy fries to the sexier fries ("These are literally just poutine," Ian says again).

When we get to the end of the last basket, Joan holds out a final fry to Olivia like she's presenting her with a gift. "It's time. We don't have candles but make a wish."

Olivia giggles, taking the fry. "Do I say it out loud?"

"Not if it's about getting laid later," Ian says.

Joan snorts. "She doesn't have to make a wish about that."

Olivia elbows her. "Okay, okay. I wish that we all find exactly what we're looking for before I turn thirty-one." She stuffs the fry in her mouth.

Ian raises his glass with a grin. "Vague and New Agey, ten out of ten."

Olivia just shoots him a look.

But I feel like my stomach is tying itself in knots around the fries. Not because I just lost my job or because my rent is about to go through the roof. Not even because the idea of trying to find a new job or a new apartment makes me want to hide under the table.

It's more that I can't picture Olivia's next birthday party. I have no idea how I'm supposed to get through the next year. I don't know how Ian and Joan are raising their glasses like none of this freaks them out—like they got some instruction manual that I missed.

I know I could probably get another grant-writing job, at least eventually. I know I could probably find *some* new living situation.

But I must be the most shallow, selfish human alive, because honestly . . . I don't want that. I don't want to sit at another job that feels like nothing, doing something I've convinced people I can do, going through motions that don't feel like mine.

"Maybe I should just move back to Oak Falls." It slips out of my mouth before my brain catches up.

For a second, there's silence.

Ian stares at me over his beer. "You're joking."

"Wait, *Oak Falls* Oak Falls?" Olivia says. "Illinois? Are you serious?"

Joan frowns. "You said you hated it there."

I open my mouth, ready to say, *That's not true.*

But maybe it is. Did I tell her I hated Oak Falls? That I hated the town where I grew up? That I hated Illinois?

I guess I probably did. I wanted out when I graduated from high school. I was ready to go anywhere else. I'd gotten a taste of life outside of Oak Falls when I went to a boarding school in upstate New York for the first semester of senior year of high school. I didn't apply to any colleges in Illinois, even though my mom told me I should. A state school as a safety net.

But even Chicago felt too close. I didn't want to be able to drive home for a weekend.

So maybe I did hate it when I left.

But some little piece of me feels annoyed. Defensive. I don't know if I was joking or not, but it gets under my skin that Ian assumed I was. I don't know why the thought suddenly crossed my mind—*what if I just left New York and moved back to Oak Falls?*

Maybe it's because you could probably rent a whole house in Oak Falls for what I'm paying for my tiny studio apartment. The tiny studio apartment I wouldn't have been able to afford in a month even *before* I lost the job I can't even convince myself I'm sorry I lost.

"Darby." Olivia sets her beer down, looking at me intensely. "We'll figure this out. I'll hit Craigslist for apartment listings. I mean, it worked for Ian."

Ian lives in a studio in Williamsburg, which Olivia did, in fact, find for him on Craigslist. I'm pretty sure he can only afford it because one of his games actually sold kind of big last year.

"Or I can ask around at Legal Aid," Joan says. "See if anybody needs a roommate."

Now I really want to hide under the table. It's not like my friends haven't helped me out before. I mean, Olivia and Ian helped me move into my current apartment. Joan brought me a whole bag of cold meds when I got really sick last year, literally delivering them on her motorcycle like the badass lesbian goddess of sinus relief. We're all one another's emergency contacts. But somehow . . . this feels different.

"No, it's okay. I don't really want to live with strangers." I feel like I'm making excuses. "Anyway, you don't have to fix my problems."

"Living with strangers is like a rite of passage, though." Joan leans back against the leather upholstery of the booth. "Honestly, it's amazing you haven't gone through it yet."

Heat creeps up my neck. "I like having my space." But it feels petty as soon as it leaves my mouth. Like I'm expecting too much out of New York. Joan lived with three strangers until she moved in with Olivia. And the two of them still live with one of Ian's ex-boyfriends. Which *should* be weird, given that Olivia and Ian used to date, but honestly, our whole friend group is a walking queer stereotype. Of course Olivia and Joan live with Ian's ex. Of course Joan and Ian are friends.

"Nobody in New York has space," Olivia says. "That's why Central Park exists." She grins, but when I don't grin back, she sighs. "Okay, sorry. We'll figure this out. Brainstorming study hall this weekend? We could crash the Think Coffee by NYU like old times."

She waggles her eyebrows at me, but this doesn't make me feel any better. I don't want to think about *old times*—Olivia and Ian and I holed up in a corner of Think, surrounded by hordes of other students, looking up internships and job openings and master's programs and feeling like anything was possible.

"Yeah," I say, but it comes out flat. "Sure."

"Darb, come on." Ian gives me a look that clearly says, *I love you, but* dude. "You can't leave New York unless it's for someplace that really slaps . . . like London."

"Ooh, or Paris," Olivia adds. (She's been dreaming about going to Paris for as long as I've known her.)

"What would you even be doing if you were in Oak Falls right now?" Joan asks.

Watching Frasier *with my mom, Mr. Grumpy flopped across both our laps.*

Reading fanfic on my laptop at night with the windows open while fireflies wink in the yard.

Riding up and down the streets balanced on the back of Michael's bike because we're bored out of our skulls and there's nothing else to do.

No. Those are all things I did in high school. When I was desperate to leave because it was *Oak Falls.*

I shake my head. "You're right." Take another gulp from my glass. "I'm just being ridiculous. Ignore me. We should be talking about Olivia's birthday anyway."

Joan lets out a whoop, and Olivia beams and fiddles with her tiara. "I'm ready to be sung to anytime."

Ian shakes his head. "We are not singing to you in public."

"You are *totally* singing to me in public."

"Why are you bent on embarrassing us?"

"You are such a dick!"

And Joan starts belting out, *"Happy birthday to you . . ."*

So I start singing too, and eventually Ian joins in with a very obvious eye roll.

We sing Olivia "Happy Birthday," just like we have every year ever since I met Olivia and Ian in college, ever since Joan rounded out our group when she showed up at one of Olivia's stand-up shows.

Just like they'll all do for me in almost three weeks. Because some things are old and settled, even if Olivia insists on the location constantly changing.

But still, I can't grin without it feeling tight and forced.

I can't shake the feeling that I'm about to turn thirty, and all I'll have to show for it is an unemployment check, an overdrawn bank account, two useless degrees, and a city that's never quite managed to feel like home.

And at the end of the day, the only person to blame for any of that is me.

CHAPTER TWO

AUGUST 12

Living on the top floor of a five-story walk-up has its perks. Or . . . perk. It's marginally less expensive than living on the fifth floor of a building with an elevator.

This is not super easy to remember as I drag myself up five flights of stairs with a pounding headache. It took me more than an hour to get home from the Lower East Side, thanks to Friday-night construction on the subway that meant I waited twenty minutes for a train. Then the train was freezing, but it was still sticky and hot outside the moment I got off, and that, plus the combination of alcohol and sexy fries, has me ready to barf. Why did I think I could drink *two* whole glasses of beer?

I manage to unlock my door and for once I'm thankful that my apartment rings in at a grand total of two hundred and fifty square feet, because once I drop my bag, it only takes me seven steps to cross the whole place and face-plant in my bed.

Ugh.

For a blissful minute, I just lie there, pretending nothing else exists. Just me and my old IKEA bed that's definitely sagging in the middle. Whatever. It's comfortable.

But I can't actually stay here, because my air conditioner is too far away for me to reach, and my apartment feels like an oven, even at ten o'clock at night.

So I push myself up and off the bed and stagger over to the AC unit stuffed into the single window at one end of my apartment, cranking it to high. Ditch my shoes. Peel off my shirt and throw it at the laundry hamper stuffed into the corner. The same laundry hamper I've had since college. It's short and wide—exactly the wrong shape for New York City. In New York City, everything is narrow but tall, including apartments. My studio might be only two hundred and fifty square feet, but it's got ten-foot ceilings. The Craigslist ad listed this like it was a big selling point: *Soaring ceilings give spacious and airy feel.*

Honestly, when I moved in here, I thought the tall ceiling was a big selling point too. I was right out of college, starting my master's program, and yeah, this apartment was tiny and a fifty-minute subway ride to NYU, but it was *mine*. It was the beginning of a new life. Just like New York City was the beginning of a new life when I got to college. The very definition of *possibility*. Here, finally, I could be myself—all parts of myself—and get lost in the noise and the crowd and the sense that everyone around me was *doing something*.

But now . . .

Now it's like the noise gets louder every day, and my apartment just gets smaller. I mean, my kitchen is barely even a kitchen. It looks like the adult version of one of those kitchen play sets you get as a kid—the kind where the sink, microwave, and oven are all sort of attached into one thing, maybe with a tiny strip of counter and a single cabinet, if you're lucky.

I drink a glass of water, which makes me feel slightly less gross, and rub my temples, looking down at my messenger bag sitting on the floor. I could leave it for tomorrow. I could collapse on my bed and ignore everything until the morning.

But somehow, I'm quite sure that if I leave it, full of everything I brought home from the RoadNet office, I'll just feel worse unpacking it tomorrow.

So out comes my NYU mug, which I only brought because everyone else at RoadNet had mugs that said STANFORD or HARVARD or COLUMBIA. Out come all my notebooks. My folders of random handouts from random meetings. Fancy graphs promising profits that clearly never showed up. Where am I going to put all this stuff? I don't feel like I can just ditch it. Some of it I should probably shred.

And who knows when I'll find a shredder now, so . . . under the bed it is.

I put my bed up on riser blocks when I moved in here because that's the real secret to existing in NYC-size apartments: hiding stuff under your bed. Put your bed up on risers and you can hide even more stuff.

And honestly, hiding stuff—in this case, all the evidence of my latest fail—sounds great right now.

I reach under my bed and pull out the first cardboard box I find. Every box under here is a leftover moving box. I kept hanging on to them, just in case. Which I guess was smart after all, since unless I magically get a great-paying job in the next three weeks, my thirtieth birthday will be spent moving.

I open the box flaps and stuff in the notebooks and folders, pressing it all down on top of a winter jacket and a few random books.

Halfway through shoving the box back under the bed, I notice the fading black text on the side.

IN BETWEEN BOOKS
OAK FALLS, IL

My heart does a funny little skip. In Between Books. The independent bookstore I worked at the summer after junior year of high school, the summer after senior year, and plenty of weekends in between. It was Oak Falls's only bookstore, owned by this weird old guy named Hank, who wore yellow-tinted glasses and probably only hired me because I was hanging around so much anyway. In Between Books was one of the places Michael would ride his bike to, with me balancing on the back. We'd spend hours just lurking in the bookstore, sitting on the floor between the shelves and paging through stuff like it was a library.

Probably super annoying, actually, but Hank never seemed bothered.

I pull out my phone, pull up Google, type *Michael Weaver* . . .

But I don't hit search. Just like I haven't hit search in years.

Because why would I want to search for the guy who used to be my best friend until my seventeenth birthday party? The guy who decided, once I got back from my semester in upstate New York, that he'd moved on and didn't care about me anymore?

That last semester, senior year of high school, it was just me and In Between Books. Me sitting behind the counter in my oversize clothes, with my short hair, picking up any extra shift Hank wanted to give me because I didn't have anything else to do. Reading whenever there weren't any customers around—which was a lot of the time—because at least getting lost in a story about somebody else was a distraction from all the ways I felt out of place and alone.

A person everyone else saw as a girl, who knew, even back then, that *girl* felt all kinds of wrong.

I didn't do anything about it until I got to college. Until I met Olivia, and then Ian, and suddenly the idea of buying a binder, of coming out, of going to the LGBT center in Manhattan and actually *transitioning* . . . none of it seemed so insurmountable, so paralyzing, anymore.

I tap the backspace key. Erase Michael Weaver from the search bar. Push myself to my feet, toss my phone onto the bed, and pull an old stretched-out T-shirt over my head.

I forgot that I stole boxes from the back room of In Between Books. The last summer I worked there, I'd sneak one out with me after every shift and use them to pack for college. And then, at the end of that summer, I packed all those boxes into the back of the absolute beater of a station wagon my mom had gotten me for graduation, and I drove to NYU.

I've been back to Oak Falls, to my mom's house. I went home for some breaks in college. But then the beater station wagon died, and plane tickets were expensive, so I called my mom on the phone instead. She never complained.

And then one summer I got an internship at a newspaper. And the next summer I worked at a magazine. And then I was going to grad school, focusing on those dreams of teaching, working in publishing, maybe writing something myself, and then . . .

I don't even remember all the *and thens*. But I never went back to In Between Books, even when I visited my mom those few times in college. It felt like a piece of a previous life, and I was trying very hard to live in my new life.

My mom visited me occasionally in New York. But she wanted to do all the touristy things, and I was completely mortified, because people who live in New York *never* do the touristy things. So eventually, we stopped doing that too. And now . . .

I pull out my phone again. This time, when I pull up Google search, I type *In Between Books*.

In Between Books
33 Main Street
Oak Falls, IL

According to Google, it's still there.

I go to the list of contacts in my phone and, before I can second-guess myself, tap on *Mom*.

Three rings. And then she answers: "Is this Darby's butt?"

This was not the answer I was expecting. "Mom?"

A second of silence. "Oh! Darby!"

"Did you just ask about my butt?"

"I thought you butt-dialed me!" She sounds defensive, like this is a perfectly reasonable excuse.

I can't figure out whether to laugh or be vaguely offended. "Mom. That's not a thing. Nobody butt-dials anyone anymore."

"Oh, that's definitely not true. Just the other day I was talking to Jeannie Young—you remember Jeannie Young? You knocked over one of her flamingos when you were learning to drive. Anyway, Jeannie told me just the other day that she butt-dialed her grandson by mistake."

This is far too much information for my brain to take in through the booze and the headache. "Who has flamingos?"

"Jeannie Young. You remember Jeannie! You used to sell her sexless cookies."

"Oh, god." My face turns into a furnace. I was in Girl Scouts for a couple years as a kid, until my mom decided it was too far to drive to the closest troop. When I came out, I asked her to use *he* and *him* even when she talked about me as a kid, and she took this so seriously that she refuses to reference any girl things in my past. But she also hasn't absorbed the term *gender neutral,* which means Girl Scout cookies have become *sexless cookies.*

At least when she talks to me. I really hope she doesn't refer to them this way to anyone else.

"Jeannie finally got rid of that hideous flamingo herd, by the way," my mom says. "We had a few months of peace and then you'll never guess what she replaced them with."

I rub my forehead. "What?"

"Penguins!" My mom sounds incensed. "She's got these incredibly tacky penguins on spikes in her yard now. She even put up an inflatable penguin with a Santa hat last Christmas. I don't know where she gets these things. It's not like the garden center has such ugly stuff." She sighs. "Anyway. So you didn't butt-dial me. What's wrong?"

"Why do you think something's wrong?"

"Because you never call me, Darby."

She doesn't say it with any malice. Or even like she's trying to guilt-trip me. It's just a casual observation.

But I feel guilty anyway. Because it's true. I haven't called her for . . .

Well, I can't actually remember the last time I called her. Which isn't a good sign.

"Sorry, Mom. I guess I've been—"

"Busy." She says it lightly, but it makes me feel worse—because it's exactly what I was going to say. "It's all right. What's that god-awful noise?"

"Oh, crap. Sorry." The AC is still roaring away, cranked to its highest setting. I must sound like I'm inside a cement mixer. "One sec . . ." I flip the dial and the unit quiets with a shudder. We're suddenly left with silence. Or as close to silence as you ever get in New York City. There's a siren going somewhere outside, and another train pulls into the subway station a block away with brakes shrieking.

"Well," Mom says. "If everything's all right, maybe we could chat tomorrow? It's getting a bit late now. Mr. Grumpy and I were just about to go to bed."

"Oh. Right." It's an hour earlier where she is, but my mom has always been an early-to-bed-early-to-rise type. Probably all the years of being a teacher. "Sorry, I wasn't even paying attention . . ."

"That's all right." A pause. And then she says, a little tentatively, "You sure you're okay, Darby?"

Yeah.

Fine.

It's what I've always said before. The only exception was when I finally came out to my mom. Sometimes, I feel like we're still recovering. Like we used up everything we had on that conversation, and now anything beyond canned responses is just overwhelming.

But this time, before I can think better of it, I say, "The company I worked for is folding, so I'm out of a job. And my rent is going up. And I'm just sick and tired of New York, or maybe I'm sick and tired of myself, and this isn't really where I thought I'd be when I turned thirty."

It rushes out, absolute word vomit. I try to add a laugh, just to sound at least a *little* fine, but it comes out panicked, a good octave higher than usual.

"I'm sorry, sweetheart," my mom says quietly. I hear a weird little grunt in the background, and she adds, "Mr. Grumpy says he's sorry too."

That makes me laugh for real, at least for a moment. Mr. Grumpy is the truly ancient basset hound my mom still has. We got him when he was a puppy. He must be going on fifteen now. She sends me pictures of him sometimes—the black and brown has faded to gray on his face and he looks saggier than ever.

He's not really grumpy. He just always had sort of a resting grump face. It's probably all the forehead wrinkles.

"What are you going to do?" Mom asks.

Isn't that the million-dollar question. "I don't know."

"You know, I was going to call you." She sounds tentative again, which doesn't fit her. My mom is not generally a tentative person. "But since I've got you now . . . I've got some news too."

The first thing that crosses my mind is that Mr. Grumpy has some fatal cancer. He's sick. He's got weeks left and for some reason she's only telling me *now* . . .

"I'm downsizing."

My brain screeches to a stop. "What?"

"I've decided to sell the house. It's more house than I need, really, and I'm by myself and getting older. And they just built these new condos right off Main Street, near the park. They've got elevators, and they allow dogs, so I went to see one and it was very nice, so . . ." She clears her throat. "So I decided to buy it."

I can't seem to take this in. "You bought a condo?"

"Don't sound so shocked! I've been thinking about downsizing for a while. And this way I won't have to look at Jeannie Young's penguins anymore."

Well, at least she knows what her priorities are. "Sorry, I just . . . you never told me."

"Oh, I didn't need to bother you with all this."

I'm not sure how to feel about that. It's weird to think about my mom making decisions about the place I grew up without me. But then again . . . why should she need to get my permission? It's her house.

And I left.

"You can bother me," I say, but it sounds hollow, even to me.

"I was going to tell you," she says. "Because I'm going to have to get rid of a whole bunch of your stuff to fit in the condo."

"What stuff?"

"Stuff! Books, school papers, stuffed animals . . . your bedroom still has plenty of stuff in it, you know. And then there's the basement. There are skis down there! I don't even remember when we went skiing. Did we go skiing?"

I have absolutely no memory of ever going skiing. "Mom," I say, "do you remember In Between Books?"

She pauses. "What about it?"

"Is it still there?"

"Of course it's still there!"

Something tugs in my chest, sharp and painful. I was ready to believe Google was wrong. That In Between had gone under, thwarted by Amazon and the fact that even twelve years ago it barely had any customers on a good day.

I look back down at the old cardboard box. "What if I came home to help you move?"

More silence. My heart thuds in my ears.

What am I doing?

"Oh," my mom says. "You want to come here?"

She says it like *here* is the north pole. Or a swamp. Or the sewers.

Was I really that eager to get out of Oak Falls? Was I really so ready to leave that I made her feel like I thought the whole town was crap?

Did I think the whole town was crap?

"Well, just to help you move," I say. "And, you know, while I figure things out. I mean, I don't have anything else going on right now."

I hear another snuffle-snort from Mr. Grumpy in the background. Finally, my mom says, "You can come home anytime, Darby. I'd love to have the help, and maybe it'll be nice to see the house again before I move. And I could show you the condo! It's quite nice. There's a whole garage under the building, so I won't need to shovel in the winter anymore—"

And she's off, rattling on about this new condo building as though it's not closing in on ten o'clock where she is, and she hadn't *just* said it was getting late . . .

But I'm barely listening.

I just offered to leave New York City.

I just offered to go back to Oak Falls.

And I think I want to go.

My friends are going to kill me.

CHAPTER THREE

AUGUST 20

I told Olivia first, and she reacted about like I would have expected:
"Darb, I love you, *but are you fucking joking?*"

I had waited to call her, at least, until the next day. Because part of me was sure that I'd wake up and realize the night before had been some weird booze-induced fever dream. But I checked my phone, and there was *Mom* under recent calls. There was the box from In Between Books, still sitting half-exposed on the floor.

"I feel like you're going to regret this," Olivia said.

But it was the harsh light of day, or whatever the saying was, and my AC was already on full blast because the temperature was rising outside, and I didn't regret it.

"I just need to get out of New York," I said. "I need a break to figure things out."

"You know what this is," Olivia said, with extreme confidence. "Your Saturn return."

One of my greatest shortcomings in life is that I am not an Astrology Queer, and I had no idea what this meant. "Sure," I said, because I didn't want to argue. "But I'm still going."

I couldn't figure out how to tell Ian and Joan. Send them each a text? Call them both? Just assume Olivia would tell Joan herself?

In fact, Olivia saved me the trouble of telling either of them, because she dropped the bomb for me in the group chat practically as soon as she and I got off the phone.

OLIVIA HENRY
Darby's moving to Oak Falls.
He's actually deserting us.

IAN ROBB
Wait what

OLIVIA HENRY
Saturn return!!! I've been warning you all!!!!

JOAN CHU
Darb are you serious?

IAN ROBB
Not everything is about planets, Ollie

OLIVIA HENRY
That is such a Capricorn thing to say, Ian

ME
Guys, I didn't say I was moving to
Oak Falls. I'm just moving out of my
place for now and going back to
Oak Falls to help my mom move.

JOAN CHU
Sure you don't want me to try to
take your landlord to court?

Ditching my apartment turned out to be ridiculously easy. Technically, I was breaking my lease a month early, but the management company was perfectly happy for me to get out ASAP so they could raise the rent sooner.

Ditching my furniture was easy too. I thought, for a second, about getting a storage unit—but even getting one for a month would have cost more than all of my furniture combined. And even though I didn't want to quite say it out loud . . . I had no idea where I would be in a month.

And anyway, it was the end of August. Swarms of college students were already descending on New York, and a lot of them needed stuff. So off went my desk, chair, narrow dresser. Off went the bowed IKEA bed and the risers. I even sold the noisy old AC unit to some poor freshman moving from Florida, who was horrified to discover New York still acted like built-in air-conditioning wasn't a thing.

Everything else got packed into the boxes I'd saved under the bed. Ian helped me load it all into the cheapest rental car I could get—a compact hatchback, which, after all the boxes, pretty much only has room for me, and I won't exactly have great visibility in any direction except forward.

And now the rental car is parked on the street in front of my building (a miraculous stroke of luck), locked (I checked approximately ten times), my apartment is empty except for a pillow and some blankets on the floor, and I'm sitting on a chair at Olivia and Joan's place in Queens. Because after a few days of waiting (not at all subtly) for me to change my mind, my friends seemed to finally realize I was serious and decided they should probably throw me a going-away party.

Even though I've said I'm not really *moving*. But when you don't have an actual exact return date . . . I guess that's almost the same thing. As Ian reminded me several times while loading up the rental car.

I'm still leaving them.

It's Saturday evening, only a week after Olivia's birthday bash, and the pizza box on the coffee table is almost empty.

"This is depressing as shit," Ian says from his spot on the floor.

We managed to laugh our way through the pizza, catching up on everything that had happened during the week that *wasn't* the huge elephant in the room. Joan got underestimated in court and handed some landlord's lawyer his ass on a silver platter. Ian's designing a game that's like *The Sims* but with dogs. Olivia's pretty sure a Real Housewife came into her Starbucks. For an hour, it's almost like everything is normal.

But now the pizza is mostly gone and so are the other conversation topics, and there's just the elephant.

"Who wants ice cream?" Olivia pops up from the couch, where she was sitting next to Joan. "I got mint chocolate chip, one of those ones with marshmallow bits, and vanilla because Ian is the most boring human on earth."

"An excellent vanilla is artistry!" Ian says, looking offended.

"Yeah, we know." Joan reaches over and pats his head. "You're pretentious. I'll have marshmallow bits."

"Vanilla, marshmallow bits . . ." Olivia glances at me, and I swear her expression cools off by several degrees. "Darby?"

I push myself out of the chair. "I'll come help you."

She opens her mouth but doesn't say anything. She just turns and heads for the narrow galley kitchen. It's a typical New York City kitchen—bigger than my single-wall kitchenette but still with a narrow stove, a narrow refrigerator, and a small sink. There's barely enough room for both of us at the same time.

"Bowls are in the cupboard." Olivia isn't looking at me.

I've been here plenty of times. I know where everything is. "Ollie, can we talk?"

She opens the freezer, which means I'm now looking at dirty limericks made out of magnet words instead of her face.

Okay, then. I open the cupboard and reach for bowls. "I know you're mad . . ."

"I'm not mad." Her voice is muffled behind the freezer door.

"You've been texting me about Saturn returns for the last week."

She reappears, holding two tubs of ice cream, and plunks them on the counter. "Because that's clearly what you're going through, and I thought if you knew more about it, you'd understand what you're feeling and not freak out as much."

"Who said I'm freaking out?"

She goes back into the freezer. "You're moving back to *Illinois*, Darby."

"It's another state, Olivia, not the moon."

"I told you a Saturn return can manifest as a big breakup, or leaving your dream job, or blowing up your whole life, and that's exactly what you're doing. I mean, come on—remember how I freaked out a few months ago about, like, everything?"

I pull open a drawer and grab several spoons. "I remember you thought about leaving stand-up for like a week."

She slams the freezer door again, holding a third ice cream tub. "That was a big deal for me."

"I'm not saying it wasn't."

"I just feel like you're setting your whole life on fire without even thinking about it." Her voice is rising. "I don't see why you can't just get a new apartment and a new job, and call that a fresh start and stay here rather than running off to a fucking *cornfield* to have a quarter-life crisis."

"I told you, my mom is moving. She has to pack up her whole house. She needs help."

"Yeah, and if you were just going for that, you'd have a plan to come back. But you don't. So we both know that's not the real reason."

That grates on me. "Why do I need another reason?"

"Because people don't give up their apartments and sell all their stuff just to go help their moms move house." She wrenches the lid off the nearest ice cream tub—pretentious vanilla. "Kinda feels like you're just ditching all of us along with your apartment."

"I need a break from New York!" My voice is rising too.

"Why? New York City has everything and instead you want to kick your friends to the curb and go to bumfuck nowhere with a bunch of assholes who think trans people shouldn't even exist!"

It lands like a slap. Or a gut punch. "You have no idea what Oak Falls is like. You're just . . . looking at it the way everybody out here does. Like it's some redneck shithole. That's always what you've thought."

She looks incredulous. "It's what *you* thought!"

"No, it's not."

"Oh, so you were just making shit up that time at Veselka, first semester?"

Now I'm annoyed. "No, I—"

"You told me you moved out here because New York City was the place you could be yourself. We're all here because this is the right place for us. So, fine—I haven't tried to learn a whole lot about some backward place in the middle of the country. I don't see why I need to, because I live here and so do you!"

"Yeah, and I'm fucking broke. I'm tired all the time. It's loud and crowded, and my apartment was tiny."

Olivia lets out a frustrated sigh. "Look, obviously New York isn't *perfect*. But I just don't get why you'd leave and ditch all of us just to move back to someplace you hated so—"

"Of course you don't get it!" I'm practically shouting now. "None of you have ever gotten it, because you're all from cities. You all belong in New York. I don't seem to belong fucking anywhere."

Silence.

Olivia stares at me. "Where the fuck did any of this come from?"

"Never mind."

"Never mind?"

But I don't want to talk anymore. I'm suddenly intensely, overwhelmingly angry and somehow horribly depressed, all at the same time.

"I'm just gonna go," I say.

Olivia opens her mouth, but nothing comes out.

I turn around and stalk back into the living room, where Ian and Joan are still sitting right where we left them, staring at me because of course they heard everything that happened. It's not like there's ever any privacy in New York, even inside.

"Darby . . ." Olivia jogs out of the kitchen after me.

But I'm already pulling on my shoes. "Look, I just need to go. I'll text you guys from the road or something."

And before I can think better of it, I leave Olivia's apartment. It's immature and selfish, and I'm straight-up throwing a tantrum, but I can't stop myself. I feel like some sort of dam has finally broken—one that's been cracking for years—and the flood is driving me forward. Part of me hopes Olivia will come running after me. Even though I don't know if I'd stop if she did.

But she doesn't.

So I don't.

I go all the way to the subway. All the way back to my building, past the packed-up rental car, up the five flights of stairs. And then I lie on the blankets on the floor of my empty apartment, staring at the ceiling, waiting for my breathing to slow down.

CHAPTER FOUR

AUGUST 21

It's thirteen and a half hours to Oak Falls, and (despite the rental car starting to beep at me with an obnoxious message on the dashboard that says, *Do you want a break?*) I drive it all in one go.

It's partly that I was wide awake at five this morning, so I figured why wait around? I might as well get on the road and really beat the traffic.

Plus, once I was out of the city, I just wanted to keep going. Like if I got a little farther, I'd stop going over and over everything Olivia said, everything I said, everything everyone else didn't say.

And also, at a certain point, I kept going just to spite the rental car.

When I stopped for gas, I got coffee. When I got hungry, I bought a sandwich and ate it while driving.

And I kept checking my phone. Ian texted while I was following a semitruck through the rolling hills of Pennsylvania: *Let us know when you get there.* I got a *Drive safe* from Joan while I was stuck in the line for a tollbooth in Indiana.

I didn't text back. I didn't know what to say.

The third time my phone buzzed, I was at an oasis near Chicago—one of the rest stops that spans the freeway like a bridge full of fast food. I fumbled my phone out of my pocket, hoping maybe this time the text would be from Olivia.

But it was my mom.

> Got your bed all made up and ready
> for you. Make sure to look for penguins
> because I would like to know if you
> also think they are hideous.

It took me a minute to remember that she was talking about decorative penguins on sticks and not actual penguins who might be roaming the suburban streets of my hometown.

The sun is going down and my back feels like someone kicked it by the time I exit the freeway and hit the county roads. The speed limit is still fifty-five and there are two lanes in each direction, but there isn't nearly as much traffic on these roads. The big billboards are gone and the stuff I pass is everything that walks that line between suburban and rural: a sprawling clinic with an ER and a parking lot that probably fits a hundred cars, a big chain grocery store, a massive lumberyard. Compared to New York, everything is weirdly huge here. Islands of civilization in the middle of a whole lot of cornfields.

The cheerful Google Maps lady is telling me what turns to take, but once I cross into Oak Falls, I switch her off. I know all of this by heart, even in the gathering twilight and even after all this time.

Oak Falls doesn't have some super cute sign with a super cute catchphrase to tell you when you've officially arrived. Probably because Oak Falls isn't a tourist town and never aspired to be one. There's no pristine lake or massive forest or anything else to draw people here. So the only sign is a plain white affair with plain black letters: OAK FALLS, POP. 8,073.

There's a back-roads route I could take to my mom's house—or . . . a *more* back-roads route, since everything is practically a back road in Oak Falls. It's the route I took when I'd come home from college, because I was so done with Oak Falls that I didn't want to see any more of it than was absolutely necessary.

But now, I turn the hatchback toward Main Street. The streetlights are on when I get there, casting pools of yellow light over the pavement and the sidewalks. They're small streetlights—not even as tall as the two-story buildings around them, black poles with lights on top shaped like globes. The streetlights in New York are at least twice that height, skinny and silver and utilitarian, blending into the urban landscape around them.

I slow down, creeping along at ten miles an hour. It's not like there's anyone behind me to get annoyed.

The buildings lining Main Street are mostly made of red brick, all attached to one another in a row. It's picturesque in a way that screams Middle America—or at least "stock image for one of those Ten Best Places to Live When Chicago Is Too Expensive" listicles. Most of the storefronts are dark, and I don't really look too closely at any of them. Just scanning, looking for . . .

In Between Books.

I pull the car over to the curb, into an empty space right in front of the store. Turn the key and the engine sputters to silence.

The store is closed. It's almost eight thirty. The plastic sign hanging in the door says, WILL RETURN 10:00, and some of the lights are off. But now that I'm here, I have to look. I have to at least peek in the window.

I open the car door. For once, it's a good thing I'm so short, because I have a feeling I'd be even more sore if I was actually the height of an average guy. I glance up and down the street, but I don't see anyone coming, so I stand with my back to the car and rub my butt in an effort to get the blood flowing again.

My legs are stiff as I go up to the store. It looks like most of the other storefronts along Main Street—a big square window in a brick wall next to an old wooden door with panes of glass in its top half. The letters on the store window look new: IN BETWEEN BOOKS is arched across the window in white frosted letters, instead of the peeling vinyl stickers that I remember.

I lean forward, peering through the glass. The front table display is exactly where it's always been, stacked with the newest releases. Beyond, I can see rows and rows of shelves. Even the clock on the wall above the door to the back room is the same—made out of an old copy of a Sherlock Holmes novel, with gold numbers stuck to its burgundy cover and hands that look like fountain pens.

All the way at one end of the store is the cash register, under a hand-painted sign that says, CHECKOUT.

There's someone behind the counter—in the process of closing up, I guess. A kid in an oversize hoodie, with short, scruffy hair, a pale face, and wire-frame glasses . . .

My heart suddenly thuds, and my stomach feels like it's fallen down ten stories.

I wore oversize hoodies all the time in high school.

I had wire-frame glasses.

I must have closed up the store dozens of times, and I always turned half the lights off, just like this, even when I was still working, because it was weirdly cozy to be alone in a half-dark space with all those books . . .

This kid, the dimness of the store, the books stacked on the display table—it all reminds me so much of *back then* that for a second, I can smell the faint mustiness of the books. I can hear the *tick-tick* of the clock above the door to the storage room. I can feel the slight greasiness of the cash register keys under my fingers. The way the cash drawer constantly stuck halfway when you tried to close it. I remember exactly how muted the colors of book covers became when I'd unpack boxes of books in that half-light of closing time. The way the stool I sat on behind the counter had one leg that was shorter than the other three, and it always tilted precariously. The way the edges of the bookshelves cut awkwardly into my back when I sat in the aisles with Michael, reading books for hours . . .

I squeeze my eyes shut and turn around, rubbing my eyes under my glasses. My bigger, plastic, tortoiseshell, *modern* glasses because I'm not in that bookstore anymore. I'm not sixteen anymore.

But for a moment, I could swear I was. I could swear I was right back there, and it all felt *real*.

Good job, Darby. This is what being on the road for almost fourteen hours straight will do to you. You arrive in your old hometown and you're exhausted and all caught up in weird nostalgia feelings, and you see some random teenager who kind of looks like you and you flip out.

What am I doing here?

I should go to my mom's house. Quit lurking outside this bookstore like a total creep. The store's closed. I can come have nostalgia feelings about it tomorrow.

I turn for the car—and bump right into someone.

It's not a very hard bump at least, but I definitely stepped on a foot that was not mine and mashed my glasses.

Whoever the person is says in a low voice, "Ope, sorry—I didn't mean . . ."

"No, my fault." I jump back and look up and . . . "Oh, shit."

The guy in front of me raises his eyebrows. He's taller than me, but not really *tall*—maybe five-foot-nine. He's wearing a checkered short-sleeve button-down and dark, nice jeans. His auburn hair is cut classic and neat, but it's also vaguely curly in a way that makes it look a little rumpled, like he's been running a hand through it all day and hasn't bothered looking in a mirror. His nose is still slightly big, but it looks like it belongs now, and even though it's getting dark outside, I know his deep-set eyes are actually, really, honest-to-god gray, just like I know he used to wear glasses and he once had a whole collection of Pokémon T-shirts . . .

Because the guy standing in front of me—the guy I just walked right into like a fool—is Michael Weaver.

"Sorry?" he says.

Oh god. He has no idea who I am. Of course he doesn't. I've been on T for ten years. I'm almost sinewy (if you don't look too closely), my face shape is different, my voice is different. I look like the older brother of the person he knew. The person with different clothes, different pronouns . . .

Different everything.

"No, I'm . . . I'm sorry." I take a step backward. "Wasn't watching where I was going. I should, uh . . . I should go."

He's staring at me. I see the moment everything suddenly clicks into place. And then he says, "Darby?"

Well, fuck. I was ready to turn tail and run. Because the thought of trying to explain was way too overwhelming. And anyway, this is the guy who decided to ignore me our last semester of high school.

I try to force a grin. It feels like a grimace. "Yeah. Uh. Hi."

"You're . . ." He's fumbling. "Um . . ."

"Trans?"

"Here."

My face heats up. My pulse is racing. I take an awkwardly large gulp of air, trying to slow down my heart. "Yeah. I, um . . . My mom is moving. I came to help her pack up." I nod, like somehow this is going to provide more emphasis.

"Oh." He's still staring at me, but I can't read the expression on his face. It's like he's seeing me and not seeing me at all. "Right. I think I heard that from Jeannie Young."

"Jeannie Young?"

"Yeah." He hesitates. "You know, with the penguins." Now he looks flustered. "Or . . . I think it was flamingos when you were here—"

"Yeah, no, I know Jeannie Young." I can't tell him that my real question was why on earth he was talking to Jeannie Young. Does he just do that now? Talk to all the adults who have been here, the whole time we were growing up, because he still lives in this same small town and sees them at the grocery store?

"I'm . . . sorry." Michael rubs the back of his neck, which makes me notice his arms, and how much less lanky he is than the last time I saw him. He's not gawky anymore. He's *actually* sinewy. "Is it . . . or, I mean . . . do we need to be reintroduced?"

I blink and make myself stop staring at his arms. "What?"

His forehead wrinkles. He looks like he's in physical pain. "I called you by the name that I knew and then I realized maybe you . . ." He waves a hand, a little desperately.

"Oh." He's worried he just deadnamed me. "It's still Darby."

His shoulders lower. "Right."

"I just, um . . . I kept it. You know, because it was technically after my uncle and stuff, even before, so—"

"Yeah, I remember." I think I see a smile cross his face. The same slightly crooked smile he had in high school. It's so familiar that for that second, he looks exactly the same as the gawky guy I once knew, even with his neater hair and without his glasses.

And then the smile is gone. "I should, uh . . ." He waves a finger vaguely in the direction he was going.

"Oh. Yeah." I step out of his way.

"Nice to see you." But he's not even looking at me.

"Yeah. You too." I turn and head back to my rental car. Just to make clear that I'm going someplace too. That I have someplace to go.

I get back in the car, but I still have an excellent view through the windshield of Michael Weaver walking down the sidewalk, leaving me behind.

MY MOM WASN'T kidding about the penguins.

Jeannie Young has always lived in the beige single-story ranch next to my mom's split-level, but even if I'd somehow forgotten this fact, it would have been obvious which house was hers. There's a literal penguin flag flying next to the front door. There are also plastic penguins on stakes in the yard (at least ten), a birdbath (held up by a penguin pedestal), two very realistic and presumably life-size penguin statues on either side of the walkway, and a collection of stone baby penguins lining the front steps.

The front door of my mom's house flies open as soon as I pull into the driveway and out shoots my mother, in polka-dot pajama pants, a bathrobe, and Crocs, arms outstretched, barreling at top speed toward the car.

I manage to get out just before she plows into me, wrapping me in a hug. My mother is one of the few people I know who is noticeably shorter than me—she's pretty much the definition of petite, with a graying pixie cut and bright-red round glasses.

"Darby! You're home!" She lets me go and stares deeply into my eyes. "Aren't they ugly?"

"What?"

"The penguins." She turns and glowers at the yard next door, hands on her hips. "Isn't it just the tackiest, most horrid thing you've ever seen? You know, I'm worried they're going to lower my property value."

"Mom!" I glance around. "Jeannie could hear you."

She just snorts. "Jeannie barely hears anything anymore. I keep telling her she needs hearing aids but she won't listen. Probably because she doesn't want to hear what anyone thinks of her penguins!" Mom turns her attention to the hatchback rental car. "You fit everything in *that*?"

"My apartment was small." It comes out a little defensive. "And I sold most of my stuff."

She looks at me—a long, shrewd look. "I see. Well." She soldiers past me and opens the trunk. "Let's get what you need for right now and we can worry about the rest tomorrow."

I feel uncomfortably like I've just come home from college on a break. "Mom, you don't need to carry my stuff."

"Oh, don't be silly. I can handle a suitcase. Load me up."

I do not, of course, load my mother up. I give her one suitcase with rolling wheels. And then I grab my messenger bag, my pillow, and a trash bag I'm pretty sure has clothes in it, and close the trunk. Beep it locked. Not that anyone probably steals anything around here. It's Safe. As my mom kept saying whenever she came to visit me in New York.

"Did you hit any of that construction on Thirty-Six?" Mom heaves the suitcase across the threshold into the house. "I swear, they just keep digging the road up and then sitting around and not doing anything. It's a highway, not a sandbox!" She sets the suitcase down and shouts, "Mr. Grumpy!" Turning to me again—"He's getting a bit deaf these days."

I hear the *click-click* of dog nails, and Mr. Grumpy rounds the corner from the kitchen into the living room. His long ears are practically dragging on the floor, and he's wheezing, but his tail wags when he sees me.

I drop the bags and squat down. "Hey, Grumpypants."

He waddles into my outstretched hand, butting his head against it, tongue lolling out of his mouth.

"You want some water? A snack? I just made a frozen pizza for dinner myself, because I need to get to the grocery store, but we've got crackers, apples, some cheese . . ." Mom disappears into the kitchen, leaving me alone with Mr. Grumpy, looking around the house where I grew up.

It looks . . . the same. Same off-white wall-to-wall carpeting, though Mom has tried to hide it with a big blue-and-white-striped rug that's new. She's still got the same light-brown sofa and armchair set, the same honeywood coffee table, the same bookshelf. Even the books on the bookshelf are familiar—a mix of classics like *Pride and Prejudice*, *The Three Musketeers*, poems by Emily Dickinson, and volumes of Shakespeare, and kids' books that went in and out of her classroom when she was teaching fourth and fifth grade. *A Wrinkle in Time*. *The Witch of Blackbird Pond*. *The Phantom Tollbooth*. Some more I don't recognize—books she must have acquired after I left for college.

There's a TV on a table against the wall. That's new. When I was growing up, Mom relegated the TV to the basement.

"So?" Mom pokes her head around the wall separating the living room from the kitchen.

I jerk, pulling myself out of memories of watching episodes of *Buffy the Vampire Slayer* with Michael. We'd rent the DVDs from the video store on Main Street, make a bag of microwave popcorn, and sit in the basement on an old futon. We watched the whole series that way.

"Sorry," I say. "What?"

"Snack?" Mom says.

"No, I'm okay." I didn't stop for dinner, but I can't tell if I'm hungry or not. I'm too unsettled.

"All right." Mom stands awkwardly in the doorway between the living room and the kitchen, arms folded, fingers tapping idly. "Well, would you like to watch *Marble Arch Murders* with me?"

That snaps me out of my thoughts. "What's that?"

"An English show on PBS every week at nine. They do great murder mysteries over there, you know. It's about an old lady solving crime in London. It's nice to see someone my age on TV."

"Since when do you watch TV?"

She looks a little offended. "I always watched TV. Don't you remember watching *Frasier* with me?"

Well, yeah. That last semester of high school. When I had no friends and nothing else to do, and Mom decided that TV wasn't so bad after all, at least not if both of us were watching it in the basement and it was reruns of *Frasier*.

"Yeah, I just . . . didn't realize you watched anything else."

She sniffs. "I watch the news and murder mysteries. I have cable now. It's too expensive. I should get rid of it. But I like Rachel Maddow." She switches on the TV and sits down on one side of the couch. Mr. Grumpy immediately puts his front paws up on the cushions and she reaches down, wrapping her hands around his butt, and hauls him up next to her. "Come sit with us!" She points at the remaining couch cushion on the other side of Mr. Grumpy.

I glance at the TV, playing an upbeat credits sequence featuring an old lady in a purple wool coat traipsing through the streets of London and looking suspiciously at things. "That's okay. I'm just gonna take my stuff to my room. Maybe take a shower or something."

"Okay." My mom shrugs and then gives me a big smile. "Good to have you home, sweetheart."

I manage to smile back at her. But it feels stiff. Like I'm rusty. "Yeah. Thanks."

She settles in with her show, absently stroking Mr. Grumpy's head, so I pick up my bags and wheel the suitcase down the carpeted hallway. Up the few steps and then around the corner into my childhood bedroom.

Just like the living room, it also hasn't really changed. I guess I don't know what I expected. Did I think my mom would turn it into a crafting room or a yoga studio or something?

But my room looks the same as I left it. Guilt washes over me. I haven't been back here for years, but Mom's still got the pastel-striped comforter on my twin bed. The light-blue carpeting has faded a little with age, but the off-white walls are still covered with pictures of wolves that I cut out of the free calendars my mom used to get in the mail. The pages from magazines of random celebrities and bands I thought I was supposed to care about are still there too, along with a grainy rendition of the *Mona Lisa*, printed on regular printer paper, because I guess I thought I needed some real art.

There are some gaps on the walls. Gaps where I'm pretty sure there used to be photos from high school. I took down every picture with Michael in it after I got back from boarding school, when it was really apparent our friendship was over. I took down everything else the first time I came home from college. I walked into my room with a proper guy's haircut, wearing a binder, and immediately got rid of anything that was a reminder of the old me. The girl me.

I ditch the suitcase and the trash bag of clothes and wander over to my dresser, pulling open the drawers. Except for a random jewelry box and a container of hair ties, they're empty. Like my mom expected me to come back and need them again.

I sit down on my bed, rubbing my stiff knees, and glance out the window. It's dark outside now. Too dark to really see anything except my own face reflected back at me.

God, that kid—the one behind the counter of In Between Books . . . that kid really looked like me. *Reminded* me of me.

But that's all it was . . . just a kid who reminded me of myself, who looks kind of like I used to look. Whatever kid works there now when they have summers off from high school. Whatever kid closes up the store, locking up the register. I guess that kid likes working in a weird half-light too.

What was Michael doing, walking down Main Street past the bookstore on a Sunday night? What does he *do* in this town where we grew up, and where he just . . . lives now?

What did he think, seeing me after all this time?

I rub my eyes again. I should go out and watch TV with my mom. It'd be a distraction. Maybe old ladies solving murder mysteries would be fun.

But it felt weird to see my mom doing what she clearly does every week. Just her and Mr. Grumpy. Carrying on with their lives when I haven't called or talked to her in months.

It's weird to see all the things that happen that I don't even think about. To see the things that have changed when I'm also surrounded by all the things that haven't.

So I don't go out to the living room. I pick up my phone and open the group chat. I should text my friends. I told them I would. They're my friends.

But everything I yelled and everything Olivia yelled is still too close. Too loud. I can't tell them how weird I feel, sitting here. It'll just be proof they were right—this was a terrible idea.

In the end, I just fire off a quick *Got here*. And then I heave myself off the bed and head for the shower, trying to tell myself *this is fine*.

CHAPTER FIVE

AUGUST 22

I wake up the next morning to Mom blasting NPR in the kitchen.

It takes me a minute to figure out what the noise is. I blink my eyes open and lay there with that groggy, vaguely ill feeling that you get when you wake up too fast after sleeping terribly.

"Good morning, I'm Steve Inskeep and you're listening to Morning Edition . . ."

Groan.

I forgot about this. Mom listening to NPR at full volume every morning while she makes her coffee and granola, and simultaneously reads the local paper like the multitasking monster she is.

I sit up, the old twin bed creaking around me, and grab my phone off the nightstand to check the group chat. Ian sent a thumbs-up emoji in response to my text.

There's nothing else. Nothing from Olivia.

I drop my phone on the bed and rub my eyes. I don't know what time it was when I finally fell asleep, but I'm pretty sure I had weird dreams. Dreams where I wandered around my old high school, trying to remember my class schedule. Dreams where I was riding Michael's bike, looking for Michael. Dreams where I was staring through the window of In Between Books, looking for myself.

My mom raises her coffee mug in greeting when I go down the hall to the kitchen a few minutes later. "Morning!" she says brightly. "I made a whole pot of coffee in case you want some."

I shuffle toward the coffee maker on the counter and open the cupboard.

Horrifyingly, Mom seems to have kept every single mug I painted at the birthday parties I had from age seven through seventh grade, when I decided I was too cool to paint mugs, and most of my friends decided they were too cool for me. I grab one. What even *is* this? It looks like a shapeless blob with eyes.

"So I thought we could drive over to the condo later," my mom says, voice raised above the din of the radio. "I was going to meet my real estate agent over there for a final look. You want to come?"

I pick up the coffee pot. "Sure. Sounds great."

"Now that you're home, we should go through your room too. Like I said on the phone, there's not as much room in the condo, so I'll need to get rid of some things." She stabs her spoon into her bowl of granola. "I was thinking of asking Michael Weaver if he wants any of my old classroom books."

I miss the blob mug and spill coffee all over the counter. "Oh?" God, it's everywhere. Where are the paper towels?

"You remember Michael Weaver? You used to—"

"Yeah, I remember Michael Weaver." (Aha. Paper towels, next to the sink.) "I ran into him last night, actually."

That gets her attention. She turns around in her chair at the white-tiled dining table in one corner of the kitchen. "You did? You didn't tell me that."

I sop up the spilled coffee. It takes three paper towels. "I'm telling you now."

"Well, how was it?"

"Um. Fine." I pour coffee into my cup, properly this time, trying to ignore the acid feeling in my stomach. "Awkward."

"Oh, I'm sure it wasn't awkward." She waves a hand dismissively and turns back to her granola. "You guys have so much in common. You should hang out while you're here! You know he's gay now?"

I choke on a mouthful of coffee. Cough and hack until my mom turns back around and fixes me with a frown. "Why are you so shocked? People turn out to be gay all the time."

"I'm not . . ." I take another sip of coffee in an attempt to soothe my throat. It's too hot and burns all the way down. "How do you know that?"

She looks thoughtful. "I don't really remember. He's been out a long time now. Not that he's loud about it, but he doesn't hide it either, you know? He was dating a fellow from Chicago for a while, I think, but they broke up a couple years ago. Anyway, he teaches ninth grade. That's why I think he might like those books from my classroom. I suppose some of them are kind of young, but he'll know who to hand them off to. How'd you run into him?"

My head is spinning. *Michael's gay now.*

Michael.

The guy I grew up with. The guy I did cannonballs off the diving board at the pool with. The guy who would try to explain the plotlines of Marvel comics to me during lunch and played trombone in our truly shit high school marching band.

Did he know in high school?

Did he know and not tell me?

"Um." I focus on my mom, trying to pull my thoughts together. "I stopped at In Between Books. Just to see it. I mean, it was closed, but . . . I ran into Michael. On the sidewalk."

Because I wasn't watching where I was going. Because I was so deep into some weird, intense flashback, all because of some random kid in an oversize hoodie and glasses . . .

I stare into my coffee, watching the bubbles collecting at the edges slowly pop. I can't shake this unsettled feeling from last night, from whatever dreams I can't quite remember.

I need to go back to the bookstore. When it's *open*, so I can walk in and see what it looks like now, and what kid works there, so I can stop being stuck in these weird nostalgia feelings. It would be fun to see it again. See what's changed.

So I can remind myself that things *have* changed.

"When did you want to go to the condo?" I ask my mom.

"I told Cheryl I'd meet her there at two. Why?"

"I'm just . . . gonna go out for a bit. Look around Main Street and stuff."

"Okay." She picks up an iPad from the table. "Give Jeannie's penguins the stink eye on your way out, would you?"

I BORROW MY mom's Jeep, since the rental hatchback is still full of stuff. The Jeep is an old Grand Cherokee from the era when a car was cool if it had a CD player, and the odometer reads well over a hundred thousand miles now, but it's got four-wheel drive, which matters for Illinois winters, and I have a feeling my mom will drive it into the ground.

I roll the windows down as I drive past ranch houses and split-levels with wide grassy lawns. It's already warm and sunny, and the breeze funneling into the Jeep is humid and smells like grass clippings. In the middle of Manhattan, the air probably smells like garbage right now. Actual garbage. It's the New York City smell of summer.

I hear birds. A lonely cicada buzzing in the trees. A lawn mower roaring in the distance. No hum of traffic. No car horns. No rattle and shriek of subway trains.

It's barely a ten-minute drive to Main Street. I pull into a free parking spot down the street from In Between Books, five minutes after ten o'clock. The stores up and down Main Street are all open now. In the light of day, I recognize a lot—the credit union, Frith & Schneider Insurance, Ethel May's ice cream parlor, Floyd's five-and-dime that's part hardware store, part craft store, with a smattering of used romance books for good measure. But Prime Pie Pizza is gone, replaced by a Subway. There's something called the Oak Café that looks scarily similar to a Manhattan brunch joint. And where Main Street Video used to be, there's a hip-looking coffee shop. Several women with strollers are sitting at the patio tables out front.

I take a deep breath and get out of the Jeep.

The sign on the door of In Between Books is flipped to OPEN. The lights are clearly on inside.

So I pull open the door and walk in. A bell overhead jingles, so familiar it makes me shiver. The first thing that hits me is the smell—the slightly musty smell of books and paper and old worn carpet. It's almost comforting, that smell.

The store looks just like I remember it looking when I worked here. Gray carpet. Ugly bands of fluorescent lighting overhead. Here's the table of newly released books. There's the newspaper stand with the *New York Times*, the *Chicago Tribune* . . . even the local *Oak Falls Sun* is still there.

And then there are all the shelves. The aisles between them are so narrow that it's not really possible for more than one person to walk between the shelves—which is why I'm sure it was actually annoying, the way Michael and I would just sit in the aisles and read books. The signs on the shelves are still hand-drawn, labeling each section: TRAVEL, FICTION, POETRY, CHILDREN'S . . .

Nothing's changed at all.

That's why I had some weird flashback moment last night. The store looks the same, *and* I saw some kid who reminded me of myself. Of course it was going to mess with my head.

I let my breath out, slow and shaky.

"Can I help you find something?"

I turn toward the counter. There's a kid sitting behind it at the cash register. Maybe sixteen or seventeen, with kind of shaggy short hair and oval wire-frame glasses, wearing a baggy *Veronica Mars* T-shirt and looking at me with raised eyebrows.

The hair stands up on the back of my neck.

This is the kid I saw through the window last night. The kid I think I dreamed about. It has to be.

But now it's the middle of the morning, and I've had coffee, and I'm awake, and I'm standing in the middle of In Between Books . . .

And this isn't a kid who looks like me. This isn't a kid who reminds me of me, because I'm not staring through a dirty window in some dim half-light. I can see clearly. Those are the glasses I had in high school. Those are my freckles, over my nose—the nose that never felt particularly delicate to me, the nose I stopped worrying about the second I came out, when suddenly it fit right in with the rest of me. Those are the round black studs I wore in my ears constantly, the studs I got from the Hot Topic in the mall in Monroe, some trip where Michael also picked up some Pokémon T-shirts. That's my messy brown hair, with that cowlick in the middle of my forehead that I *still* haven't totally figured out . . .

This isn't a kid who looks like me.

This kid *is* me.

The version of me that worked at the bookstore. High school me.

I'm staring at myself.

CHAPTER SIX

No way.

Absolutely not.

The kid behind the counter can't possibly be me. Because the last time I worked in this bookstore—the last time I looked like this kid—it was the summer before I went to college, and that was 2010.

It's obviously not 2010. So unless my seventeen-year-old self somehow time traveled ahead twelve years . . .

But this kid—this kid who is absolutely-definitely-100-percent Not Me—is still looking at me, eyebrows raised, waiting. As though nothing strange is happening at all.

"Um." My voice comes out a squeak. I cough. "I'm good. Thanks."

And I do the first thing that occurs to me: I walk very fast into an aisle between two bookshelves where the kid behind the counter can't see me.

My pulse thuds in my head. My heart is going a mile a minute. I lean back against the shelf behind me, trying to slow my breathing down, blinking, because my vision is suddenly full of black spots.

What is happening?

I'm hallucinating. I have to be hallucinating. Maybe my mom put something in the coffee this morning. Cannabis is legal in Illinois now. Maybe my mom watches TV *and* does a whole lot of weed.

Not that weed has ever made me hallucinate. I've only gotten high a couple times, because I'm boring, and that was way back in college. So I suppose I could have forgotten the finer details of what it felt like, but

I'm quite sure I never hallucinated something like this. Something that felt so *real*.

So maybe I'm dreaming. Maybe I'm actually still asleep in my mom's house. Or, hell, maybe I never even left New York. Maybe the last week was a really intense fever dream.

I pinch my arm, *hard*. But all that does is make my arm hurt. I watch the pink mark slowly fade. Either I'm not dreaming, or I just pinched myself in the dream. Now that I think about it, I don't know why pinching yourself is supposed to help you determine if you're awake or asleep.

I lean around the end of the bookshelf, just far enough to see the cash register.

The kid who looks like me is still sitting behind the counter. No, not looks like—*is me*. Sitting there, reading a book.

I have the same feeling, straight to my core, that I get when I look at old pictures of myself. That certain knowledge that, yes, that's me, even if I look like a girl. Even if I feel, almost, like I'm looking at a stranger. Like I'm staring into a life that never quite belonged to me.

Why is there a teenage version of me in here?

I lean back and focus on the shelf of books in front of me. They're travel books. Guides to Venice. London. Los Angeles. *Notes from a Small Island* by Bill Bryson.

I'm in the travel section.

I grab a book off the shelf. Travel books are updated all the time. I remember that from when I worked here. There were new editions out practically every year. This book is a Fodor's guide—a thick paperback about India. I flip the cover open and turn the first page, looking for the copyright information.

First published: *2009.*

Okay. Well, obviously this one is old. Out-of-date. How much demand is there for a guidebook about India in Oak Falls, anyway? People in Oak Falls are not big world travelers. Maybe this book has been sitting on this shelf since it came out in 2009.

But I know that's impossible. No bookstore would keep stock around that long. And In Between Books is not a very big store—we were always clearing space for new books.

I put the India guide back on the shelf and pull out the Fodor's guide to Florida instead. Oak Falls residents definitely go to Florida. Jeannie Young used to spend the winter in Miami. She paid me five dollars a visit to water her plants twice a week.

First published: *2009.*

My heart is hammering again, so hard it's rocking me back and forth where I'm standing. I go through several more guidebooks, and they're all from 2009, except for one about Arizona, which is from 2008. Every book in this section is old enough to attend the seventh grade.

I look around the store. My eyes catch on the table of new releases right near the entrance. It's in full view of the counter, which means there's no way to get to it without the teenager—without *me*—seeing me. And if I see me, then . . .

Then what? Would I recognize myself?

I don't know. I mean, I probably wouldn't expect my older self to look like a guy. By the time I left for boarding school, I definitely knew that *girl* felt wrong for me. I think I even knew—in a back corner of my mind that I didn't fully acknowledge—that I wasn't a girl. But I didn't really let myself picture what a not-girl version of my future might look like. It seemed impossible, in Oak Falls, to even get myself *into* that future.

So . . . okay. I probably wouldn't recognize me now. I mean, nobody really spends time, at seventeen, thinking that much about what they might look like when they're about to turn thirty, right? Even if they *don't* want to change genders.

But still. Last night, Michael Weaver recognized me.

Maybe that doesn't mean anything, either. Michael could have looked me up online, Google-stalking me the way I've almost Google-stalked him countless times. He could have seen my Instagram. Or the LinkedIn page I should really get rid of because it's never once been useful. Or RoadNet's website, if that's even still up.

Something flutters behind my solar plexus at the thought of Michael Weaver Google-stalking me. Deciding I was worth *looking* for, even in an online way.

This is ridiculous. *Just go look at the new releases.*

I take a shaky breath and walk, as slowly and casually as I can, to the table in the middle of the bookstore. At the counter, the younger version of me just keeps reading.

I pick up the first book on the table that catches my eye, because it's a book I remember reading in high school. *The Last Olympian*. I flip back the cover.

First published: *2009*.

This is going from weird to unhinged.

I open more book covers—*The Help, When You Reach Me, What Alice Forgot* . . .

They all say 2009.

I get that feeling in my stomach again—the same feeling as when Greg Lester told me RoadNet was folding. Like I'm plunging down a roller coaster. But this time it's worse. This time it's like I'm plunging off a cliff.

I look around the store again, at the gray carpet, at the book clock ticking away, at the handwritten signs on the ends of the shelves, labeling each section. It's all just like I remember.

Exactly like I remember.

Like no time has passed at all.

The hair stands up on my arms and I feel suddenly cold.

I have to get out of here.

I head for the door without looking at the counter. One foot in front of the other. I reach out, find the doorknob, push open the door, the bell jingling overhead . . .

And then I'm outside, back on the sidewalk. Warm, humid summer air washes over me. Across the street is the coffee shop—the one that replaced the video store. The sign hanging from the lip of the roof reads MAGIC BEANS, which might be the world's worst coffee shop name. The women with strollers are still sitting at their café table.

I fumble my phone out of my pocket so I can check my calendar. Check the date. Check the *year* . . .

My phone screen is black. No matter how many times I press the power button, it won't wake up. It's completely dead, even though I charged it overnight.

Great.

I look back at In Between Books. But from here on the sidewalk, I can't see anything through the big picture window. There's too much glare. All I get is the reflection of Main Street.

And I can't quite make myself go up to it, like I did last night, and peer in. I can't make myself go back through the door, either.

I should go back to my mom's house. Have another cup of coffee, or pet Mr. Grumpy, or go out to the yard and touch literal grass. Ignore whatever just happened. Maybe my brain can work it out in the background if I let it stew in my subconscious. Don't people solve problems that way?

At the very least, I can go home and raid my mom's kitchen and make sure she really didn't add anything to that coffee.

I rub my eyes under my glasses and start walking. Okay.

Okay.

CHAPTER SEVEN

AUGUST 22

The house is unlocked when I get back, which is a good thing, since I realize, as soon as I pull the Jeep into the driveway, that I completely forgot to ask my mom for a key.

The house also seems to be empty. I toss the car key onto the table by the door. Nobody's in the living room or in the kitchen. "Mom?"

There's no answer. I go down the hall to my bedroom (my suitcase and the trash bag of clothes are still there, which is more comforting than it should be), and then to her bedroom. It looks the same as it did when I lived here. Same floral quilt on her bed. Same photo collection on her dresser—a picture of my uncle Darby in his air force uniform, a black-and-white photo of her parents on their fiftieth wedding anniversary, my old school pictures . . .

Another shiver goes up my back. This is not helping.

I stick my fists in my eyes, trying to push away whatever the hell I saw in the bookstore, and go back down the hall to the kitchen. I'm about to try the basement when I glance out the window and see my mom, half-way up a stepladder in the backyard under the big maple tree, which still has a tire swing hanging from one of the biggest branches. Mr. Grumpy is sitting at her feet, tongue lolling out of his mouth, looking anxious. Or maybe that's just the forehead wrinkles.

I push my way out the back door. "Mom!"

She turns her head and looks down at me. She's wearing sunglasses and a wide-brimmed straw hat, but otherwise she's still in her pajama pants and bathrobe. "Oh, hi, Darby! Did you just get back?"

"What are you doing up there?"

She points to the tire swing. "Cheryl says I've got to get this thing down before we show the house. I'm trying to remember how we got it up here in the first place."

I look at the tire swing. And then up at the branch. Force myself to focus. "It's rope. I think you'll probably have to cut it down."

"Yes, yes, I suppose." But she's not looking at me. She's not even looking at the tire swing. She's standing on her toes on the stepladder, peering over the tall wooden fence that runs around our yard.

"Mom, are you spying on Jeannie Young?"

She looks back down at me and the ladder wobbles dangerously. I reach out and grab it. "Don't be ridiculous," my mom says. "I'm spying on her penguins. She's got more back there, you know. I think their numbers have grown since last week."

This is too much for my brain. I have a sudden, very strong urge to go inside and crawl back into bed. Give up on today and try again tomorrow. "Can you please come down off the stepladder? I'm worried you're going to fall."

She snorts, but she climbs down, one foot at a time, until she's back on the ground. I could swear even Mr. Grumpy looks relieved.

"I can climb a ladder," Mom says defensively. "I've been taking care of this house all by myself without you telling me when it's safe to climb a ladder. I cleaned the gutters just a few weeks ago!"

I run a shaky hand through my hair. "You're right. I'm sorry." A twinge of guilt cuts through the swirling cloud of *what the fuck*. Of course she's been taking care of the house by herself. And I have no idea how it's been going because we never talk about that. Just like we never talk about anything. Because I hardly ever call her.

"Well, I'm back now," I say. "So I can get the tire swing down."

I half expect her to fight me on this, just on principle, because my mom is stubborn. But she shrugs. "That's true." She starts back toward the house. "I'll leave the ladder for you, then. I should take a shower! Can't go see my new condo in my pajamas." And she disappears through the back door.

Leaving me with Mr. Grumpy and the tire swing. I let my breath out and look up at the branch overhead. The tire swing hangs vertically, held up by a thick rope looped through the tire and over the tree branch. The rope is so weathered, it's almost white. I reach up and pull half-heartedly at the knot above the tire. Unsurprisingly, it's not remotely effective. If the rope has stayed knotted for this many years, there's no way it's going to budge now. I'll have to get a saw. There's probably one in the basement somewhere, but I can't make myself go look. It's one step too many for my overloaded brain.

Instead, I grab hold of the rope and swing my legs through the tire swing. My momentum sets the swing in motion, and Mr. Grumpy hastily backs up out of the way with an alarmed grunt.

I stare across the backyard. It's green in a way nothing in New York City is. Central Park comes the closest in the height of summer, if you're standing out in the middle of one of the rolling lawns. But even so . . . there's something different about the grass here—the depth of the green, the saturation of it. The way it sits against the sky, which is almost completely cloudless and just *blue*.

Now that I think about it, I realize this is the color I think of when someone says *blue*. This kind of clear, pure blue that seems to go on forever.

The rope creaks against the branch, and the sound is so familiar, I shiver. For a disconcerting moment, I feel like I'm still in high school. Sitting here on this tire swing, listening to the rope creak against the branch, because I'm seventeen and Michael isn't talking to me anymore and my mom is still at work and I don't know what else to do except sit here, swinging slowly back and forth . . .

I slide through the tire and wriggle free of it. Mr. Grumpy looks up at me. His tongue is still hanging out of his mouth. His ears drag on the grass. In the sunshine, he looks grayer than ever.

Because I'm almost thirty. Not seventeen.

I pull my phone out of my pocket, ready to text Olivia and Ian and Joan. Who cares if Olivia's mad at me? Who cares if they all are? I need Ian to tell me about some random thing he read online about how brains can make up weird stuff. I need Joan to laugh at me. Honestly, I'd even take Olivia texting me a big old *told you that you shouldn't have left New York* . . .

But my phone is still dead. Obviously. Because I haven't plugged it in.

I close my eyes. I need to stop thinking about this. All of this.

I'm going to see my mom's new condo. I'm going to help her pack stuff up. I'm going to watch her random British murder mysteries and sit on the couch with Mr. Grumpy.

I am *not* going to think about whatever just happened in that bookstore.

IT'S A FIFTEEN-MINUTE drive to the new condo. Nothing in New York time, and Actually Pretty Far in Oak Falls time. You could probably drive from Strickland Farms at one end of Oak Falls to the Solutions Bank at the other in under half an hour.

Mom insisted on bringing Mr. Grumpy, saying he needed to see the condo too, so he could get used to it. She also said he didn't like sitting in the back seat because it made him lonely, which means he's sitting on my lap in the passenger seat, hanging his head out the window, ears flapping and drool flying in the breeze.

The cicadas are really going now, and the air streaming into the Jeep is hot. It's sunny here in a way New York never really manages, simply because all the tall buildings get in the way. Manhattan streets are practically always in the shade, but here I actually have to squint against the glare of the cloudless blue sky.

The new condos are right off Main Street, Mom tells me, near Krape Park and the baseball field, which means she'll be able to walk to the band shell for the musical every summer *and* walk to the coffee shop. Which will be great, she says, because she won't have to deal with traffic.

"Look at this!" She waves a hand at the three cars ahead of us, waiting at a stop sign on Main Street. "Middle of a summer day. I knew there would be traffic. I should've taken the back roads."

Is she joking? "Mom. There's no such thing as traffic here."

"Oh, yes, there is. You've seen the coffee shop. Things are getting hip!" She shakes her head as we inch up to the stop sign. "Young families moving in, and the coffee shops and traffic come with them. The other day, I couldn't even find a parking space here! I had to park on a side street!"

I open my mouth to explain the concept of actual traffic to my mother, using, say, Midtown Manhattan as an example, and change my mind. It wouldn't do any good, and anyway, I suppose it's probably all relative.

There are multiple people out on the sidewalk in the middle of a Monday. I remember looking out of the window of In Between Books on any given weekday and Main Street would be dead.

I rub my eyes under my glasses and stare fixedly out the front windshield. *I'm going to see my mom's condo. I'm not thinking about In Between Books.*

I don't look at it as we drive past.

The new condo buildings are on a tidy new boulevard that didn't even exist when I was growing up. The sign reads STARRY HILL DRIVE, which seems both whimsical and misleading since this road is as flat as the rest of Oak Falls.

Mom turns the Jeep into a freshly paved parking lot between two identical brick buildings with pointed roofs. Like a lot of Midwestern architecture, the condo buildings can't seem to figure out what style they're going for. But they definitely look *new*. Their brick corners are crisp and perfectly straight. The white-sided balconies are glaringly bright. It's all a far cry from the worn brick storefronts of Main Street that date back to the 1800s, or the ho-hum midcentury ranch houses that make up most of Oak Falls. The condo buildings are three stories . . . which is tall for around here. And they just sit here in the middle of . . . well, nothing. Past these buildings, Starry Hill Drive just stops, with a sign that says, DEAD END. Past that, there's just a big field. And a for sale sign.

"They've been selling land around here for more development," Mom says, when she notices me looking at it. "I'm guessing it'll be more condos. Or a subdivision. Come on, let's not keep Cheryl waiting!"

I clip Mr. Grumpy's leash onto his collar and follow my mom through the parking lot as she leads the way to a glass door set under a white wooden archway. She heaves the door open. "We're here, Cheryl! Sorry we're late!"

"Phyllis!" A tall woman in a gray business suit, with dyed blond hair that can only be described as helmetlike, clicks across the spotless lobby toward us. "No worries at all. I see you brought Mr. Grumpy! And . . ." She looks at me and seems to lose her train of thought.

"Cheryl, you remember my son, Darby." Mom squeezes my shoulder. "He came all the way from New York to help me move. Can you believe how long it's been since he and Natalie took ballet together?"

Oh, *right*. Natalie Linsmeier. She definitely called me a dyke in high school. And not in the reclaimed-by-queer-people way.

"Oh, it's been so long!" Cheryl quickly pastes on another smile. There's no way she doesn't know I'm trans. Mom never made an effort to hide it after I came out, and I didn't ask her to. Anyway, news travels fast in Oak Falls. There's basically nothing to do except gossip about your neighbors.

But still. I guess knowing something and *seeing me* are two different things. I wonder if I look like Cheryl expected. If I look more or less normal than she thought a trans guy would look.

"So?" Cheryl turns her dazzling smile on my mom. "Are you ready?"

"Yes, yes." Mom waves her hands at Cheryl, but she's practically on the balls of her feet. I can't remember the last time I saw her this excited. "Let's go!"

We take a shiny new elevator up to the third floor and Cheryl leads us down a carpeted hallway to a door sporting the number *12* in polished brass. She unlocks it, holding the door open for us.

Inside, the condo is big and bright, with white walls, high ceilings, and an enormous arched window at one end of the living room, plus a sliding door that leads out to a balcony. A sleek modern fireplace sits nestled in one wall. The floor is carpeted, but it's much newer and cleaner than the carpet at my mom's house.

My mouth actually falls open. In New York, you'd have to get deep into Brooklyn or way into Queens before you'd find a condo like this for less than a million dollars. And it definitely wouldn't be brand-new.

"So, everything's just been painted," Cheryl says. "But look around, and let me know if you think we need touch-ups anywhere . . ."

Mom doesn't need to be told twice. She grabs my arm and pulls me through the condo, pointing out stainless-steel appliances that are at least a decade newer than anything in her house, a bathroom that's half the size of my entire studio, and the view of Krape Park from the master bedroom. The second bedroom is smaller, with a single window, but from up here, I can see over the trees to the steeple of First Church, where it sits at one end of Main Street.

"Well?" Mom says. "What do you think?"

I look around the room. "It's nice."

She frowns. "Darby, I know I haven't seen you much recently, but I can tell when you're not telling me something."

A stab of guilt goes through me. I'm not being excited enough, and I know it . . . and I can't seem to do anything about it. "It's nice, Mom. Really. It's just . . ." I fish around for a word. "Different."

Different than the house. Different from what I pictured—even though now that I'm here, I have no idea what I pictured. Maybe something less shiny, less brand-new, less blank. Or maybe it's just that my mom has always existed in her outdated split-level house, and even though it's weird to be back there, sleeping in my old bedroom, it also never occurred to me that one day I wouldn't have it.

Which feels incredibly selfish, now that I think about it.

"Well, I want different," Mom says firmly. "Anyway, you'll have a nice view. Plus, this is the top floor, so the rooftop deck is very accessible. There's a grill up there and one of those outdoor firepits."

I'm pretty sure the only thing my mother has ever grilled is a cheese sandwich, but now doesn't seem like the time to bring that up. And anyway, I'm hung up on *You'll have a nice view.*

Does that mean, like, *a nice view when you come to visit?*

Or *a nice view because this is your new bedroom since you don't have your life together and will obviously be moving in with me?*

"So . . ." Cheryl appears in the bedroom doorway. "Everything looking good?"

"Yes, very good," Mom says.

"Well, in that case, we're all set for closing." Cheryl beams. "I'll meet you here on Saturday to hand off the keys. And for listing your house—Labor Day weekend still okay?"

All thoughts of the small second bedroom evaporate. "Labor Day weekend?" I look at Mom. "That's in, like, two weeks."

Cheryl looks between us, uncertain. "Well . . . as I told Phyllis, it could be very beneficial to have the holiday weekend for an open house. Get some interest going before everyone's busy with the beginning of the school year . . ."

"Yes, Labor Day weekend is perfect," Mom says. She waves a hand at me. "Don't worry, Darby, we'll get everything packed up. Especially since you're here to help."

I open my mouth to say that's not really what I was worried about, but Mr. Grumpy lets out a whine from his spot on the floor.

Mom sighs. "He probably needs to go outside. Darby, would you take him? I might have to get him something for the balcony," she says to Cheryl. "He needs to go out more often now . . ."

I leave Mom and Cheryl to their discussion of movers and open houses and staging ideas, and pull Mr. Grumpy toward the door, perfectly happy to have an excuse to escape. I suddenly don't want to spend another minute in this blank, perfect space, trying to imagine myself in that bedroom, or my mom watching her British murder mysteries in this living room, under this massive arched window, like this makes any sense as *home*.

CHAPTER EIGHT

AUGUST 22

The condo building doesn't really have a yard, so I pull Mr. Grumpy across the street to the grassy median running down the middle of Starry Hill Drive. He makes a very lazy attempt to hike his leg against a tree and then wheezes his way over to a sunny patch and sinks down with a contented grunt.

I sit down next to him in the sliver of shade offered by the skinny new trees planted here and pull out my phone. It's still as charged up as it was a few minutes ago, so maybe whatever happened this morning was a fluke.

I turn the phone over and over in my hands, chewing my lip. And then, on an impulse, I google *In Between Books*. The store has a website, but the only thing on it is IN BETWEEN BOOKS in big blue letters against a plain white background, followed by the hours and location. The only option on the menu is SHOP NOW, but when I tap on that, the page just says COMING SOON!

This is not helpful. I want an image of the inside of the store—something recent. Something to tell me whether it really looks exactly the same as I remember. If it really hasn't changed.

But even using Google Image Search, the only picture I find is the storefront, from the online version of the Oak Falls newspaper. It belongs to a bitty article about In Between Books getting a new front window and ditching the old peeling letters that I remember. I try zooming in on the image, hoping I'll be able to see through the window. But there's too much glare on the glass, and this zoomed-in, the picture quality is grainy anyway.

Maybe it's because my thoughts are still stuck in the bookstore, on that kid behind the register who couldn't possibly have been me, or maybe I'm just desperate for a distraction, but before I even realize what I'm doing, I type *Michael Weaver* into Google. And this time, finally, I actually hit search.

The first thing that pops up is his LinkedIn page. There's no picture, but I'm pretty sure it's him. Graduated from the University of Illinois Urbana-Champaign. Teacher at Plainview High School in Oak Falls. It has to be him.

The second result is from Plainview High School's website. The page listing all the teachers. The back of my neck tingles as I scroll past name after name that I recognize. Teachers I had who are still there, like Mr. George (who's completely bald now, according to his picture), Mrs. Koracek-Smith (who used to just be Ms. Koracek), and Mrs. Siriani (who either dyes her hair or hasn't updated her picture in a decade because she looks exactly the same). But apparently Keegan Turner is the band director now—he used to paint mugs at my birthday parties and played trombone with Michael in band. Rebecca Voss was part of Natalie Linsmeier's crowd, and I mostly remember her constantly chewing gum and looking bored, but now she has glasses and a sharp bob, and teaches history.

And there, at the bottom of the page, is Michael. He looks quietly professional in his picture—sitting against a blue background, wearing a checkered button-down a lot like the one he was wearing when I bumped into him. No glasses. A very small, only slightly crooked smile. His auburn hair is neatly combed—barely any hint of rumpled curls.

I tap on his name, and a short bio appears: he grew up in Oak Falls, he went to Plainview himself, then to college, then got a teaching degree and now here he is. Professional. Upstanding. Adult. He looks . . . *functional.* Like someone who has a 401(k) and probably actually goes to the dentist every year.

"Darby!"

I look up. Mom is standing in front of the condo building, waving at me. I push myself up and tug Mr. Grumpy back across the street.

"Ready to go?" Mom asks.

"Yeah. Sure. Where's Cheryl?"

"Oh, she already left. Off to show another house!" Mom shakes her head. "She says the real estate business around here is better than ever, and I'd believe it."

We get back in the Jeep and the windows go down again. Mom turns the other way on Main Street, muttering something about *not going through that traffic again*. We loop around behind First Church to West Avenue, the back-roads route that follows the edge of Oak Falls. We drive past Dr. Nilsen's big white house, with its four massive columns. It's one of the oldest houses around—the original farmhouse from back when a whole lot of Oak Falls was farmland. Now the original farm has been broken up and sold off, turned into subdivisions, and just the old farmhouse is left, owned by Oak Falls's only dentist. The houses out here sit on larger lots, and the roads that wind between them are narrow and don't resemble any kind of grid.

I'm turning my phone over and over in my hands again. "Hey, where does Michael Weaver live these days?"

I try to sound as casual as I can, but I still see Mom's eyebrows go up from the corner of my eye. "Right up there," she says, pointing through the windshield.

Wait, seriously?

I follow her gaze. She's pointing at a two-story house with white siding, sitting far back from West Avenue at the end of a cracked driveway. The expansive front yard is a little overgrown and the mailbox is leaning, but the house is kind of cute, in an old farmhouse type of way. It's got a big front porch with several lawn chairs, the overhanging roof held up by white posts.

It also looks vaguely familiar. "Isn't that Michael's grandma's house?"

Mom looks surprised that I remembered. "Yes, it is. Betty died a number of years ago. Michael lives there now with a couple roommates. You remember Liz Forrest?"

"Yeah." And I wish I didn't. I wish I couldn't still picture a spindly girl with long, layered dark hair and a penchant for leather wrist cuffs and a lot of necklaces.

Liz Forrest was my replacement. When I got back from that semester of boarding school, she was Michael's new best friend.

"She's one of the roommates," Mom says. "I wish I could remember the other girl's name . . . you wouldn't know her. She's not from around here. Indiana, maybe? That reminds me!" Mom reaches over and whacks my arm. "I need to remember to give Michael all those old books from my classroom. Help me remember to write that down, Darby. *Give Michael books.*"

"Yeah," I say, but I'm barely listening.

I REALLY THOUGHT Michael and Liz might be dating. By the end of my first week back at Plainview, I was really starting to wonder. I couldn't see why else they'd be spending literally every single minute together. Anytime I saw them in class, they were sitting next to each other. At lunch, the two of them sat at our old table, and based on his hand gestures and the Marvel comics on the table between them, I was pretty sure Michael was explaining the plot of whatever issue he'd just read— just like he used to do with me.

In fact, everything they did together was stuff Michael used to do with me. Michael drove Liz to school in his dad's old pickup truck. In homeroom, they scribbled notes to each other. I even saw them together at Main Street Video after school one Friday when Mom and I were picking out a movie to rent. They didn't notice me, which probably had less to do with them being distracted by each other and more to do with the fact that as soon as they walked in, I deserted my mom and hid behind the shelf of kids' movies, where I figured I'd be safe.

But the real kicker was the Saturday they came into the bookstore. I'd been back for two weeks—the longest two weeks of my life. Michael hadn't said a word to me. It was like I was invisible. Like he'd forgotten we were ever friends.

I was re-alphabetizing a shelf, with the hood of my sweatshirt pulled up because it was blowing snow everywhere outside and the store was drafty. The bell over the door jingled, I turned around, and there they were, scuffing snow off their winter boots.

They were both bundled up in coats and hats and scarves. Liz's long hair was sticking awkwardly out over the shoulders of her puffy coat, and Michael's glasses were completely fogged up.

"Okay, where are these comics," Liz said, looking around. "I want pizza."

"Just a sec," Michael said. "I have to pick them up."

Liz looked up at him and laughed. "Can you even see where to go?"

"I can see," Michael said defensively, starting for the counter.

I was pretty sure he couldn't see, because he hadn't noticed me at all. Neither had Liz, but she had no reason to notice me. She wasn't my friend.

My heart tried to jump halfway up my throat. I'd been hoping Michael would stop by the store. If he was explaining Marvel comics to Liz at lunch, then I figured he must still be picking them up from In Between, which meant there was a chance he'd come to the store when I was working. And I thought—or at least I hoped—that if he came to pick up a comic while I was working, and I was the one who handed it to him, then maybe he'd remember all the other times I handed him the latest Marvel comic . . . and things would stop being weird.

I left my shelf reorganizing and slipped back behind the counter just as Michael reached it. Just as his glasses unfogged.

He stared at me. Any lingering hint of his crooked smile vanished. His face was totally blank. He might as well have turned into a statue.

"Hi," I said.

"Hi," said Liz. She sounded awkward, and I suddenly wondered if Michael had *told* her something. Something about me, about why he was ignoring me.

I swallowed and ducked down behind the counter to the shelf where Hank always put the comics when they arrived at the store. They were so much slimmer than any book, he was worried they'd get lost in the back room.

I straightened up and set the comic on the counter. "Here you go."

Michael just kept staring at me. Blankly. He fished some cash out of his coat pocket and laid it down on the counter. Which meant there was no risk of us touching. I wondered if he'd done that on purpose.

I glanced down at the counter and realized he'd put down exact change. I picked up the bills and the coins, and saw the comic move from the corner of my eye. When I looked up, Michael was already turning away, tucking it inside his coat, and Liz was giggling at him. They pushed their way out of the bookstore, letting in an icy blast of air.

He hadn't said a single word to me.

* * *

As soon as we get back to the house, Mom makes a beeline for the base-ment. "I know I've got some boxes down there," she says. "Better figure out how many, so we can buy some more and get packing!"

I unhook Mr. Grumpy from his leash and head to my room, the book-store and Michael and Liz still banging around in my brain. I need a door to close, because I'm about to google something completely ridiculous.

I sit down on my bedroom floor, pull out my phone, and google *time travel*.

Time travel is the concept of movement between certain points in time, according to Wikipedia.

Clocks on airplanes and satellites travel at a different speed than those on Earth, according to NASA's website.

Time can't exist without space, and space can't exist without time, accord-ing to some website called How Stuff Works.

Next Star Trek *movie promises to clear up some big time-travel questions!*, according to Vulture.

Well, that's not particularly helpful or relevant.

But actually, none of it is. Most of the results are guys complaining about movie plots on YouTube or incredibly long physics papers behind paywalls. And the rest are fluffy pop-science pieces in *USA Today* or *Na-tional Geographic* about Jules Verne or wormholes or singularities. The only real conclusion seems to be that time travel *might* be possible go-ing forward, theoretically anyway, but certainly not backward. Beyond that . . . there is no conclusion.

I toss my phone onto the bed.

I didn't time travel back to 2009. And some teenage version of me didn't time travel to the present. I hallucinated something super weird. That's the only *real* explanation, because nobody can travel through time. Everything I just read told me that.

I feel like this should be comforting.

It's not.

CHAPTER NINE

AUGUST 23

Which means I have to go back to In Between Books.

I spent the rest of yesterday helping my mom track down boxes, heating up a frozen pizza, and sitting on the couch with her, watching an old English lady in a peacoat solve crime while Mr. Grumpy tried to eat our pizza.

And I did all of it like I was in a daze. My brain kept spinning around the bookstore, looking for something—anything I could remember—to make it make sense. Like somewhere there'd be a clue to explain everything, if only I could find it.

I couldn't find it. So I have to go back.

This time, I park the Jeep almost a block away from In Between Books, like the bookstore is a sentient being and it's vitally important it doesn't see me coming. Across the street, the glass door of Magic Beans is propped open. The same two women with strollers are sitting at a café table, next to a chalkboard sign with the specials written on it.

I told Mom I wanted to try the coffee shop. Get a sense of "the new Oak Falls." She interpreted this as me getting on board with the condo, which is the only reason I'm here skipping out on helping her go through random crap in the basement.

Get out of the car, Darby.

I lock the Jeep behind me and check my phone. 10:15 a.m. The battery is at 97 percent.

Okay. Here goes.

I pull open the door of In Between Books. The bell jingles, and I step inside.

The store looks just like it did yesterday. Fluorescent lights. Gray carpet. Table of new releases. The magazine stand. But the only thing I really care about is the counter, and it's empty. There's no one behind it at all.

My breath rushes out and my stomach unwinds, and for a second, I think my knees might actually buckle.

Maybe I really was hallucinating. Or maybe someone was playing some weird, twisted trick on me, even though I have no idea how a trick like that would even work, much less who would actually play it.

I turn and look over the table of new releases. They're all the same as yesterday. The same new-in-2009 books.

Wait a minute . . .

I go to the magazine stand, pick up a copy of the *New York Times*, and scan the date at the top of the front page.

Sunday, August 23, 2009.

The front-page photo is a big beige house. Underneath it, the headline reads "A Cul-de-Sac of Lost Dreams."

My skin prickles.

Next to that is the smaller headline "Marines Fight with Little Aid from Afghans." I scan the text of the articles. It's all about the housing crisis and the war in Afghanistan, except for a random article near the bottom of the page with the headline "Debating Just How Much Weed Killer Is Safe in Your Water Glass."

I stuff the paper hastily back onto the stand. This has to be a prank. I mean, an article about weed killer in drinking water?

Actually, the more I think about it, the less unbelievable that one sounds.

I look at the other newspapers on the stand. But the *Chicago Tribune* and the *Oak Falls Sun* have the same date: Sunday, August 23, 2009. The front-page story in the *Sun* is about breaking ground for a big new health clinic—the fully built, been-there-for-years health clinic I drove past on my way into town.

My stomach is plunging off a cliff again.

August 23, 2009, was nine days before I left for boarding school. Eight days before I ruined everything with Michael.

"Can I help you?"

I turn around, and there, just coming out of the storage room, is me. Or . . . my younger doppelgänger. This time, the doppelgänger is wearing an oversize ringer T-shirt, jeans, Converse sneakers, and a terribly uncool digital watch.

I remember that watch. I wore it everywhere for years. Until I got a smartphone in college and decided I didn't actually need a watch anymore.

"Oh, I'm fine." My voice, at least, sounds more chill than it did yesterday. Sort of. "I was just, uh . . . looking at the papers." I flap my hand at the magazine stand in a way that is decidedly not chill.

"Okay. Let me know if you need anything." Doppelgänger Darby slips behind the counter and hops up on the stool, picking up a book.

I step back, so I'm half-hidden behind the newspaper stand, and pull out my phone, hands shaking. I need proof. Some kind of proof that I can take home and show my mom, so she can either explain who this weird kid is that looks just like me, or say that somehow, impossibly . . . yeah, that's teenage me. Either way, a picture will help me prove I'm not losing my mind by myself.

But as soon as I unlock my phone, a message pops up: *Low Battery.*

Seriously? It was just at 97 percent right before I walked in here. I look at the battery icon in the upper corner of the screen. It's red. Next to it: *3 percent.*

And before I can even open my camera app, the screen turns black. I press the power button, but there's no response. The phone is dead. Again.

Now what?

I shove it back in my pocket and chew my lip, looking between the newspapers and Doppelgänger Darby, still reading behind the counter. And then I take a deep breath and leave the shelter of the magazine stand. The only way I'm going to figure anything out is by talking. To myself. "Um, excuse me?"

Doppelgänger Darby looks up.

"Are these all, um . . . today's paper?"

My younger doppelgänger blinks. "Yeah. Did you want . . . a different paper?"

"No, no. All good. Just . . . curious." I try for a casual grin, but it feels more like a grimace.

My doppelgänger gives me a slightly confused smile and goes back to the book.

I rack my brain, trying to think of something that you'd only know if you were actually *in* Oak Falls in 2009. Something that some present-day kid who inexplicably looks exactly like me wouldn't know.

"Hey, do you have any idea how long the video store is open today?"

Younger Me looks up again. "Uh, I'm not really sure . . ." And my doppelgänger turns and looks out the window.

So I do too. Automatically.

For a second, I straight-up forget to breathe.

Outside the big picture window of In Between Books is the video store. Right across the street, exactly where the coffee shop should be. The café tables are gone; so are the women with strollers. Instead of the MAGIC BEANS sign, there's a sign that reads MAIN STREET VIDEO in blocky orange letters that look like they're trying to impersonate Blockbuster. Because back when Main Street Video opened, Blockbuster was still a thing that existed and was worth impersonating.

I move closer to the window, like some gravitational force is pulling me. Farther down the street, the Subway is gone, and Prime Pie Pizza is back.

"Are you okay?" It's Doppelgänger Darby, from behind me.

"Yeah, I just . . ." I focus on the window itself. The old peeling vinyl letters are still there, spelling out IN BETWEEN BOOKS backward.

My breath is suddenly too loud in my ears, but I can't seem to get enough air. I walk, with a kind of hyperaware calm, back to the bookstore's entrance. Open the door. Step out onto the sidewalk . . .

And there's the coffee shop. The women with strollers. Subway.

What. Is going. On.

I fumble behind me until I find the doorknob and back my way into the bookstore again. The door closes in front of me. I lean close to the glass panel in the door and look across the street. There's Main Street Video again. It looks real. *Really* real. I can practically see the outlines of shelves through the window.

"Darby!"

I jump.

Someone walks out of the storage room, gray hair a tousled mess, wearing a very loud Hawaiian shirt and yellow-tinted glasses.

It's Hank. The owner of In Between Books. The guy who hired me. Who let me and Michael sit in the aisles and read books, whether we bought them or not.

I open my mouth, with no idea what to say, but Hank isn't looking at me. He's looking at the kid behind the counter.

"Just talked to the plumber," he says. "He's gonna come look at that bathroom faucet tomorrow afternoon. Can you show him the problem when he gets here?"

"Yeah," the kid behind the counter says. "Sure."

"Great." Hank turns around and disappears into the back room again.

Wait a minute. I remember this.

I remember this because *I* broke the bathroom faucet. It was old and falling apart, and a piece of it literally just came off in my hand when I tried to turn the tap. But I was so stressed out about it that I lied and told Hank a customer broke it. I was afraid if he knew it was me, I'd get fired.

All he did was shrug and say something about how that faucet had been on death's door for years.

I feel dizzy. And too hot. And vaguely sick.

I turn around, push open the door again, and escape onto the sidewalk.

CHAPTER TEN

AUGUST 23

I make it to the curb and sit down, so abruptly it hurts. My heart is pounding. Black spots eat at the edges of my vision again. Forget roller coasters or cliffs, my stomach has actually disappeared.

Time travel, especially backward, according to everything I googled, is impossible.

But the newspaper dates, the broken faucet, the books on the table, Hank . . .

All of that really, *really* seemed like 2009.

I run a hand through my hair and pull out my phone again. It's still dead. Useless as a brick. I think, for a second, about going back into the bookstore and yelling that someone had better explain what the hell is going on. Just to see if anyone pops out with a camera and yells, "Gotcha!"

No. I'm too shaky for that. I feel like passing out is not out of the question. Like my brain might just give up and switch off due to an overload of . . . everything. I need coffee. Or something to eat. Or both.

I push myself up, dust off my pants, and head for Magic Beans.

The wooden door of the coffee shop is propped open by a chalkboard easel sign listing seasonal coffee specials. The smell of coffee wafting out is so strong that for a minute I just stand on the sidewalk and breathe it in. It's grounding.

The women with strollers are still sitting at one of the café tables. I glance sideways at them. It's a little hard to tell with the baseball hats and sunglasses, but I'm pretty sure I don't know them, which is kind of a relief. Maybe they're the new people Mom keeps talking about, moving to Oak Falls.

Inside, Magic Beans looks like it aspires to be a coffee shop in New York. The worn carpet of the video store is gone, exposing scuffed wood floors. The drop-ceiling tiles with their ugly fluorescent lights are gone too. The ceiling is higher now, revealing pipes snaking along it. There's a big steel-and-wood counter where the old video store counter used to be, glinting under a row of pendant lights shaped like globes. The only hints of Main Street Video are three framed movie posters behind the counter—*Singin' in the Rain, Ghostbusters,* and *Casablanca*—hung against an exposed brick wall, which has to be fake, or an addition, or something, because Main Street Video definitely did not have an exposed brick wall.

"Darby?"

I turn.

Michael Weaver is sitting at a small table just past the counter. He's got a laptop in front of him, and his hands are hovering above it like he was mid-type. His hair is more rumpled than it was when I ran into him outside the bookstore, and instead of a button-down, he's wearing a gray T-shirt and beat-up jeans.

The T-shirt just makes me notice his arms again. And the way his shoulders are so much broader than they used to be. Not like he's spent hours at a gym—just like he's filled out. Grown up.

And he's looking at me. With a kind of hesitant surprise.

My mouth goes dry. It takes me a minute to find my voice. "Hi."

Behind the counter, the barista asks, "What can I get you?"

I tear my eyes away from Michael and turn to the barista. She's about my age, black hair pulled into a messy ponytail, a folded bandana tied around her head.

She doesn't look familiar at all. So, not someone I went to high school with, at least. "Uh . . ." I scan the menu on the wall behind her, trying to ignore the fact that I'm 99 percent sure Michael is still looking at me. "Just a latte, please."

I pay with a credit card and then stand awkwardly while she heads to the espresso machines. I really wish my phone wasn't dead. Then I could look at my phone, instead of glancing around the coffee shop, trying to decide if I should make eye contact with Michael or if that would be weird. Or if looking around the coffee shop, obviously *not* making eye contact with Michael, is weirder.

Finally, I have to look at him. Because I could swear I've looked everywhere else and my latte still isn't done.

He's gone back to looking at his laptop. My stomach sinks. It feels almost like a reflex. Like even though I haven't seen Michael for more than a decade, my automatic reaction is still to feel disappointed any time he decides to ignore me.

"Here you go." The barista with the bandana slides a white cup and saucer across the counter toward me, a flower drawn in the foam.

"Thanks." *Crap.* I should have asked for a paper to-go cup. In New York, to-go cups are the default. In New York, everyone is moving too fast for anything else, unless you're at one of the coffee shops where people sit with laptops. And then they ask you if you're staying or going.

I could go sit outside. It's bright and I'm not wearing any sunscreen, which means I'll resemble a tomato in under ten minutes, but at least I'll look less like I'm *obviously* trying to avoid Michael . . .

I swear that's what I mean to do—balance my cup and saucer and head for the door. Who cares if it means I'll end up staring at In Between Books? But instead, somehow, I'm suddenly turning to Michael. "I'm sorry I was so awkward the other night."

He looks up. His eyes meet mine and he drops his hands to his jeans, shoulders hunching up. It's exactly how he looked every time he was nervous in high school. Shoulders rising to his ears like he wished he could turn into a turtle. "No, it's . . . it's fine," he says.

Right. Okay.

I should leave, right? I should turn around and go outside, like I meant to—stare at the bookstore, continue spiraling, and leave him alone.

But he's still looking at me. And I can't seem to look away.

He jerks, like he suddenly realized he's staring, and gestures to the seat across from him. "Do you want to sit for a minute?"

I look at the chair. And then back to his face. Is he being serious?

He sounded friendly. He's looking at me again, and he looks like he means it.

"Um. Sure. Thanks." I set the cup and saucer on the table and sit down, pointing at the laptop. "Are you working on something?"

"Oh." He looks down at his laptop like he forgot it was there and then closes it. "Just lesson plans for the semester."

Oh, god. I have committed the cardinal sin of the Midwest: I misread an invitation and actually accepted. He was inviting me to sit down to be polite. I was supposed to recognize that he was busy, and say something about how that was so nice but I had something to get to, even though I don't.

I really should have gotten a to-go cup.

"Sorry," I say. "I didn't mean to interrupt you. I can let you get back to it—"

"No, no." He says it quickly. And then he looks self-conscious. The tips of his ears redden. "You're not interrupting. And anyway, I should also apologize. I was awkward too, and . . . I didn't mean to be so abrupt. I just . . . wasn't expecting to run into you."

That makes two of us. "Well, I don't live here."

The corner of his mouth turns up. "Right. Yeah. You're in New York now, right?"

My fingers tense around my cup. What do I say to that? *Well, I was, but now I'm having an existential crisis so I'm living with my mother?* "I'm . . . taking a bit of a break. Exploring my options, I guess. My mom is moving, so I came back to help."

Exploring my options? I might as well have just said I got fired. It obviously means the same thing.

But all Michael says is "Yeah, she told me she was moving."

I blink. "She told you?"

"I ran into her at the grocery store right after she bought the condo," he says, like this is a completely normal occurrence. Which I guess it is. Because Michael is an adult now, and grocery shops, and obviously runs into everyone else in Oak Falls there, including my mom.

I try to picture them in the checkout line, having a casual conversation.

I wonder if he ever asks about me.

"Oh," I say.

"So how is it?" he asks. "Being back?"

I rub my hands on my jeans. My palms are sweating. "A little weird." Understatement of the millennium. "Things have . . . changed and not changed."

"Yeah." Michael glances up at the pendant lights and then at the counter of the coffee shop. I suddenly notice how much sharper his jawline looks. And that the freckles that used to cover his nose are practically gone.

"This place has been here for a while now," he says. "But the Subway only moved in a couple of years ago. At least In Between Books is still hanging on." His ears turn pink again. "Which you obviously noticed."

Wait.

Michael has been inside the bookstore since 2009. Of course he has—he lives here. He knows what it looks like now. Whether it's actually really exactly like it was back then.

"Yeah," I say. "I haven't stopped in yet." A lie, but Michael doesn't know that. Unless he was spying on me from inside the coffee shop, I guess, but that doesn't seem very likely. "Is it different?"

Michael fiddles with the handle of his coffee cup. "Kind of? It is and it isn't." He glances at me with a hint of that crooked grin again. "Like everything else here."

That wasn't as helpful as I was hoping. "How's Hank doing?"

"He's getting older. Obviously." Michael shrugs one shoulder. "He's got pretty bad arthritis now. His daughter said he's not really in the store much anymore. He uses a cane, but even with that . . . I think it's hard for him to be on his feet for that long."

Cold seeps through my skin. The Hank I saw did not have a cane. And he didn't look a day older than the last time I saw him.

I try to push that out of my mind. "Does he have someone helping him?" I ask. "I mean, in the store?"

Another smile tugs at Michael's mouth. "Like annoying high school kids who sit in the aisles and read stuff?"

"Yeah." I smile, barely. "We were annoying."

"Super annoying." Michael glances at me, and the chasm between us—the years of distance and silence—doesn't seem quite as wide as it did a minute ago. "And yeah, Hank has a few regular employees. At least a couple of high school students during the summer."

"That's good." Although it doesn't tell me anything about whether one of those high school students could mysteriously look exactly like me. And there's no not-weird way for me to ask that.

And I don't want to. I want to ask something that will close the chasm a little more. Something that will let us keep talking, pretending like we can erase that last year of high school.

Michael lets his breath out. "Well," he says, with that finality that's basically Midwestern for *time to go.* "I've got a teacher meeting at Plainview, so . . ." He picks up a backpack from the floor, slipping his laptop into it. His eyes come back to mine. "It was really nice to see you."

"Yeah." Everything inside me sinks. "You too."

He slings the backpack over his shoulder and stands up, picking up his coffee cup and saucer. And then he hesitates. His shoulders hunch up and he turns back. "We're having some friends over to our place tonight. My roommates and I. It's this thing we do every month—drinks night. You should come by . . . if you have time."

This is a pity invite. It's clearly a pity invite, and he's extending it because I'm here and it's polite. This is the moment when I wave my hand and say, *Oh, that's so nice but,* and come up with some excuse that doesn't exist—like I should have when he asked if I wanted to sit down at this table in the first place—because Michael doesn't actually want me to show up at his house, and I'm supposed to know that.

But I can't do it. The tug in my chest is too sharp and too strong.

"I'll be there," I say.

To his credit, he doesn't look thrown. He just gives me a slight smile and readjusts his backpack on his shoulder. "Okay. Well. People will probably start showing up around seven."

I nod. "Seven. Sounds good."

He looks at me for another moment, and I wonder if he's going to say something else. But in the end, he just turns and slides the cup and saucer onto the counter, holding up a hand, waving to the barista. "See you later, Tash."

"Bye, Mike!"

No one, in all the years I remember, ever called Michael *Mike*.

But he doesn't seem to think it's anything unusual. He just walks through the door and out onto the sunny sidewalk.

CHAPTER ELEVEN

AUGUST 23

It's almost seven thirty when I pull the Jeep off the side of the road out-side Michael's house, rumbling up behind three other cars. Out here on the edge of Oak Falls, the roads don't really have curbs—they're just asphalt slapped on the ground, and they're also narrow. Which means the only way to really park is to pull half off the road.

I kept telling myself I wasn't actually going to drive over here. I told myself I wouldn't know anyone except Michael, I'd probably run into Liz, and everyone else in attendance would have heard all sorts of horrible stories about me and why Michael kicked me to the curb senior year of high school. The whole evening could be one long parade of *Oh, so you're Darby?*

But here I am. Because I made the mistake of telling my mom that Michael had invited me, and she said that was *nice*, and what was I sup-posed to do with that?

And anyway . . . I want to go. Michael invited me, and I can't stop hoping that that alone means *something*. Maybe it is a pity invite, but that's still better than him ignoring me.

I glance out of the Jeep's open window at Michael's house. The front porch is crisscrossed with string lights, and I can dimly make out people sitting in lawn chairs. A murmur of conversation floats across the yard.

Okay. This looks pretty low-key, right?

I tug on my light-pink polo shirt, flapping the fabric. The air outside the Jeep is cooler now that the sun has gone down, but I'm sweating.

I shouldn't have spent so long deciding what to wear. I mean, I didn't want to risk being the first person to show up, but looking at the five cars parked in his long driveway, plus the three sitting on the road with me, I'm beginning to think I'm going to be the *last* person to show up. I wasted too much time trying to guess what kind of party this was. The I-just-came-from-work kind? The casual-but-fun kind? The lol-I-threw-this-together-but-miraculously-look-super-cool kind?

I must have tried on half a dozen different options before ending up in the same polo shirt and jeans I started with. It was the only outfit that didn't seem to say, *I'm looking for the unemployed-and-living-with-your-mom party.*

Why did I wear a pink polo shirt? I might as well have written *Hi, I'm from the East Coast and super pretentious* on my forehead. I'm peak prep.

This was a bad idea. My insides are knotted up and shivery. I should turn around—go back to my mom's house and claim I have a headache so I can hide in my room for the rest of the evening. I don't know what I would do there other than feel sorry for myself, but at least I can do that in pajamas.

I reach for the key, and I'm about to start the Jeep again and actually bail when someone glides up next to me on a bicycle.

"Hey! Are you Darby, by any chance?"

I blink, staring at the person on the bike. She's white but with a deep tan, wearing cut-off denim shorts and a T-shirt, light brown hair tied back in a braid, the end dyed a faint pink. Flyaway strands stick to her neck. "Yeah," I say. "Do I know you?"

She grins. "No. Sorry. I'm Amanda. I'm one of Michael's roommates. He said you might be stopping by, and since I didn't recognize you . . ." She pauses. "Are you leaving already?"

"Oh. No." I quickly pull the key out of the ignition. I can't bail now. Not with Amanda watching me. Not if Michael told her I might be stopping by. "Just . . . working up to going in."

Amanda nods, but she looks a little like she's trying not to laugh at me. Which is fair. "You want to walk in with me? Or are you still . . . working?"

Heat rises up my neck. "No, I'm good."

She hops off her bike while I roll up the windows and lock the Jeep, and we go up the driveway together. The crickets are starting in, but even with their hum, it hits me again just how quiet it is. I can hear the bike creaking as Amanda walks it along next to us. The voices on the porch get closer, but it's all gentle, a wash of sound dissipating into a large expanse of space. In New York, sound reflects off everything—skyscrapers, sidewalks, the tiled walls of subway stations.

We cross into the glow cast by the string lights, and a woman with short hair shoots up from one of the lawn chairs on the porch. "Hey, there you are. Jesus, Amanda, what took you so long?"

Amanda leans her bike against the railing of the porch steps. "Connie kept changing her mind about her color. Took ages to finish it."

"Yikes." The woman meets Amanda halfway up the porch steps and kisses her, quick and familiar. "Do you need to change? Are you covered in hair bits?"

"So many hair bits." Amanda wrinkles her nose. "I might just jump in the shower real quick." She gestures to me, still loitering on the porch steps behind her. "This is Darby, by the way."

The woman Amanda was just kissing looks at me for the first time, and her face goes slack with surprise. "Oh my god. Darby Madden?"

Holy shit. It's Liz Forrest. I almost didn't recognize her without her long, layered hair or her necklaces or her leggings and UGG boots. Her hair is cut short now, and she's wearing rolled-up jeans and a loose tank top. She has a tattoo of flowers on one shoulder.

And she was just kissing Amanda.

Liz is queer.

I force my brain to work and pull my face into a smile. Or at least something that feels like one. "Hey. It's been a while."

"Yeah. Wow. It's been ages." She smiles, and it looks genuine enough. Like maybe she's not still thinking about that awkward snowy Saturday at In Between Books. Like it's not weird that I'm here on her porch steps and also trans.

I certainly didn't expect her to be queer, so maybe we're even.

"Come on in and grab a drink." She opens the screen door and holds it for me.

I feel weirdly disoriented as soon as I step inside. Pieces of this house are sharply familiar—the popcorn ceilings, the little round window in the entryway, even the coat hooks on the wall. It's not like I hung out at

Michael's grandma's house all the time, but at least a couple of his birth-day parties were here, and there was that time we got a group together to go see the *Star Trek* reboot the summer before senior year of high school, and the only car that would fit all six of us was Michael's grandma's old Buick with its front bench seat, so she let us borrow it . . .

So I've been here, at least a few times. I hadn't expected to remember it so strongly, but I do—which means I notice what's different too. The stale pall of cigarette smoke is gone. There used to be paisley wallpaper all over the front entryway and up along the staircase that Amanda is currently climbing. Now the walls are painted light blue.

And the living room is full of people.

This is definitely a gathering rather than a party. There's no music. And it's really just a few knots of people standing around, talking and holding beer bottles or cocktails in mason jars. Not enough of a crowd to count as a real party.

And I definitely did not need to look this put together. Nobody here is trying to look cool. Nobody here is *trying* to look like anything. One guy is actually wearing cargo pants. And not in a sloppy way—in a very functional, I-probably-wear-these-for-my-job way. He's got a carabiner of keys and a pocketknife dangling from a belt loop, and he's wearing a green trucker cap that says JOHN DEERE.

I swallow. My mouth is dry again. What kind of gathering did I just walk into?

"This way." Liz leads me down the hallway to the big eat-in kitchen. The dining table in the middle of the kitchen is cluttered with bottles of booze, bowls of pretzels, popcorn, crackers, a plate of cheese slices, and a whole bunch of empty mismatched mason jars.

And leaning over the table, stirring a drink, is Michael, still in the same beat-up jeans and gray T-shirt he was wearing this morning.

"Hey, Mike," Liz says, opening a cooler next to the table and fishing around in the ice for a beer. "Look who I found."

Michael looks up and pauses, the slim cocktail stirrer in his hand hovering above the drink. "Hi."

I can't read his expression. Amanda said he told her I might come by, but I can't tell if he's happy I'm actually here. "Hi."

Liz opens the tab on her can of Pabst. "Okay, I'm going to make sure

Amanda is actually showering and not, like, falling asleep." She glances at me. "Grab whatever looks good, Darby. There's pop in the cooler too."

I haven't heard anybody call it *pop* in years. I said pop exactly once when I arrived at boarding school. Nobody knew what I was talking about. "Thanks."

"You bet." She turns and goes back down the hall, swinging herself around on the newel at the bottom of the stairs and jogging up them in search of Amanda.

Leaving me with Michael.

Now that I'm here, I have no idea what to say to him. I can't say anything that I'm thinking—*Remember that time we shoveled your grandma's driveway when it snowed three feet, remember that birthday party when half the cake fell on this floor, what made you ditch the paisley wallpaper* . . . It's all too much; too personal, too fast. I have no idea if I'm here because once upon a time we were friends, or just because I'm someone Michael used to know who's back in town and it's the polite thing to do.

"Thanks for inviting me." It feels shallow leaving my mouth, like the most *nothing* thing I could have possibly said. It's the thing your mom makes you say to kids whose birthday party you're at when you have no idea why you're there.

"I wasn't sure you were gonna make it," Michael says.

There's definitely a version of this where Michael is making a very Midwestern dig at me. I just can't quite tell if I'm living that version. "Sorry I'm so late. In New York I'd blame the subway, but the truth is . . . I just forgot 'fashionably late' isn't really a thing here."

His lips twitch into a smile. "I seem to remember you always being unfashionably early."

I should probably cringe, but I'm too caught on Michael remembering something about me. The shivery feeling is back in my stomach. "I'm actually still unfashionably early. Most of the time."

He idly swirls his drink. "Some things don't change, huh?"

I manage a grin, but it feels tight and strained. "Guess not."

He hesitates, and I hesitate—both of us waiting for the other person to say something.

Finally, he clears his throat and gestures to the table. "Well, um . . . grab something and I'll introduce you to everybody."

Right. The part I've been dreading. My stomach has gone from shivering to churning.

It's fine. It'll be fine. Nobody in that living room looked familiar. So maybe there's nobody here I went to high school with. Maybe these friends only know grown-up Michael, and they'll have no idea who I am or why it might be a terrible idea that I'm here.

I lean down and root around in the cooler until I find a ginger ale. No way am I having alcohol tonight. Even aside from my embarrassing lightweightness, I don't think my stomach can handle it. It would be just my luck to drink booze and then vomit spectacularly over one of Michael's friends because I'm an anxious mess.

Michael leads me back down the hall to the living room, where we join the edge of the closest knot of people, the one that includes the guy in cargo pants. His scruffy face splits into a grin when he sees us. "Michael! How long does it take you to make one drink?" His blue eyes shift to me and he holds out his hand. "Hey. I'm John."

I wipe my hand furiously on my shirt and shake his hand. "Darby."

"We grew up together," Michael says.

"Oh, Darby!" John's eyebrows jump up to the brim of his hat. "Yeah, of course, we've totally heard about you!"

A jolt of anxiety shoots through me.

"You're the reason Michael's still got a stuffed Pikachu in his bedroom," John says.

I blink. That wasn't what I was expecting. It takes me a second to even clock what John is talking about.

Then I remember. I gave Michael a little plush Pikachu for his fifteenth birthday. It wasn't anything special—it had literally come as the toy in a Burger King meal. I only gave it to him because I didn't know what to do with it, and there wasn't a Burger King anywhere near Oak Falls; my mom and I had stopped at one on our way back from Chicago, when she'd gone to a teaching conference over the summer and taken me with her.

I can't believe Michael kept that plush.

"Wait, really? Pikachu?" The shorter, dark-haired guy next to John leans around him. "How come I didn't know this?"

Michael's ears are turning red. I bite my lip, trying not to smile.

"You totally knew it," John says. "Remember, we were helping Michael move that new desk he got up to his room and I knocked it off his dresser, and then asked why on earth he had a Pikachu—"

"Oh, right." The dark-haired guy nods and then holds out his hand to me. "Sorry, hi, I'm Lucas. I'm this guy's husband." He jerks his head at John.

All thoughts of Michael and Pikachu plushies evaporate out of my brain. I shake Lucas's hand, but my mind has gone completely numb. John—this guy in cargo pants and a John Deere baseball hat—*this* guy is queer? I look from him to Lucas, who isn't wearing cargo pants, but *is* wearing faded jeans and a T-shirt that says MONROE COUNTY FAIR 2019.

And it's not like either of them *shouldn't* be wearing those clothes, but . . .

But I assumed they were straight Midwestern farm guys. There's a look.

Michael clears his throat. "Yeah, so John and Lucas live on the opposite side of town, over by Strickland Farms—"

"That's where I work," John says, so I guess I wasn't totally off on the *farm guy* thing.

"And this is Bex and their partner, Erin." Michael gestures to the two remaining people in the circle. "Bex and I got our teaching degrees together."

"Oh." I look at Bex, who has short buzzed hair and a septum piercing, and is the only other person besides me wearing a shirt with a collar. It's a short-sleeve floral button-down, though. Not a polo shirt. Definitely not prep. "So you teach at Plainview?"

"No, we're over in Monroe," Bex says. "I'd honestly love to be a bit more out in the country than that, but Erin's the assistant principal at the middle school, so . . . we're good for now."

Erin snorts. "Uh, since we just bought a house, I *hope* we're good for now." Erin is taller than Bex, a willowy woman with light-brown skin and black curls that are currently piled up on her head.

"Wait, I didn't know you *bought* already; I thought you just started looking," Lucas says.

"We got lucky," Bex says.

"Well, that's great!" John says. "Now you've got it before you really get going on baby stuff."

Erin shoots me a slightly amused look. "Sorry, Darby, we just met you and we're already talking houses and babies . . ."

"It's fine," I say quickly. I'm still stuck on the fact that these people are queer. That there are other queer people *here*, in Oak Falls, the place I left. The place I couldn't get away from fast enough, because I was so sure there was no one else like me here. Because I was so sure there wasn't room for me.

"So, you live around here?" John asks me.

"Kind of," I say, at the same time Michael says, "He's just visiting."

There's an awkward silence. Bex, Erin, John, and Lucas all glance at Michael. And then back at me.

"I'm visiting my mom to help her move," I say. "I was in New York, but . . . I haven't totally figured out what I'm doing next."

From the corner of my eye, I see Michael look down at his drink. His shoulders rise.

"Well, if you want a sales pitch for Oak Falls, let us know," John says with a grin.

A strange twinge cuts through me. I have a sudden urge to tell him I don't need a sales pitch. I grew up here—I know everything there is to know about this place.

Except, if I'm being honest, I'm not sure I do. Not anymore.

So all I say is "Thanks. I'll keep you posted."

The conversation drifts to Bex and Erin's new house and the electrical rewiring they need to do. Michael shares a few tips because apparently he's rewired outlets in this house. I stand there feeling very much like a useless city queer. When the single ceiling light in my apartment kept blowing out, I called the super. I don't even know what the problem was in the end.

Eventually, Michael asks if I want to meet everyone else, and I say sure because what else am I going to say. We go through the same routine with everyone else in the living room.

And it quickly becomes clear that nobody at this gathering is straight. It's not that anyone really announces it—or even talks about it that much. It's just that Robin with the blue hair says *when Mikaela and I started dating* as an offhand comment, nudging the arm of the woman next to her. And Brianna, a tall blond woman in a tank top and overalls, mentions driving to Chicago for hormones in a story that's otherwise mostly about her cat. And by the time we've gone through the living room and we're back out on the porch, where Liz and Amanda are sitting on lawn chairs with a Black man in khakis and a Chicago Cubs T-shirt, I feel like I've wandered into some alternate reality.

I knew Oak Falls had changed. The condos, the coffee shop, Subway, the supposed traffic . . .

But this is something else. This is something that digs deep into my core until it's a dull, nagging ache. Because I can't help wondering how many of these people were here, growing up when I was growing up. I can't help wondering why I didn't find them. Why I *couldn't* find them.

And whether anything might have been different if I had.

"Did you meet everybody?"

Liz's voice pulls me out of my thoughts and I force my face into a smile. "Yeah. They're all, um . . ."

"Queer?" Liz says with a grin.

"I was going to say nice," I mumble, because I suddenly feel ashamed that Liz knew, somehow, that that's what I was thinking.

Liz shrugs. "Yeah, they're nice too, in addition to being queer. Except for Grant." She nods her head toward the guy next to her. "He's nice but he's not queer."

Grant snorts and rolls his eyes. "Hey, nice to meet you."

"Grant works with Liz at the hospital out on Highway Thirty-Six," Michael says for my benefit.

"Fellow nurse." Liz takes a swig from her beer. "Fellow night-shift sufferer."

Grant groans. "Ugh, don't remind me. I have to go to work after this. Thus the pop." He holds up a can of Dr. Pepper.

Something catches in my brain at that. "Yeah, you said you do this every month." I glance at Michael. "Is it always this many people? Or is this, like . . . a special occasion?"

He shrugs. "No, it's just whoever can come. We started doing it . . . a few years ago?" He glances at Liz, and she nods. "It's usually on a weekend but a few folks were on vacation, so . . . this worked out."

"Plus, there's not really anything else to do," Amanda says, and Liz and Grant laugh at that.

The ache settles deeper.

Grant asks Amanda how things are going at the hair salon where she works, and then he and Liz start telling stories about the weirdest patients they've gotten in the ER late at night, and I try to keep up. Nod along. Laugh with everyone else. But I'm barely listening.

All I can think about is *how did I miss this*.

And then, *I miss this*.

I want this.

Why didn't I realize that there were queer people right here? How did Michael find them? Did he and Liz know about each other in high school? Is that why they were friends?

Something twists inside me, sharp as a knife. *Why* did I assume they were dating, back then? *Why* didn't I see what was really going on?

I wish, so deeply it hurts, that I could have gone through senior year of high school with them. The three of us together. I don't know what difference it would have made . . . but I feel sure it would have made a difference.

Maybe I wouldn't have spent so much time feeling lost.

Maybe I wouldn't feel so lost now.

"Okay, I need to go inside and say hi to people," Amanda says, pushing herself out of her lawn chair. "I haven't talked to anybody else since I got home."

"I'll go with you." Liz tips her head back, draining the last of her beer, and reaches out a hand. Amanda pulls her up.

Grant wanders after them into the house with a kind of self-consciousness that makes me think he's a newer addition to this group, and he's still following Liz around as his closest friend.

And now I'm alone with Michael again, both of us standing awkwardly next to each other on the front porch. I can't decide if I should sit down in one of the lawn chairs, or suggest we could go back inside, or wait for him to say something. In the end, I just stare out into the yard. It's fully dark now—darker than it ever gets in New York—and a few tiny spots of goldish green wink on and off. Fireflies.

The ache in me digs even deeper. I missed fireflies. There aren't any in New York. Not in the city, anyway. Fireflies are one thing I know I always loved about Oak Falls. One thing that always felt faintly magical.

"Did you get a lot of fireflies this summer?" I ask.

Michael turns toward the yard, leaning one hand on the porch railing. "Yeah," he says. "I mean, about average, probably. This is pretty good for this late in the year."

I nod. We're silent again, watching the fireflies, while the conversation from inside drifts through the screen door and the open windows.

And suddenly the ache is too much. "I didn't know you were gay." It comes out choked.

His eyes jerk to me.

I swallow around the tightness in my throat. "I mean, my mom told me when I got back. But I didn't know back then, and I didn't know about Liz, either, and . . . I don't know if I was supposed to, but . . . I'm sorry. That I didn't."

I look up at him. He's looking back at me with a strange expression—like he's seeing me and not seeing me, just like that night I ran into him outside the bookstore. "I didn't tell you."

"I know."

"So . . . you didn't know." His voice is quiet and flat.

My chest tightens. "Well, I know, but . . ."

He watches me, waiting, but I don't know what to say. It's not like I told him I was trans, back then. I mean, I was barely even admitting it to myself.

So maybe he was doing the same. Maybe he really didn't know.

And yet . . .

"What happened to us, Michael?" It bursts out of me, like it's been building ever since I got back, or ever since I found that box from In Between Books shoved under my bed in New York. "I know we got in a fight at my seventeenth birthday party, but that was . . . it was ridiculous. I can't even totally remember why it blew up so big. Was that really enough to ruin everything? Was that enough to just . . . stop talking to me?"

Michael has gone very still. Like a statue, barely breathing, face perfectly blank. And then it twists with hurt. "You're asking me?" His voice is rough. Rusty.

The ache turns into desperation. "I'm just trying to—"

"Darby, I can't . . ." His eyes skip to my face and then away. "This isn't . . . I can't do this right now." He runs a hand through his hair, which just makes his curls stick up, and then looks down at his glass. "I'm gonna get a refill. I'll . . . I'll be right back."

He turns away from me, like he can't get away fast enough. Pulls open the screen door.

"Michael—"

But he's already gone back into the house. The screen door squeaks closed behind him. I twist around and look through one of the windows, but he disappears down the hall.

What just happened?

I let my breath out, shaky, and realize I'm staring into the living room. I turn back to the yard and the twinkling fireflies.

I should apologize. Go find him and tell him I was being a fool. Tell him *forget it. Never mind.*

But I know it's too late for that. I can't just say *forget it* after yanking everything back into the open.

And I can't go in there and apologize—not when he's surrounded by all his friends. I should wait here until he comes back. Then I can at least say I'm sorry. I can at least try to move on.

So I wait, slowly sipping my ginger ale.

One minute.

Five minutes.

I get bitten by at least one mosquito, but Michael doesn't come back.

I turn and look through the window again. Liz and Amanda and Grant are talking to John and Lucas. But I don't see Michael.

So maybe he's hiding somewhere. Maybe I should go look for him.

Or maybe he's leaving me out here on purpose.

God, what am I doing here?

Everything inside me wants to curl up into a ball. I've been standing on this porch for five minutes and either nobody's noticed, or they're all hoping I'll leave, and either way, the message is the same: I don't belong here. These aren't my friends.

I set the ginger ale can down on the porch railing. And then I feel guilty leaving it there and pick it back up. I'll recycle it at my mom's house.

I waver for another moment, hoping that if I just hang on for a second longer the screen door will open and Michael will reappear.

He doesn't.

So I walk down the porch steps, following the driveway through the fireflies.

It's not that easy to cry on testosterone. But when I get back to the Jeep, I have to sit for several minutes, taking deep, shuddering breaths, before I can see without the steering wheel swimming in front of me.

CHAPTER TWELVE

AUGUST 23

The house is dark when I unlock the front door, and it takes me an embarrassingly long time to find the light switch. When I finally do, I just about have a heart attack. Mr. Grumpy is sitting on the floor right in front of me, tongue lolling out of his mouth and tail thumping the carpet.

I let my breath out and reach down to scratch his head. "What are you doing up, bud?"

He just yawns and pads after me as I creep down the hall to my room. My mom's door is closed. I glance at my phone. It's almost ten—she's probably fast asleep.

I wait for Mr. Grumpy to lumber into my room and then I close the door and flip on the light. My bedroom looks exactly the same as it did when I left for Michael's, but somehow that just makes me annoyed. Annoyed at the version of me from three hours ago who was caught up in picking an outfit, like if I wore the right clothes, I could fit right in and slip back into my friendship with Michael like it had never gone up in flames.

I gather up the shirts and pants strewn across my bed and fling them into my suitcase with so much vehemence that Mr. Grumpy jumps out of the way and gives me a concerned look.

And then I sit down on the edge of the bed, glaring at the empty spots on the walls where the photos from high school used to be, suddenly furious with myself for taking them down. So what if they made me dysphoric as fuck? Maybe if I had them now, I'd be able to learn something.

Maybe if I stared at them for long enough, I'd be able to figure out why I never realized Michael was gay or Liz was queer. Maybe I'd understand *something* about what happened back then.

I know it's ridiculous. I know pictures couldn't really tell me any of those things. I know all they'd really do is make me feel worse—but maybe part of me wants that too.

I push myself up. Brush my teeth. Change into pajamas. When I turn off the light and climb into bed, Mr. Grumpy immediately sits up and puts his front paws on the mattress.

"You're not supposed to be up here," I tell him.

He whines.

I sigh and lean down, getting an arm under his butt and hauling him up onto the bed. He flops down on my feet with a sigh.

I lie back down, hands under my head, staring up at the ceiling. In this moment, I actually miss the constant background noise of New York. The shriek of subway brakes. The distant sirens. The hum of traffic or people talking or a neighbor's TV. Sure, it was claustrophobic a lot of the time, but at least it also distracted me from my own thoughts.

Here, there's only Mr. Grumpy's wheezing and the chirp of crickets outside the open window. I'm painfully aware of my own breathing. My own thoughts crashing around in my head. A series of *why why why*.

I lean over and grab my phone off the nightstand. My thumb hovers over the messages icon. But I still don't know how to reply to Ian's thumbs-up emoji. I don't know how to explain tonight. How to explain Michael. How to explain anything.

So instead, I open Instagram. I want distraction, but more than that, I want to see New York. I want to see my life in New York. I want a reminder of that noise—a reminder of everything that made me leave New York—so I can stop feeling alone in this quiet, with only Mr. Grumpy snoring and the crickets to keep me company.

My most recent post is a selfie from Olivia's birthday party, all of us crowded into the booth while Ian holds my phone because he has the longest arms. I quickly scroll past it. I need something more distant, something farther away that isn't so raw. I scroll past pictures from Olivia's stand-up shows—most of them blurry because it was too dark in the cramped comedy clubs for my old phone to focus. I scroll past a selfie of all of us at NYC Pride—Olivia and Joan with rainbow glitter on their faces, Ian in a feather boa and a mesh tank top, and me just wearing a regular old T-shirt and jeans because I was never quite loud enough for anything else.

I scroll faster and faster, past old birthday parties and picnics in Prospect Park and that time we all carved pumpkins in Ian's old apartment and then it smelled like raw pumpkin for weeks. Faster and faster until years are rolling by in seconds. Until, finally, I get to the very first picture I ever posted.

It's a selfie of me and Olivia in front of the fountain in Washington Square Park. It's sunny, and I'm wearing my old navy-blue peacoat and my oval glasses. Olivia's in a sweatshirt and a puffy vest; instead of long braids, her hair is in short twists.

This picture is from college. Freshman year. I know before I even look at the date on the post, because I lost those glasses at the end of my first semester. No wonder the picture quality seems a little grainy.

This was before I came out to my mom. Before I started hormones. Before I had top surgery. When the bubble where I existed as a trans guy was very, very small.

This was back when the only person I'd come out to was Olivia.

I TALKED MYSELF out of going to that queer meetup at least five times, including when I was literally on my way there. It was the end of orientation week and Manhattan was still hot and sticky, but at least the half-empty dorms were filling up as all the upperclassmen started to arrive on campus. I'd spent orientation feeling itchy for classes to actually get started, because it didn't take very long for me to determine I was absolutely no good at orientation. I felt behind the whole week. Friend groups formed while I was still getting lost trying to find my way back to my dorm. Parties happened that I never even knew were happening until my roommate came back well after midnight and told me she'd been at a party. It was like the beginning of high school all over again, except with a lot more booze and weed.

Plus, there was the whole thing where rooming with a girl was just making it extra obvious to me that I was not, in fact, a girl.

But even so, when I saw the flyer advertising a meetup for LGBTQ students, all genders and sexualities welcome . . . I still told myself I shouldn't go. I told myself I didn't really *know*. I told myself I wasn't sure, and it would probably just be five people and be super awkward, *and and and . . .*

But *all genders* stuck in my head.

So I went. I walked into one of the student lounges in a building I barely clocked the name of, because I still didn't really know where anything was on campus. And it wasn't just five people. It was a roomful of people. At least thirty. Some sitting on the couches and chairs in the lounge, some standing, some talking and laughing, and others hovering on the edge and watching, like me. On one wall was a very handmade paperboard sign: WELCOME LGBTQ STUDENTS, all in rainbow markers with an abundance of glitter.

I had no idea what a roomful of queer people would look like. A lot of the girls had short hair. Several of the guys were wearing very low-cut T-shirts. There were definitely more earrings than average for the general population.

A girl with short hair and long earrings climbed onto a chair, hands cupped around her mouth. "All right, everybody, listen up!" she yelled. "My name is Bree, I'm a junior, and I run the LGBTQ Student Alliance along with Rickie over there." She pointed to a tall, lanky guy with light-brown skin and gold hoops in both ears. He waved. "Since this is a meetup, we feel you actually need to *meet* people. So I'm gonna ask everybody to get in a circle, and we're gonna facilitate some meeting."

I almost walked out. I'd changed my mind. Meeting people sounded like a terrible idea. There were icebreaker activities coming—I could feel it. And I hated icebreaker activities. I'd suffered through a round of icebreaker activities when I arrived at boarding school. It was the worst.

But a circle was already forming, people lining up on either side of me. I'd somehow joined in without even meaning to. And then Bree was walking around the circle, labeling each of us a "one" or a "two," and I couldn't leave without it being really obvious. And being obvious felt worse than being part of an icebreaker activity.

So I stood there, so anxious I was ready to barf, as Bree instructed the ones to turn to the person to our right and introduce ourselves.

I was definitely disassociating. My brain felt a hundred miles away when I turned to the Black girl next to me, and said, "Hi, I'm Darby."

The room was a cacophony of voices, everyone introducing themselves, as she said, "I'm Olivia."

I bobbed my head, trying to think of something else to say so we wouldn't be awkwardly staring at each other. "So, are you—"

"I'm bi," Olivia said.

She said it like it was simultaneously easy and like she was desperate to let it out in the open.

I gaped at her. I'd been about to ask if she was a freshman, since clearly not everyone here was. Maybe she'd thought I said something else, since it was loud with everyone talking. Or maybe she just wanted to tell me she was bi because it was no big deal, because we were in New York City, because this was the kind of space where people said things like that easily.

At the end of the day, it didn't really matter, because now I had to decide what to say back. And either I could make us both embarrassed by telling her that actually that was not what I was asking at all . . . or I could share my truth with her, and try, really hard, to trust her with it.

"I'm trans," I said, at the same time Olivia said, "You don't have to tell me anything."

We stared at each other. I couldn't breathe. My lungs wouldn't expand. Had she heard me? Did I have to say it again? Would that just make this weirder?

Then her face split into a smile. "Sorry," she said, laughing. "That's cool. What pronouns?"

Air rushed into my lungs and my adrenaline crashed so hard, I felt dizzy. I'd never once let myself think this far. *What pronouns?* I'd never even thought about pronouns in my own head. I realized, with an uncomfortable jolt, that I still shaved my legs and under my arms. I wore a sports bra, and I liked that it helped me look flatter, and the T-shirt I was wearing was sort of oversize, and the jeans I had on were actually from the boys' section—but I certainly wasn't wearing guys' underwear.

I had no business using male pronouns. Did I?

But I wasn't a girl. And every time I let myself exist—even just in my own head—as a guy, pretending that was how the world saw me . . .

Those were the only times I didn't feel like a fraud.

"Male pronouns," I said, and immediately wondered if that was the right way to say it. "He, him, and his." Was that better?

Olivia nodded quickly, almost eagerly. "Okay. Cool. I just use she and her."

"Right. Okay."

We stared at each other some more. My heart was pounding so hard I could hear it in my ears, louder even than the voices of the people around me.

I'd just come out.

I'd told this complete stranger that I was trans.

And she'd believed me.

Her forehead wrinkled. "Are you okay?"

No. I felt like I was going to pass out. Or have a full-blown panic attack. I was sweaty, too hot, and my heart was trying to hammer straight out of my chest. "Yeah. I just . . . I never actually told anyone that before."

The wrinkles in her forehead disappeared. "Cool. I haven't told that many people, either."

We went through a few other introductory questions, and even though I didn't think I made friends easily—probably because I'd spent the last seven or eight months basically hanging out with myself—after coming out for the first time, everything else felt like a piece of cake. Olivia told me she was from the Bronx. I told her I was from Illinois; she had no idea where that was. We were both freshmen and even in the same dorm, just on different floors.

She was in the middle of telling me her favorite bagel place close to NYU when Bree got back up on her chair and informed us that now we were going to turn to the person on our other side, and this time we had to share a dream or a goal we had for the semester.

My palms turned clammy. I had no idea what my dreams or goals were. Up until this moment, all I wanted was to survive all my classes and get decent grades, like that would prove I belonged here. But I'd just come out. I'd literally invented a new Darby—or finally uncovered the Darby that had been there all along.

And maybe it was cheesy, but the world suddenly seemed a whole lot bigger. And I didn't feel remotely ready to share any of that with a random stranger. Coming out to Olivia was enough for one day.

Did people on the East Coast really get this personal this fast?

Judging by Olivia's face, they did not. She looked like a deer in the headlights.

She glanced at me. "Hey, you want a bagel now?"

I blinked. "You mean, like, leave?"

She bit her lip and glanced sideways at Bree. "I kind of hate stuff like this," she confessed. "I just really wanted to meet someone else queer, but like . . . this is a lot."

"Yeah," I said. Now my heart was pounding for a different reason. For the first time in a long time, I felt excited. I felt hopeful. I suppose it was probably really sad that I was so thrilled someone wanted to get a bagel with me, but I was. "Let's bail."

So we bailed. I told myself it was fine—we'd taken out a "one" and a "two," which meant nobody would be left without a partner. And anyway, Bree didn't seem to care or even notice that we turned and walked right out of the room.

I guess Olivia and I were both a little stressed out, or a little overwhelmed, or we'd just spent too much time in tiny dorm rooms desperately wishing it would cool off outside, because we bent over laughing as soon as we were out of the room.

"I don't even know what my goal would be," I said.

"Dude, I don't have goals, I live in the *moment*," Olivia said, still laughing. I couldn't tell if she was joking or not, but in that particular moment, I didn't care.

I PUT THE phone face down on my chest and close my eyes, thinking back to all the bits and pieces of things that happened after I came out to Olivia. I stopped shaving. I ordered my first binder online. Ian took me to the barbershop he went to and I got an actual guy's haircut. (The barber barely said three words the whole time. It was great.)

All of that was packed into that first semester—the semester that flew by and felt a million years long at the same time. At the end of it, I went home for Christmas, and I came out to my mom.

And then, when I got back to New York, Olivia and Ian went shopping with me. We went to the big Target in Brooklyn because it was cheap, and I bought a whole bunch of new clothes. From the boys' section. I was too short for basically everything in the men's section.

I called the LGBT center and found a therapist I could afford, because I couldn't start actually transitioning without one giving me permission and writing some formal letter. To attest I wasn't just fooling around and *going through a phase*—like constantly getting misgendered by teachers was a fun hobby.

It was awful and wonderful and terrifying, and even with *all of it* . . . I loved New York. I loved wandering around the holiday market in Union Square with Olivia and Ian. I loved taking the subway with them on the weekends—going wherever Olivia had decided we should go, since she was the only one of us who knew New York at that point. We wandered around the Met, paying a few bucks because they let students do that. We studied in Central Park. We bought pizza by the slice and crammed for finals in crowded coffee shops, and it all felt like the fantasy of what New York was supposed to be.

I rub my eyes. I can't think of any particular moment I fell out of love with the city. I can't remember exactly when the subway stopped being thrilling and started being mundane. Or when my apartment got too small and too crappy. Maybe it was inevitable. Too many years of barely affording things, getting older and feeling like there was a list of things I was supposed to be accomplishing. Buy a house, get a solid job that was also supposed to be my passion, own a car, get married, or at least find a partner . . .

It started to seem like none of those things would happen in New York. I dated occasionally—a girl in college for a few months, a guy in grad school for a bit longer—but nothing seemed to really stick. There was always some piece of me that never seemed to make sense to people.

And I don't even know if I need the partner, the house, the Dream Job in publishing or academia, or whatever I thought was my passion. I just know that I'm missing something. Like I spent the last twelve years carefully putting together a jigsaw puzzle, only to come up one piece short.

My mind wanders back to In Between Books, to the version of myself

I saw behind the counter, to the dates on the newspapers and the video store outside the window.

I pick up my phone again. The screen glows in the darkness. *Tuesday, August 23, 10:34 p.m.*

The breeze filtering through my window suddenly feels chilly.

Today, when I walked into the bookstore, it was August 23—the same date as it is today, in my present. I didn't check the newspapers yesterday; was that August 22? And will tomorrow be August 24?

Because if time inside the bookstore moves like it does out here, just thirteen years earlier . . .

Then maybe I have a chance to figure out what happened to me and Michael, even if Michael—the Michael that's here and now—won't tell me. Maybe I can ask the younger version of me in the bookstore. I can't ask exactly *that* obviously. I can't walk into the store and go, *Hey, tell me why you're about to have a huge falling-out with your best friend.*

But I can ask *something*. Maybe I can learn enough to piece things together, and if I know what made everything crumble between us, maybe I can figure out how to fix it.

And I've walked into the bookstore twice since I arrived in Oak Falls. Both times, I traveled. It seems reasonable to assume I'll do it again when I go back tomorrow.

And I'm going to go back.

I have to go back.

I set my phone down on the nightstand. Set my glasses on top of it. And then I close my eyes and repeat it to myself over and over, like something to hold on to.

Tomorrow, I'm going back.

CHAPTER THIRTEEN

AUGUST 24

I hold my breath this time, as I cross the threshold of In Between Books. Just to see if I feel the moment it happens. The moment I *travel*.

But I might as well be walking through any other doorway into any other store. I don't feel anything. The bell jingles, the door creaks closed behind me, and here I am. It's practically mundane.

Except that when I pull my phone out of my pocket, it blinks another *Low Battery* warning at me and then shuts itself off.

A shiver runs up my back.

I shove my phone back in my pocket and look toward the counter. It's empty. So I wait, scuffing the toe of my shoe idly against the floor. Maybe my younger self is in the back room like the last time I was here.

But I count out ten agonizingly long seconds, and nobody comes out of the back room.

Shit. Maybe my younger self isn't here. Was there a day I didn't work, that last week before I left for boarding school?

And then, a scarier thought: Am I even in that week?

Did I travel to some other completely random day?

I turn for the magazine stand and grab the closest newspaper, a copy of the *Oak Falls Sun*. The date on the top reads *Monday, August 24, 2009.*

The same date as today. Or . . . the version of today that exists outside the bookstore. It's Wednesday out there, but also August 24, which is what matters. I glance up at the book clock above the storage room door. The hands point to 10:30. My phone read 10:28 when I checked it before I walked in.

Which means it's the same time in here and out there. On the same date.

Time moving in parallel.

I set the newspaper back on the stand and go up to the counter, leaning my hands on it, awkwardly craning to try to peer into the storage room. But all I can see are a few boxes stacked near the doorway and a row of coat hooks.

I chew my lip, looking around the quiet store, and then I skirt the table of new releases and start walking along the row of shelves, looking down each aisle. Nobody else seems to be here. I don't see any customers browsing in any of the aisles I pass, although maybe that wasn't all that unusual for 10:30 on a Monday morning. In Between Books was usually busiest on the weekends.

Anxiety is tightening my chest when I reach the last row of shelves—a nonfiction section.

And there I am. The younger version of me. Crouching under a handwritten sign that says BIOGRAPHY, pulling books off shelves and putting them back in different places. Re-alphabetizing. Just like I was on that snowy day when Michael and Liz came into the bookstore.

Just like I *will* be. None of that has happened for this version of me.

I shiver again, even though I'm not cold.

Today, my younger self is wearing jeans, worn Adidas sneakers, and a striped polo shirt that's several sizes too big. Okay, so maybe I always had a polo-shirt-prep streak. Or I just really wanted to look like Zac Efron. I definitely remember looking at pictures of him in the celebrity magazines the bookstore stocked (because they sold, as Hank grumbled, not because he liked them) and feeling a deep desire to look like that. This younger Darby's hair even looks like I tried, very hard, to go for *swoopy*, but it's ended up at *Midwest-swamp-summer-poofy*.

I run my hand through my own hair, automatically, like a reflex, reassuring myself it doesn't look like that anymore. I may not have anything else figured out, and my hair may still wave in all the wrong directions in high humidity, but at least it looks better than *that*. Thank god for Ian and his surly barber; my mom's hairstylist never seemed to know quite what to do with my hair and never believed me that I didn't want it to look "cute and girly."

Something sharp twists in my chest. I'd forgotten about that striped polo until this moment. I bought it because I thought all the stripes might help hide my boobs. I thought the big size would help too.

I didn't know *why* I wanted to hide my boobs. Just that I did. They felt like a part of my body someone had stuck on as a practical joke.

Young Darby glances over and notices me lurking at the end of the aisle. "Hi. Can I help you?"

I quickly drop my hand back to my side. I can't tell if my younger self recognizes me from yesterday, and the day before. Young Darby's face is blank, eyebrows vaguely raised.

I swallow. *This is weird. This is so weird.* "I'm wondering if you can help me find a book."

Young Darby slides a book back onto the shelf and straightens up. "Sure. What are you looking for?"

"I don't really remember the name of it," I say. "But it's the first book in a series, and the main character is named Percy Jackson."

Young Darby's face lights up in recognition. "Oh, yeah, I totally know which book you mean."

I let my breath out in relief. I could have googled, I suppose. That might have been smart, but really, it didn't even matter if my younger self knew the exact book I meant or not. The book isn't the point. I just needed some way to strike up a conversation—some reason to talk to my younger self that wasn't creepy and weird. Young Darby has no idea who I am, and if I walked in and started asking questions about Young Darby's friend Michael, that would go to a stranger-danger place real fast.

So . . . books. The thing I could ask about was books.

And I may not remember the exact title, but I remember the Percy Jackson books. I read all of them. I was obsessed. And more important, Michael read some of them too. We read the first book in the series together the summer before we started high school, sitting in the aisle of In Between Books. I don't remember which of us found it first. But we sat there, next to each other on the floor, the edges of the shelf behind us digging into our backs, and read the whole book. It was the first time we did that—read together in the aisles of the bookstore.

"This way," Young Darby says, and slips past me, so close that the sleeve of that striped polo shirt brushes my arm. I have to resist the urge to reach out and poke my younger self, just to prove this version of me is *real*.

Young Darby heads for the children's section at the other end of the bookstore, and I follow. It's weird watching this younger Darby move through space. To see the way I tap two fingers against my thumb, idly, and realize I still do that as a mindless tic. To see the way I hunch my shoulders forward, hiding my chest, and remember the moment I realized, after I had top surgery, that I was standing differently.

Taller is what Olivia said.

"Should be here somewhere." Young Darby turns down a row of shelves near the front of the store, dragging a finger along the book spines, and then leans down and pulls out a paperback. "Here you go."

I reach out and take the book from my younger self. My eyes catch on the creases in the skin of Young Darby's wrist—the same creases I have. The particular freckle on my thumb.

Goose bumps prickle up my arms.

"Thanks." I take the book quickly, hoping Young Darby doesn't notice the strange similarity of our hands. At least mine are a bit . . . hairier.

God, this is so weird.

I look down at the cover of the book. It's instantly familiar—a wash of greenish blue, with a kid in an orange T-shirt, holding a sword, standing knee-deep in the ocean while a lightning bolt crackles over a city. My breath hitches. The book is so real and so familiar in my hands that I can practically see myself sitting in this aisle, my feet stretched out in front of me, with Michael next to me (folded up because his legs were too long for the width of the aisle), both of us reading and occasionally leaning over to see where the other one was in the story.

"Is that the right book?"

I look up. Young Darby is looking back at me with a kind of nervous expectation.

I push the memory of Michael out of my mind. "Yeah, I think this is it. I'm . . . it's for my cousin. He got it from the library and really liked it, so he told his best friend about it, and his best friend is going to read it, so I thought I'd get a copy for my cousin so they could read it together. At the same time."

I'm rambling, completely spinning a story, but I didn't plan this far.

I got up to deciding I should ask about *The Lightning Thief*, because I remembered reading this book with Michael, and then I'd figure out how to get from there to asking about Michael. It seemed hard to plan in advance without knowing what the younger version of me would say or if In Between would even have this book. I told myself I could wing it. Figure it out in the moment.

I'm regretting that now.

"Oh, that's cool." There's an edge of excitement in Young Darby's voice. "I actually did the same thing. I mean, I didn't get it from the library, but I read this at the same time as my friend Michael. We totally spent a week calling each other Percy and Grover." My younger self's face suddenly flushes. "It was kind of silly. I mean, we were fourteen, but . . ."

I bite my lip to keep from smiling. I'd completely forgotten about that, but it's coming back now. I ended up as Percy and Michael ended up as Grover because he had a very impassioned argument about how cool secretly being a satyr would be. It made my stomach tingle, every time he called me Percy—like I was getting away with something.

But I'd always liked made-up stuff. I liked books. I liked movies. I liked making up stories. It's the whole reason I was an English major in college. The whole reason I studied literature and thought about trying to get a job in publishing.

So, I told myself it was just . . . that. Make-believe. And maybe I was a little old for it. But it wasn't more than that.

"Michael seems like a good friend," I say.

Young Darby blinks at me. "Uh, yeah. I guess."

"You guys read any other books together? Or, like, watch TV shows or movies together?"

Now my younger self looks a little suspicious.

Shit. I'm totally doing the thing I was trying *not* to do—I'm taking this in a creepy stranger-danger direction. Asking way too many personal questions of this teenager I'm not supposed to know anything about.

"Sorry." I grin, but it feels shaky. "I was just thinking maybe you'd have more book recommendations or, like, TV show recommendations that my cousin would like."

"Oh." Young Darby is still giving me a bit of side-eye but seems to accept this answer. "Uh, I mean . . . Michael and I watch a lot of *Buffy*, I guess."

This isn't getting me anywhere. I don't know how to turn *Buffy the Vampire Slayer* into a question about why everything is about to crumble with my best friend. I look back down at the book in my hands. Something else occurs to me.

"What did Michael think of this?" I ask, holding the book up.

Young Darby's eyes skip to the cover and then back to me. "He liked it. It's a series—I mean, I guess you know that. We read the first few books together. Or, like, at the same time. He's more into comics now, though." Younger Me barely suppresses an eye roll.

I try not to smile. "Comics aren't your thing?"

Young Darby shrugs. "I don't know. I guess I'm just not that into superheroes."

I look back at the book I'm holding. "These aren't superheroes?"

Young Darby is quiet a moment. "I guess they always felt more like real people." A self-conscious grin and then another shrug. "Whatever. Michael still asked me what happened in the last Percy Jackson book. I spent, like, an hour when we were hanging out at the Falls explaining the book." Young Darby's face turns pink again, like that was too much to share.

My mind catches on the Falls. On a leafy canopy and the roar of water and the awkward ridges of rock under me when I'm lying on my back . . .

"Did you . . . want to buy that book?" Young Darby asks, glancing at the paperback in my hands.

Right. I did say I was going to get it for my cousin. And if I put it back on the shelf now, Young Darby will probably be a little miffed. I got so attached to this bookstore when I worked here. It felt like the one constant—the thing that had been in my life forever and never changed, not even after I came back from boarding school and lost Michael.

I let my breath out. I'm still not any closer to figuring out what happened—or what's about to happen—with Michael.

But I can't figure out what to say, and if I stand here for any longer, Young Darby is going to get suspicious again. "Yeah. Um." I wave the book awkwardly. "I'll take this."

"I can ring you up." Young Darby turns for the cash register and I follow.

My eyes drift to the big picture window as I walk up to the counter. There's the video store again. Underneath the MAIN STREET VIDEO sign is a banner that wasn't there yesterday: PLAINVIEW CHARGERS SEASON OPENER. Underneath the bright blue letters is the high school mascot—a really pissed-off blue bull. Smaller type underneath the bull reads FRIDAY, AUGUST 28, 7 P.M. RAFFLE FOR A MONTH OF FREE VIDEO RENTALS!

Football.

Michael used to be in the marching band.

It gives me an idea. "Are you going to that?" I point out the window.

Young Darby follows my gaze and looks less than thrilled. "Football isn't my thing. But my friend Michael's in the band, so . . . yeah. I'm going. We're gonna try for the month of free rentals too."

Okay. So there must not be any friction between me and Michael here, on August 24. I hated football games. It felt like every piece of Oak Falls I couldn't blend into—all in one place and turned up to eleven.

If I was going just to support Michael in the marching band, then things were fine between us. Better than fine. We were best friends.

"You go to high school at Plainview?" I ask.

"Yeah." Young Darby's voice drops to a murmur. "Unfortunately."

I look at my younger self in surprise. I know I didn't like high school. Obviously I know that. As soon as Greta Doyle showed up with boobs freshman year, which everybody immediately started talking about, it was one long slide into who was kissing who, who thought who was hot, who was cool because everyone else thought they were hot, and who . . . wasn't.

The girls I'd been friends with started dressing differently and wearing makeup and talking about boys they had crushes on, and I felt like I'd missed a step. Like they'd all discovered a secret entrance into a new kind of femininity and I was still wandering around outside the building looking for the door.

Eventually, I didn't even know how to talk to them anymore. I hung out with Michael all the time instead.

So I knew I didn't like high school. I just . . . hadn't expected my younger self to be this outspoken about it. Like it's all so much that Young Darby can't figure out how to keep it in.

"At least you've got Michael," I say, and I'm not sure if I'm trying to comfort Young Darby or myself.

"Yeah." Darby sighs. "Ten thirty-five, please."

I pull out my wallet and hand over my credit card. "Does Michael like high school?"

Young Darby swipes my card and shrugs. "I don't know. Michael's pretty good at letting things bounce off him."

Well, that's definitely not true. Or if it was at this point, it's not now. I picture Michael's face as he turned and walked back into his house, leaving me on the front porch.

That expression didn't belong to someone who knew how to let things go.

"Sorry . . ." Young Darby holds out my credit card. "This doesn't seem to be working."

I pull myself out of thoughts of Michael. "Really?"

"It's acting like the card isn't activated or something. Do you have another one or . . . ?"

Oh. *Duh.* I'm in 2009. Of course this card isn't activated. It didn't even exist; it's definitely not going to talk to the credit card company.

I grab it from Young Darby, quickly, because it's suddenly occurring to me that my name is right there on that card and my younger self is going to notice it any second, and then things will *really* get weird. "Huh. Yeah, it might be a new card." I tuck it back in my wallet. "Um, cash okay?"

The twenty I hand over doesn't seem to cause any trouble, and Young Darby counts out my change. The register lazily prints out a receipt. Young Darby tears it off and tucks it inside the book cover.

"There you go." Younger Me slides the book across the counter.

I stare at it. The transaction is over. I'm supposed to leave now. But I haven't found anything out. I've barely started. I don't know how to fix anything with Michael; I have no idea what's about to happen or why.

But every new question that pops into my head just sounds creepy.

How's everything with Michael these days?

Have you guys ever had a fight?

Is there any chance you're about to majorly hurt your best friend?

Even if this Darby didn't clock any of it as stranger danger, my younger self would probably still write me off as super weird.

I pick up the book. But I can't quite make myself leave. "I guess you're probably not excited about the school year, huh?"

I say it as casually as I can, hoping it doesn't sound like a creep-adjacent question. Hoping I can find out *something* if I can just extend this conversation for another minute.

Young Darby brightens. "Actually, I kind of am, but just because I'm not going back to Plainview. I'm going to a school on the East Coast for a semester."

My heart sinks. Finally, Young Darby sounds excited about something, but all I can think about is just how much distance that semester is going to put between me and Michael—in every sense. Just how painful everything will be when I get back.

"You won't miss your friends?" I ask quietly.

Young Darby glances out the window toward the Plainview Chargers banner, and then down at the counter, scratching a fingernail over a dent in the surface. "I guess."

I guess?

That just sends my heart sinking even further. What's wrong with me that *I guess* is the best I can muster? That makes it sound like Michael's an afterthought.

Or else I'm still just a total stranger asking a kid weirdly personal questions.

Ugh. Maybe this is hopeless. Maybe it's impossible to unravel why Michael and I fell apart when it hasn't happened yet.

No. I can't believe that. Because I'm here. Because for the third time since I've been back, I've walked into this bookstore and traveled.

There has to be a reason I'm here.

"You must be leaving for boarding school soon then, right?" I ask.

Young Darby glances up. "Yeah. September first."

I count in my head. Eight days.

So maybe I don't need to figure everything out right now. I have eight days. And if this is the third day in a row that I've walked into 2009, then it's reasonable to assume I'll be able to come back here tomorrow, right?

Young Darby doesn't seem to think I'm a creep now. I can come in tomorrow, look for another book, ask more questions. I can get to know my younger self. Maybe then it'll get easier to ask questions without seeming creepy.

As if this could get any weirder.

"Do you want a bag?" Young Darby asks.

"No, I'm good." I manage a smile. It feels marginally more natural. "Thanks for the help with the book."

Young Darby smiles back at me—and it looks genuine. "No problem."

I turn and leave the store. It occurs to me, just as I pass under the jingling bell, that I have no idea what's about to happen to this book I'm holding.

But when I get to the sidewalk, the book is still in my hands, as new and crisp as it was in the store. I open the cover and scan the receipt for the date: August 24, 2009.

The receipt is still crisp too.

The hair on my arms stands up again.

I close the book and look around at the street. I'm out in the sun again—no sign of the clouds I saw beyond the window in the bookstore. The stroller moms are gone from Magic Beans, and a couple people with laptops have taken their table.

I need to think. I need a minute to sit somewhere and be alone. I have no idea what time it is because my phone is dead, but I can't have been in the bookstore more than half an hour. I already feel wrung out.

I look back at the book in my hands. The Falls. Young Darby mentioned the Falls and sitting there with Michael, telling him the plot of the latest book in this series.

If I need someplace to be alone—maybe it's finally time to go back.

CHAPTER FOURTEEN

AUGUST 24

I don't remember exactly *when* I last went to the Falls. It was just something I did with Michael, regularly, until it wasn't. I don't even remember if we spent any time there that last week before I left for boarding school.

I remember the last time I *tried* to go to the Falls. It was the first warm day after I got back from boarding school. I told my mom I was going to take a walk in Krape Park, which was a lie, but I knew she wouldn't let me borrow her car if I told her I was going to climb up the old steps to the top of the Falls. She didn't think the steps were safe. Which they weren't. They'd been roped off, with a firm NO ENTRY sign, for as long as I could remember.

But Michael and I climbed them all the time anyway. And we weren't the only ones—at least on weekend nights or prom or homecoming. The Falls was a prime romantic make-out spot. Honestly, the fact that the steps were roped off just made it more alluring to everyone under the age of twenty-five.

The Falls are, I assume, what Oak Falls was named for, although I never bothered to actually try to find out if that was true. They're all the way at one edge of Krape Park and (since Krape Park is at one edge of Oak Falls) all the way at the edge of Oak Falls. On one side of Huron Road is Krape Park, and on the other side is unincorporated farmland. Literal cornfields.

The side of Krape Park that's closer to the rest of Oak Falls—the side that's right across the street from my mom's new condo—has a playground, a band shell, an antique carousel, and even an old fire truck for kids to play on. There's a gazebo with an outdoor grill and a ton of picnic tables. But past all that, there are trails that wind away through grassy lawns, a wildflower meadow, and a forest—which is where the Falls are.

It wasn't really that warm, the day I tried to go back to the Falls. It was what counted as warm when you'd just been through winter in Illinois. It was probably, like, fifty degrees. Half the people in town were in T-shirts.

I don't know exactly why I wanted to go back to the Falls. Maybe I just wanted something else besides the bookstore that hadn't changed. Maybe I wanted to claim it as mine, just by existing in it. Maybe I wanted to torture myself a little bit. Who knows. But I drove out in my mom's Jeep, pulled the Jeep off to the side of the road, and started down the paved path toward the Falls.

I only made it halfway. Then I saw Michael's bike, leaning against a tree.

And it hit me, with all the subtlety of a brick, that the Falls didn't belong to me. I couldn't claim them as mine, because Michael had already done that by being here the whole time I was gone. Of *course* he'd been hanging out at the Falls while I was away at boarding school.

In the back of my mind, I'd told myself he'd been avoiding the Falls. I'd told myself he didn't want to go back there without me.

But clearly, I was wrong. Just like I'd been wrong about everything else. Michael was probably up on the rock at the top of the Falls with Liz, since she'd replaced me in every other way possible.

So I turned around and went back to the Jeep. I sat in the driver's seat and cried. And selfishly, I wished Michael and Liz would come out of the park while I was there, so Michael would see me crying and feel bad. And then I cried harder because knowing I was selfishly wishing for that just made me feel worse.

I cried until my head hurt and my eyes felt puffy. Until my mouth tasted like salt. Until I ran out of energy to cry, and then I drove back home.

I didn't go back to the Falls for the rest of high school. I sat on the tire swing in the backyard instead and tried to pretend it felt as private and magical as the Falls had.

* * *

THE LONG, DRAWN-OUT buzz of a cicada is the only sound when I step out of the Jeep, except for a very faint rushing sound, like white noise— water plunging down the bluffs. I parked off the side of Huron Road, across from an overgrown sign that simply says FALLS, with an arrow pointing down the wooded trail. The rest of the road is deserted, which isn't all that surprising. The actual parking lot for Krape Park is all the way on the other side, near the merry-go-round and the playground and the parts of the park most people spend time in.

I cross the road, the paperback copy of *The Lightning Thief* in one hand. The temperature drops a good five degrees once I get into the trees. The path is dappled in sunlight and everything smells damp. The rushing sound grows louder, and then the trees clear away and there's the waterfall.

It's not really all that impressive as far as waterfalls go. It's not something you'd see a picture of online and go, *Wow, who needs to see Niagara Falls when I could see this!* It just looks like . . . a waterfall in the middle of a bunch of trees.

But for Oak Falls, it's exciting. I mean, the Falls are practically the only altitude change in the entire county. The landscape here is flat—so flat that for a science project in middle school, Michael and I once actually tried to figure out if Oak Falls was flatter than a pancake. (Result: inconclusive.)

But in this one spot in Krape Park, there's a bluff face that rears a good forty feet high, and water plunges down it, splashing over jagged rocks overgrown with moss, into a creek that winds away from the Falls and snakes off through the rest of the park. The steps are literally cut into the bluff face next to the waterfall. I have no idea how long they've been there, but they're worn and rounded now, leading up to the large flat rock at the top that Michael and I called the Lookout. A metal railing is bolted to the stone next to the steps—it looks like it's more rust than not-rust at this point.

I could sit by the edge of the creek. There's nobody here. It's private. Quiet. I might see a turtle.

But I'm overwhelmed and weirded out by *everything* and I feel like doing something a bit reckless.

So I tuck the paperback book into the waistband of my jeans and follow the edge of the creek to the base of the steps. I grab the rusted railing and give it a tug. It doesn't budge. Seems sturdy enough. I crane my head back and look up the steps to the top of the bluff, but I can't really see anything besides leaves. The Lookout is hidden behind all the tree branches.

Well. Here goes.

The steps are slippery under my sneakers. Mist washes over me, leaving droplets on my glasses. The roar of the waterfall fills my ears, and my hands feel damp and grimy by the time I finally reach the top. There's a dicey moment where the railing ends and I have to sort of scramble to pull myself onto the Lookout, but I make it.

And there, sitting on the rock in front of me, wearing running shoes and shorts and a ragged T-shirt, is Michael. Because apparently the universe is having a great time fucking with me.

We stare at each other.

How is he here?

Why is he here?

"Um." My heart thuds and I gasp for breath. That climb was definitely harder than I remember. "Hi."

He pulls out a pair of wireless earbuds. "Hi."

It's jarring to see him here after I was just in the bookstore, trying to ask questions about him. I feel guilty, like I was gossiping about him behind his back. "Sorry. I didn't know you were up here."

"No, it's fine . . ." He looks ruefully at his earbuds. "I didn't hear you coming."

"Well, I can go." I think. I lean forward, looking back down the steps. They look a lot steeper from up here. Clearly it's *possible* to get back down—Michael probably wouldn't have come up here if it wasn't, and obviously we used to go up and down all the time. But in this moment, I can't exactly remember how.

"No, don't," Michael says. He rubs the back of his neck self-consciously. "I was just taking a break from my run. You're . . . you don't have to go."

I look back at him, taking in the muddy running shoes and the T-shirt and shorts again. "You *run?*"

He blinks at me, and then he cracks a smile. "Well . . . it's more like jogging."

"Okay. You *jog*?"

He huffs out a laugh. "Yeah, I know. But I actually kind of like it now. It's a nice way to . . . think." He glances up, eyes meeting mine, and I'm pretty sure we're both remembering that the Michael I knew hated running. He had to jog around the football field in band camp, and he always complained about it.

"Do you still play trombone too?" I ask.

He pulls a face. "God, no. I quit as soon as I got to college."

I smile, but it feels a little tight. Seeing him here at the Falls, even this filled-out, grown-up version of him . . . I momentarily forgot we were anything except two people who'd known each other for ages and used to hang out up here and goof off. But now last night is creeping back into the space between us, hovering in the air like the mist rising off the Falls.

"Listen, Michael . . ." I shift awkwardly; the paperback book rubs against my back, and I pull it out of my waistband. "I'm sorry about . . . what I said. Yesterday. It was really nice of you to invite me over and introduce me to your friends, and I ruined it. We don't have to talk about it or anything, I'm just . . . sorry."

He looks at me, and his face is guarded, carefully blank, but something goes through his gray eyes. That same unreadable thing.

"It's okay." He looks away, down at the earbuds he's fiddling with, rolling them around on his palm. "And . . . I'm sorry too. I kind of deserted you."

I try to shrug. Try to deflect. "I had my ginger ale."

His mouth quirks up, but he looks self-conscious. His eyes land on the book in my hands. "Did you come up here to read?"

I look down at the copy of *The Lightning Thief*. It's hazy through my glasses—the water itself has mostly evaporated, but it definitely left spots. "Oh. Um. I don't know. I just picked this up from In Between on a whim and . . . felt like coming up here."

He frowns at the book. "Wait, that's . . . Is that Percy Jackson?"

My eyebrows jump in surprise. "Yeah. You remember?"

He glances up at me, and his face doesn't seem quite so guarded now. "Percy Jackson? Of course I remember." He holds out a hand, almost tentatively. I hand him the book, and immediately realize the receipt is still tucked in the pages—the brand-new, crisp receipt with a 2009 date on the bottom.

But Michael doesn't seem to notice. He just flips slowly and gently through the pages. A smile creeps across his face. "Man, I haven't thought about this in ages. You finished the series, right? I think I remember you recapping the last book."

Something twists in my chest—tender and painful at the same time. "Yeah. I read the last book the summer before . . . I left."

He pauses. Chews his lip and then closes the book. "Right."

He holds the book out to me, and I take it. I can feel us getting close again to whatever was off-limits last night. Whatever it is he doesn't want to talk about.

I swallow. "So . . . what about you? You still read Marvel comics?"

He snorts, and the tension seems to dissipate again. "I have absolutely no idea what is happening in the Marvel universe these days." He leans back on his hands. "Honestly, I think my students know more than I do. I'm officially old."

"What about Pokémon?"

He opens his mouth and hesitates.

I raise my eyebrows. "You still know stuff about Pokémon, don't you."

"Okay." He points one of his earbuds at me. "Yes, but only because that stuff sticks with you. Although . . ." He lets his breath out. "I might still have some of my action figures."

"And a plushie, apparently."

His ears redden. "And a plushie."

"That's practically a Pokéshrine."

It makes him laugh—a real laugh, deep and easy, and everything inside me lifts. "I mean, I was gonna go with . . . mementos, but sure."

"Mementos? Next you'll be calling them heirlooms."

He shrugs. "They could be valuable one day. I keep meaning to bring one to school—win some cool points with my students."

I raise an eyebrow. "Pokémon is cool now?"

He sticks out his lower lip. "Pokémon was always cool."

That makes *me* laugh. He's pouting. For a second, I could almost believe the two of us are sixteen again.

And then I kind of run out of laughs, and he seems to realize he's pouting at me and sucks his lip in. We both turn and stare out over the Falls.

"You still come up here a lot?" I ask.

He pulls his knees up and wraps his arms around them. "I guess. I mean, not every day, but I still like to come up sometimes."

"You think your students ever come up here?"

He grimaces. "I made a decision never to consider that a long time ago."

I grin. "Fair enough." My grin fades and I know I probably shouldn't ask the question that's in my head, but I can't help it. "You ever come up here with anyone else?"

I'm asking about Liz. And I'm asking about *back then*—senior year.

He looks at me, and once again I can't read his face. I can't tell if he knows what I'm really asking—or trying to ask.

He shakes his head. "No." He looks back out over the Falls. "Just by myself."

I nod. That answer doesn't make me feel better the way I thought it would.

"Did you ever come back here?" he asks.

It feels like a jab—poking at me. But I guess it's fair. I just poked at him. "What do you mean?"

I know what he means, and I don't even know why I'm trying to pretend I don't, so I'm not surprised when he says, "Did you ever come back here when you got back from boarding school?"

"No. I guess I forgot about it." I say this still staring into the mist rising above the Falls, because I can't bring myself to look at him and lie. But I also can't bring myself to tell him the truth. It feels too vulnerable to admit that I had a complete meltdown just because I found his bike. Maybe I'm worried he'll think I was childish, crying for that long in my mom's Jeep. Or maybe I'm worried if I tell him, I'll feel childish.

All he says is "Oh."

Does he sound disappointed? Am I just trying to tell myself he does?

We're quiet for a while, the white noise of the Falls filling the air.

Then he leans on his hands again and tips his head back, looking up at the dappled sunlight filtering through the leaves. "How's the packing going?"

Right. Topic change. We're getting too close to That Subject again. "Uh . . ." I try to pull my thoughts together. "Well, I discovered my mom kept all the embarrassing mugs I ever made."

He glances at me with a hint of a grin. "She kept the birthday mugs?"

"Every single one."

"Just be glad you don't live closer." He sighs. "My parents have been gradually unloading all my old crap onto me for years. They can't decide what to do with it, so now I have to."

"And . . . have you?"

"Not at all. Now it's sitting in *my* basement."

"Let me guess . . . band uniforms?"

He grunts. "So many band uniforms."

My mind drifts back to the banner I saw through the bookstore window, strung up over Main Street Video. "I still can't believe how many football games I sat through just to watch that shit band play halftime."

"Hey!" He shoots me an offended look. And then he shrugs. "Actually, yeah, we were totally shit. So was the football team, though."

"Yeah. You complemented each other nicely."

"Ouch." But he's smiling. "Actually, speaking of football . . . the season opener is this Friday. You should come."

For a second, I just stare at him. "What?"

"Plainview season opener," he says. "High school football? Friday night?"

"Yeah, I . . ." But I actually have no idea if I knew what he meant. Michael inviting me to a football game wasn't exactly something I expected to happen. Mostly because neither of us are in high school anymore. "You're going?"

"Well," he says, "I'm a teacher, so . . . yes, I generally go. Anyway, it's kind of fun. You know, now that I'm not actually on the field trying to play trombone."

I feel like my mind is trying to catch up, bumping over Michael teaching at our old high school, Michael going to football games as a teacher, Michael inviting me to go with him . . .

"Just a thought," he says.

Just a thought isn't something you say when you're extending a pity invite, right?

Just a thought feels like he's really asking—like he's letting last night go and trying again. Like maybe I didn't ruin everything after all.

"Yeah," I say. "I mean, if you're going . . ."

"Give me your phone number." He fishes his phone out of the pocket of his shorts. "I can text you the details."

He holds his phone out to me, unlocked. It feels weirdly intimate to take it. Like even though I'm obviously *not* going to look through Michael's text messages or his photos or this random app called AccuWeather (why isn't the regular weather app good enough for him?), I could. It's all there. Little bits of who he is, on a phone in my hands.

I enter my name and phone number into his contacts and hand the phone back.

"I'll text you," he says again.

I nod. Try to be casual around the fluttery feeling in my chest. "Great. Thanks."

Silence hovers between us, and then he slaps his hands on his knees— another Midwestern gesture for *time to go*—and pushes himself to his feet. "I should probably finish this run and get home."

"Yeah. Sure." I inch backward on the rock so he can get past me.

"See you," he says.

"See you."

And then he tucks his earbuds in and carefully swings his legs over the edge of the rock, turning around and going down the steps like a ladder, one hand on the railing. He disappears from view pretty quickly behind the bluff face because the steps are *steep*. But I catch a glimpse of him through the trees once he's on the ground—jogging off down the same trail I walked in on.

So, he really does run.

I let my breath out, picking up the paperback copy of *The Lightning Thief*. I flip through the pages the way Michael did, slowly enough to catch familiar names as they pass by.

I should probably go too. Head back to the house and help my mom pack. I don't even know what time it is since my phone is dead.

Maybe I need to get an actual watch if I'm going to keep going back to the bookstore. Of course, then again, would a watch work any better than my phone? Maybe its battery would also die.

I groan, rubbing my eyes under my glasses. This is clearly not going to be a break. Even the white noise of the Falls can't shut out all the questions banging around my brain.

But I can't quite make myself leave. I climbed all the way up here. I want a minute to just *be here*. On the Lookout. Like I'm reclaiming it, as shallow and petty as that sounds.

I lie down on my back and squint up at the leaves overhead. It's not comfortable. The rock is hard and uneven under my back. I'm suddenly way too aware of my shoulder blades.

I close my eyes anyway, trying to unearth memories of being up here with Michael. Even trying to conjure up images of Michael up here by himself.

Like maybe between those two things, I'll be able to overwrite all the times I pictured him up here with Liz, that last year of high school, like recording over a videotape.

CHAPTER FIFTEEN

AUGUST 25

It's raining in the morning—the kind of summer rain that plunges the temperature by ten degrees in twenty minutes and smells like dirt and makes the air and the kitchen floor and every surface I touch feel vaguely sticky.

Mom and I stand on the front stoop, holding coffee mugs, and watch the rain for a while, Mr. Grumpy sitting between us.

"Well," Mom says, with a sigh, "I guess we won't be cutting down the tire swing today."

I look at the puddles forming in the front yard. "Yeah, I'm not going out in that."

Mom leans around me, squinting at Jeannie Young's yard. "On the plus side," she says, "at least you-know-who won't be adding to the penguin herd today, either."

I follow my mom's gaze to Jeannie's yard. I'm pretty sure Jeannie hasn't actually added to the penguin herd since I've been back. Not in the front yard anyway.

Although, then again, there are so many penguins already, I probably wouldn't notice if a few more showed up.

"I think you're going to miss the penguins when you move," I say.

Mom just huffs and stalks back inside.

I keep putting off going back to the bookstore, waiting for the rain to stop. But it rains all morning, so I help Mom pack things up to donate—clothes she doesn't wear anymore, old coats, random kitchen tools and dishes, the skis from the basement.

"I still don't remember ever buying skis," she says, as we haul them out to the garage. "Or going skiing."

"Maybe they came with the house," I say.

She considers. "I suppose that's possible. Like the underwear in the laundry chute."

We set the skis down. "I'm sorry . . . the what?"

"You know . . . the laundry chute!"

The laundry chute was a feature of our house that I was always kind of disappointed didn't work when I was a kid. It seemed so cool—you open this little door in the hallway and fling your laundry in, and it goes down a chute to a basket at the bottom. You never have to carry a laundry basket down to the basement.

"Hang on," I say. "You told me we didn't use the laundry chute because it *didn't work*."

"Well, it didn't," she says. "There was very old underwear in the way. And I certainly wasn't going to touch it."

"Mom, you're about to sell this house."

She gives me a very innocent look. "And then it will be the new owner's problem."

It's still raining when we pause to make sandwiches for lunch. And still raining after lunch, so we sort through the books and CDs in the living room. (She won't part with any of her CDs, even though I try to explain that she can put all that stuff on her phone now.)

By the time we've divided the books into two piles—books going to the condo and books my mother is planning to dump on Michael and his classroom—the rain is finally letting up, turning first to a thin drizzle and then disappearing completely. But there's a small lake in the back-yard, and my mom decides she's run out of steam, so we put off cutting down the tire swing. She sits down on the couch to read, Mr. Grumpy flopping beside her, and I steal her keys and head for the Jeep.

I drive to the bookstore with the windows down, letting in damp air that's so cool, I actually shiver. The tires make a *whooshing* sound on the wet pavement, and the edges of the sky are deep, rich blue. I can see dark vertical streaks in the distance—rain falling very far away.

The clouds are clearing off when I pull up in front of the bookstore. It's almost three o'clock. I hope Young Darby is still here. I didn't always work until closing since I was technically part-time. And anyway, Hank knew I was going to leave for a semester, so he'd hired a couple other people to help keep the store running, and by the end of August, I was splitting time with them.

I pull open the door and walk in under the jingling bell.

For once, the store isn't completely empty. My first thought is that people came in to get out of the rain—before I glance out the big picture window onto a bright, sunny street and realize that of course it's not raining *here*.

Not completely empty still isn't close to *crowded*. A couple people are browsing the table of new releases, there's a guy at the magazine stand, and a woman who looks vaguely familiar in the travel section.

I squint at her. I think she might be a substitute teacher at Plainview.

I suppose it makes sense that there are more people here in the afternoon. Especially at the end of summer. Oak Falls isn't exactly a place where people head out for vacations like clockwork, the way they do in New York, where the whole city empties out in August. But Michael's family used to go camping occasionally. Other kids in school went up to the Wisconsin Dells or down to Disney World.

But it's late in August now. The first football game is on Friday. Anybody who's been on vacation is probably back.

I glance toward the register. Young Darby is sitting behind it, elbows resting on the counter, reading a book. The box fan is set up on the chair again, sending a musty breeze through the store. I tug on my shirt, flapping it to cool myself off. It's definitely warmer in here than it was outside just now.

Even though I technically had all morning to think, I still haven't come up with any brilliant questions to ask my younger self. All I've got is what I had yesterday: strike up a conversation and try not to act like a creeper. At least Young Darby vaguely knows who I am now; hopefully I seem like a nonthreatening presence.

All the same, maybe I should browse for a while just to be safe. So it looks like I came here for the bookstore, and not just to talk to the kid behind the counter.

Behind me, the bell over the door jingles again.

I turn toward the sound automatically—and my mouth goes dry.

It's Michael. Standing just inside the door, pulling crumpled dollar bills out of the pocket of his cargo shorts. He's wearing geeky black glasses and a Captain America T-shirt. He's lanky. Gawky. His nose is a little too big for his face again. His vague curls are an overgrown mess.

This is sixteen-year-old Michael, and he's so familiar, it's like someone punched the air out of my lungs. *He's here.*

Of course he's here. He came by the bookstore all the time while I was working, especially in the summer.

It seems obvious now—why *wouldn't* he be here—but it never once occurred to me until this moment that he would be. That I might actually see him here. Maybe because I haven't seen anyone else enter or leave the bookstore . . . at least not yet, not while I've been inside it. Every time I crossed the threshold, I felt like I was stepping out of reality into a remote, removed bubble. Not the real world, even if I knew, in the back of my mind, that it was 2009 and I was about to ruin my friendship with Michael. All of that was certainly real.

But also, time travel, especially backward, is supposed to be impossible. My brain wasn't exactly focused on working out every single rule of how any of this was happening, because none of it was supposed to be possible in the first place.

I turn back to the table of new releases, my mind spinning. *Don't stare at Michael.* I pick up a book and flip open the cover. But I don't read it—I don't even know what book I'm holding. I watch Michael from the corner of my eye as he goes up to the counter.

Young Darby looks up from the book and breaks into a grin. "Hey."

"Hey." Michael lays the crumpled dollar bills on the counter. "You have it?"

Young Darby slides off the stool and crouches down behind the counter, emerging a second later with a thin, brightly colored booklet, presenting it to Michael like it's some kind of rare treasure. "*Lockjaw and the Pet Avengers*, number four, baby."

"Sweet." Michael takes the comic and opens it carefully, eyes scanning the pages. "Oh man, I'm so excited. This is gonna be *epic*."

Young Darby's eyebrows go up. "Seriously? *Pet Avengers*?"

"What?" Michael sounds defensive.

"Nothing." Younger Me shrugs. "It's just, you know . . . the Avengers. But pets. Seems kind of *un*epic."

Michael sticks out his lower lip—the same fake pout I saw at the Falls yesterday. "You're making fun of me."

"I'm just saying!"

My chest tightens, watching how comfortable my younger self is with Michael, and how comfortable Michael is with me. The way they lean close to each other, elbows on the counter, Young Darby rocking slightly on the wobbly stool.

Michael stops pouting and his mouth turns up into a familiar crooked grin. "Okay, but I think this series is actually really inventive once you get into it. It's weird, but it's fun."

"*It's Weird but It's Fun: The Michael Weaver Story,*" Young Darby deadpans. I wince.

But Michael just laughs. "*I Incessantly Make Fun of My Friends: The Darby Madden Story.*"

Okay, I deserved that.

Young Darby snorts and picks up the crumpled dollar bills, sticking them in the cash register. "So how long before I find out what happens in the epic finale?"

Michael sets the comic down on the counter and slowly pages through it. "You could just read these yourself, you know."

"You could read the last Percy Jackson book yourself too."

Michael shrugs. "I like our trade. You recap Percy Jackson; I recap *Pet Avengers.* It's like our own personal Television Without Pity."

Young Darby does an eye roll, wrestling the cash register drawer closed. "Yeah, except Percy Jackson is good, so I don't have to be snarky about it."

I'd completely forgotten about Television Without Pity. It was one of Michael's discoveries. A group of people with usernames like Couch Baron literally just recapping episodes of television online, sometimes for twenty pages. Usually with a lot of sarcasm. The recaps were too long for me—I'd check out somewhere around page seven.

"They're not all snarky," Michael says. The fake pout makes a brief reappearance. "Some of the *Buffy* recappers really liked the show. They only get snarky about, like, the actually *bad* episodes."

"I know, I know. You've said that." Young Darby finally gets the cash drawer closed with a slam. "What are you going to do when I go to boarding school anyway? Recap comic books to the lunchroom at large?"

I clearly mean it as a joke. My younger self looks up with a grin, and Michael smiles back, but it looks less comfortable. Strained. "Um, about that . . ."

"What?"

"Well, it's not really related. But there was this thing I wanted to do, before you left . . ." Michael hesitates, shoulders rising up to his ears. He and Young Darby look at each other. The fan whirs through the stillness.

My heart creeps up my throat. I don't know why, but I feel like the air has turned thick.

Michael looks back down at the comic. His shoulders lower. "I was just gonna ask if you want to watch some *Buffy* before you go." His voice is low. "Like . . . the greatest hits, or something."

"Oh, sure." Young Darby nods. "I'm off at four. We could go to the video store."

What?

I look at Michael, still studying the comic book in front of him. That isn't what he wanted to say. Whatever it was—whatever it *really* was—it was clearly a lot bigger than that.

But my younger self doesn't seem to notice.

And Michael just goes along. "Yeah, okay. We could see what episodes they have."

(They'll probably have all of them. They always did. I'm pretty sure nobody was renting the *Buffy* DVDs except us.)

"I was just joking, you know," Young Darby says, a little more seriously. "You can totally write me your own TWoP recaps for whatever comic you're reading if you want. After I leave. I mean, I'll have email."

"Yeah. Totally." The corner of Michael's mouth turns up, but it looks half-hearted.

"Or there's Facebook. And I'll have my cell phone." Young Darby pauses, thinking. "Although texting a whole Marvel recap seems like a pain in the ass."

That makes me smile, a little. I didn't get a smartphone until college, and Michael didn't have one, either—at least not in August 2009. We both had old flip phones and texting anything long was a chore.

Michael nods, but he doesn't look that enthusiastic.

Young Darby sighs. "It's just a semester."

"Yeah, I know." Michael sounds tired. I get the sense they've had this conversation before.

"And I wanted you to apply too." Now my younger self's voice sounds hurt. Or bitter.

"I *know*." And Michael sounds frustrated. "Look, it sounds cool and stuff, but I told you, it's just . . . really far away. And, I don't know . . . I kind of want to stay here."

Young Darby snorts. "Yeah, who *wouldn't* want to stay here."

It's an annoyed mutter, but it digs into me, sharp and unsettling.

Michael leans away, pulling into himself, shoulders hunching up again. "It's not all bad," he says, and it sounds like something he's said before.

Young Darby pulls a face. "For you, maybe."

God, what's *wrong* with me? That sounded almost mean.

Michael's shoulders go higher, his chest caving in. But Young Darby is stubbing a thumb against the counter, frowning at it, and isn't looking at Michael at all.

I'm tempted to walk over and shake myself. *You're being a dick.*

The bell over the door jingles again. I turn to look. So does Michael.

In walks Natalie Linsmeier, holding hands with Brendan Mitchell. My skin prickles—she looks just like I remember her. Long blond hair parted on the side, long eyelashes, a small nose. She and Brendan were crowned homecoming king and queen this year, and nobody was remotely surprised. Natalie sailed through everything with a kind of confidence that made me both extremely annoyed and kind of jealous.

I glance at Young Darby. Even now my younger self looks like this day has definitely taken a turn for the worse.

Natalie pulls Brendan toward the counter. "Hey, Darby. Do you have the new Hunger Games book yet?"

Young Darby gives her a look that suggests this isn't the first time somebody's asked this question. "No, it comes out next Tuesday. We've got the first Hunger Games if you want that."

"Oh, great." Natalie turns without looking at Michael and tugs Brendan off across the store. "I haven't even read the first one yet, but, like, *every-body* else has read it now, so I need to catch up. Rebecca told me the second one was coming out and I don't want to get behind."

"Uh-huh," Brendan says, like he has no idea what's happening, which he probably doesn't. I'm not sure I ever saw Brendan with a book.

I look back at Michael and Young Darby. Young Darby is looking at something on the computer, but Michael is staring after Natalie and Brendan, and his face looks so unguarded and vulnerable that my breath catches.

I don't know what that look means, but it makes me ache.

"I'm gonna go." Michael turns back to the counter and picks up the comic. "Meet at the video store after you're done?"

Young Darby glances up from the computer. "Yeah, sure." A flash of anxiety goes across my younger self's face. "You can just hang out if you want. I mean, I'll be off in, like . . . half an hour."

Michael's eyes dart to the other end of the bookstore, where I can hear Natalie still talking to Brendan about *The Hunger Games.* "Um . . ." He chews his lip. "Yeah, I think I'm gonna go get a slice at Prime or something. I'll see you in a bit?"

He's already straightening up, like he can't wait to leave.

Young Darby shrugs. "Okay. See you in a bit."

Michael turns, holding his comic with both hands, like it's some kind of protective shield, and heads for the door.

Natalie lets out a peal of laughter just as he opens the door. He looks toward them again—wherever they are in the aisles—and then leaves. The bell jingles. The door creaks closed behind him.

What was that about?

I look down at the book I'm still holding, open to the first page. Natalie and Brendan didn't even seem to notice Michael. Why was he looking at them like that? Like some tiny piece of his world was about to end?

And why was Young Darby being such an asshole?

My mind goes back to Olivia, asking with shock why I'd want to move back to someplace I hated.

I close the book and set it back down on the table, glancing up at the book clock above the storage room. It's just after three thirty. I'd better do this now if I'm going to.

I walk up to the counter and say, as casually as I can, "I didn't know this store had comic books."

Young Darby jumps a little, eyes moving from the computer to me. "Um . . . we don't?"

I do my best to look confused. "Sorry. I thought I saw someone picking one up."

Young Darby stares blankly, and then it clicks. "Oh. Yeah. Well, we don't really have them usually, but we can order just about anything, so . . . That was my friend Michael, actually. He orders pretty much every new Marvel comic."

So Young Darby definitely remembers me from yesterday and remembers that Michael came up. "I didn't mean to eavesdrop," I say, carefully, "but I heard you mention that you're going to boarding school, and, uh . . ." *Here goes.* "I did that too. I mean, I went to boarding school in high school, just for a semester."

Young Darby looks interested. "Oh, really? I'm going to this program in upstate New York. Is that where you went, or . . . ?"

I hesitate. It's tempting to say yes. But how likely is it that some random stranger my younger self doesn't know would just *happen* to have gone to the exact same boarding school program?

I'm too afraid of making Young Darby suspicious. "No, I went to a place in Connecticut," I lie. "It was cool, though. Kind of a big change."

"Yeah, exactly." Young Darby sounds enthusiastic. "That's why I want to do it. Just, like . . . go somewhere else."

"Right," I say, but something in my chest is tightening again. Did I really just *miss* how tense Michael got the minute the subject of me leaving came up?

For a second, I think about saying fuck it and telling my younger self everything. Telling this kid, *Don't get in a fight with Michael whatever you do.* Hell, maybe even saying, *You're trans! Figure it out already!*

But I bite my lip. Keep it in. I've seen *Back to the Future.* I know messing with my own future is a phenomenally bad idea. Or at least—I have every reason to assume it would be.

And anyway, why would Young Darby believe anything I say? I'm a stranger. I'm not supposed to know this stuff, and if I had to explain why I know it . . .

Then what? I try to convince this version of me I'm from the future? I'm sure that would go well.

So all I say is "Yeah. Just a semester."

"Did your cousin like *The Lightning Thief*?" Young Darby asks.

Now it's my turn to stare blankly until my brain catches up. "Oh. Yeah. Big hit."

But before I can come up with something else to say, the floor creaks behind me, and I hear Natalie Linsmeier giggle. She and Brendan have reappeared, and she's clutching a book. I recognize the black and gold cover of *The Hunger Games*.

They're clearly heading for the register, so I step back, out of the way. Natalie sets the book down and pulls her wallet out of a small fringed purse. "You're literally going to be the only person at school who hasn't read it," she says. Clearly talking to Brendan.

"I don't really read," Brendan says, like this is very cool.

I retreat to the magazine stand, glancing up at the clock. It's 3:40. Any minute now, Hank will probably show up to take over, and Young Darby will fill him in on how the day's been going.

Natalie is counting out cash for the book while Brendan stares out the window. Young Darby looks ready for them to leave.

I could wait. Talk to my younger self again as soon as Natalie's bought the book.

But I don't know what to say. I'm too stuck on Michael's face as he watched Natalie and Brendan. Too stuck on the edge in Young Darby's voice—*for you, maybe.*

Too stuck on just how much my younger self seems to be missing. And I don't know how to change that. Or if I should.

I still have no idea what's going to blow everything up between me and Michael, but I'm beginning to think Michael might have a good reason for getting upset.

I don't know what to do with any of this. And I can't figure it out in the next twenty minutes.

On impulse, I turn for the door. I don't have forever, but I'm not out of time yet. I've got days still to go before Young Darby leaves. I can come back tomorrow.

CHAPTER SIXTEEN

AUGUST 26

I mean to go back the next day. I really do.

But Mom ropes me into a trip to the grocery store—the big County Market that's out by the health clinic—and on the way back, she wants to swing by the Strickland farm stand because "corn season's practically over, Darby, and we need to enjoy it." And my mother picking out ears of sweet corn takes at least fifteen minutes. She has a whole method. I still don't get it.

And then once we're back at the house, I get pulled into sorting through things in the bathroom, and then in the pantry, and then it's suddenly the middle of the afternoon and I'm standing in the middle of the kitchen with a plastic bag full of expired spices when my phone vibrates in my pocket.

I heave the plastic bag onto the counter and pull out my phone. It's a text message from an Oak Falls area code.

> Hi, it's Michael. Game starts at 7 tonight if you're still interested. Let me know if I can give you a ride.

"Mustard probably stays good for a while, right?" my mom says.

I blink, looking up from my phone. "What?"

"Mustard." She's standing by the pantry, holding up a yellow plastic bottle. "It's two years past expiration but I haven't opened it yet."

"God, no, Mom, get rid of the mustard."

She looks disappointed. "Fine. Who are you texting?"

I erase everything I just entered into the message window, which is fine because it was terrible anyway, and stuff my phone into my back pocket. "Just . . . Michael texted me. About the football game tonight—he's going and wondered if I wanted to come."

"Oh, I was meaning to ask you about that!" Mom throws the mustard into the trash can across the kitchen, suggesting that in another life she could have been a professional basketball player, if they took women who were five-foot-two. "I'm going with all my old teacher friends. I was going to ask if you wanted to come along."

"Since when do you go to the football game?"

"Since always!" She pauses, considering. "Actually, that's not true. I started going after you went to college. It's a nice way to get out of the house. I mean, everybody goes."

Well, I don't know about *everybody*. Oak Falls supposedly has eight thousand people in it, and the football games weren't *that* well attended.

But the bleachers were usually more full than not, even though the team sucked and the marching band was unintentionally avant-garde. Maybe she has a point.

Mom picks up the plastic bag of spices from the counter and heaves it into the trash can. "What did you tell him?"

I jerk out of vague memories of bright lights and bad hot dogs. "Who?"

"Michael!"

"Oh." Nothing. Yet. "Um . . . I guess I'll probably go."

"Great!" Mom beams at me. "Ask him if he needs a ride. I'm happy to swing by. We can pick him up."

Is she serious? "He's a grown man, Mom, I don't think he needs a ride."

"It can't hurt to ask! It's practically on the way."

She's not going to drop it now that she's had the idea, so I give in. Pull out my phone and type out a text.

ME

Thanks for the info! Definitely still interested. And my mom wants to know if you would like a ride. Sorry.

Three little dots pop up. Michael typing.

Haha, that is very kind of Phyllis, but I'm all set. See you there!

I can't decide whether to be vaguely bummed that he won't be picking me up tonight or weirded out that he just called my mom by her first name. Which is an incredibly grown-up thing to do and I guess makes perfect sense because they run into each other all the time around town. And it doesn't stop it from being strange.

I clear my throat. "He's good on a ride. I'll just meet him there."

Mom shrugs. "Okay, then." She pulls out her own phone. "Well, in that case, I'm going to text my teacher group chat. They'll all be thrilled to know you're coming."

They will?

I guess I never expected my mom *not* to talk about me to her friends, but since I haven't seen her friends for years, I also never had to think about it until now. I suddenly feel very unprepared for this football game.

Something else occurs to me. "Since when do you know what a group chat is?"

Mom looks offended. "I learn things! Jeannie's grandson told me all about group chats the last time he was here. Jeannie had him over to help with that horrible inflatable penguin last Christmas . . ."

And she's off, ranting about just how garish and over-the-top Jeannie's penguin-themed Christmas display was, and how much traffic there was on our street because half the town drove through to see it.

I go back to my phone and add Michael's number as a new contact, typing his name into the boxes. Something warm blooms in my chest. I haven't had Michael's number since I got a smartphone. None of my contacts survived the great flip-phone-to-iPhone migration. It wasn't as big a disaster as it could have been. I wrote down a bunch of the phone numbers in my flip phone ahead of time, just in case.

But when I got to Michael's number, I skipped it. I told myself it was time to let it go. I wasn't Oak Falls Darby anymore. I was New York Darby. Somebody new.

I can't help smiling to myself, just a little bit, as I slip my phone back in my pocket. It's just a phone number.

But all the same, it feels kind of grounding, and kind of hopeful, to have it again.

I FEEL DECIDEDLY less grounded when we pull into the parking lot of Plainview High School.

Even if I didn't remember every single inch of the route to Plainview (which I do), the white glow radiating into the sky from all the football lights and the distant thrum of the drumline make the location of the high school pretty obvious. The sun is sinking low when Mom turns the Jeep into the big parking lot that sits between the high school and the football field. The parking lot is already half full, most of the cars clustered at the end closest to the field, and it's only 6:45. But Mom still hauls Mr. Grumpy out of the Jeep like we're in a rush.

"We need seats in the front," she says, clipping the basset hound's leash to his collar. "Mr. Grumpy doesn't like the stairs. Honestly, neither does Susan Donovan. They're bad for her hip."

Plainview High School is long and low, a rambling two-story beige brick building with an American flag flying out front in the middle of the wide lawn. It's peak Midwest architecture, spreading out like someone squashed a LEGO brick. The air smells like rubber and metal and popcorn, and the ground turns dry and dusty as we get closer to the bleachers. The drumline is out on the field, loud enough that the sound vibrates my sternum. The bleachers are slowly filling up, a sea of trucker hats and T-shirts and shorts and flip-flops. People talking and laughing over the noise of the drums.

"Ah, there they are!" Mom waves and hurries toward the front row of the bleachers, dragging Mr. Grumpy with her. "Darby, come on!"

I follow her to a group of people who are waving back. *Oh, god.* I recognize Mrs. Siriani, my high school physics teacher, as well as Mr. George and Mrs. Koracek-Smith. Looking at them on the Plainview website was weird enough. This feels surreal. They've all faded a little, gotten older, but as soon as Mrs. Siriani says it's nice to see me again, it's like I'm right back in physics. Her voice sounds exactly the same.

Mom tells them all how I'm here helping her move and then starts talking about the condo and all the packing. I'm just starting to wonder how rude it would look if I pulled out my phone and tried to text Michael when someone taps me on the shoulder.

I jump, twisting around, and there he is. Wearing a Plainview High School T-shirt and jeans. Hair relatively neat. Looking at me with an easy, lopsided grin.

"Hey," he says, "you made it."

Mom turns around and lights up with a smile when she sees him. "We did!" She looks back at the group of teachers on the bench. "Is there room for three, you think?"

"Oh, I'm actually sitting up there with some friends," Michael says, jerking a thumb over his shoulder. "I've got a spot saved for Darby—if you want to join us." He looks at me.

My stomach does a strange flip. "Yeah. It was, uh . . ." I look back at the teachers. "Nice to see you."

Mom gives my arm a squeeze, so at least she doesn't seem to think I'm deserting her. I turn and follow Michael.

"We're just up here," he says, pointing vaguely up the bleachers.

"Are your parents here?" I ask, and immediately wonder why I asked that. His parents didn't even always come out when he was in marching band. Mom's presence must be throwing me off.

He just smiles. "No, they're out visiting Lauren in Iowa this week."

"Oh. Lauren's in Iowa?"

"Yeah. She moved out there from Springfield a while ago. Her husband went back to help out on his family's farm."

Lauren is Michael's older sister, who I mostly remember lifeguarding at the pool when she was home from college for the summer. Whenever she wasn't lifeguarding, she was hanging out with her friends at the mall over in Monroe. We didn't see her all that much.

"Darby!"

I look up. In the second-to-last row of the bleachers, Amanda is standing up, enthusiastically waving her arms in the air. Next to her is Liz, busy leaning forward and talking to people farther down the row.

My stomach drops.

Sitting on the bleachers next to Liz is Rebecca Voss. She looks just like her picture on Plainview's website—sharp bob and glasses. And next to

Rebecca is a blond woman in a loose T-shirt, her hair in a high ponytail. Natalie Linsmeier.

The two guys next to them are familiar too. It takes me a minute to recognize Cody Garvin—his sandy hair is short now instead of swoopy, and he's wearing a very ordinary polo shirt, no popped collar in sight. But next to him, Brendan Mitchell looks almost the same—boring haircut, Gap T-shirt, cargo shorts. Like he walked out of a frat in 2014.

Since when is Michael friends with these people?

But he just holds up a hand to Amanda, like none of this is out of the ordinary. We slide in on the end of the bench, Michael next to Amanda, me next to Michael.

My insides have turned into a squirm of anxiety. It didn't even occur to me that I might run into people I went to high school with. Which . . . *why didn't I think of that?* I've stalked Facebook. Or I did—back when I had Facebook. I know plenty of people I went to high school with never left Oak Falls. Or if they did, they didn't go that far.

But I was just so focused on Michael . . .

"You guys remember Darby?" Michael gestures to me, and I manage a wave and something that feels like it might be at least related to a grin.

Rebecca, Natalie, and Cody all come back with variations of *Hey* and *How are you* and *It's been so long*. All I get from Brendan is a what's-up chin jerk.

At least none of them look confused. So either they stalked me on Facebook too, or they already know I'm trans because everyone in Oak Falls knows.

I rub my hands on my jeans, palms sweating.

A cheer goes up around us and the marching band kicks in, the bright brassy sound ricocheting off the bleachers and echoing into the air. They actually don't sound terrible. I must look surprised because Michael leans over and says in my ear, "They've gotten a lot better since Keegan took over as band director."

Right. Keegan. I saw him on Plainview's website. I guess it's nice to know he's doing a good job.

The football team runs out onto the field while the cheerleaders wave blue and yellow pompoms on the track next to the band. Cody and Brendan cup their hands around their mouths and yell, "Go Chargers!" Even Michael claps his hands.

Maybe he has to. He's a teacher. Showing support for the football team is probably required, especially in Oak Falls.

I suffered through enough football in high school to understand the rules. More or less anyway. Coin toss. Oak Falls wins it. Kickoff. The cheering dies down and the marching band troops off to wait for halftime.

Rebecca passes down a bucket of popcorn. "So, Darby, Liz said you're helping your mom move." She leans out and looks at me. "Are you back in Oak Falls now?"

"Oh. Uh . . ." I shake my head when Michael holds the bucket of popcorn out to me. My stomach is still churning way too hard for popcorn. "I'm not sure. Things are kind of open-ended."

"Your mom's house is over on Creek Road, right?" Now Natalie's leaning forward, raising perfectly shaped eyebrows, looking at me like she never called me a dyke in high school. "That's a nice area. You ever think of just buying your mom's house? You know, like Michael did?"

Michael shifts uncomfortably. "I inherited my grandma's house," he says.

Natalie doesn't seem to hear him. "Probably beats New York City prices, right?" She brushes her bangs out of her face. "I saw something online about how expensive those cities are. And just to *rent*, which is basically throwing money away."

I suddenly hear Joan's voice in my head, saying mildly, *But tell me, Natalie, how do you* really *feel?*

"It's definitely cheaper here," I say. Because it is, and wasn't that one of the reasons I was so fed up with New York? "But, I mean . . . it's pretty easy to get around. And there's a lot to do."

Why am I making excuses for the city I was so eager to get out of?

"You didn't worry about the crime?" Cody says, taking the bucket of popcorn Michael passes him.

I feel vaguely annoyed. "No."

"I think I'd just feel weird not knowing who my neighbors were," Cody says. "Here, I know I've got this guy down the street." He elbows Brendan and both of them laugh.

Now I feel frustrated. For one thing, having Brendan down the street actually sounds kind of terrible. But also, I recognized my neighbors in my apartment building, even if I didn't know their names. And honestly, sometimes it's kind of nice just how much New Yorkers ignore you. If you get lost on the subway, five people will give you directions. But you could have a full-on snot-nosed sobbing meltdown and nobody would even look at you. Like New Yorkers have way too much secondhand embarrassment to get involved, which somehow gives you room to be as embarrassing as you want.

Not that I have any personal experience with that. Because I definitely don't.

"What did you do in New York, Darby?" Rebecca asks.

"Um. I worked at a start-up." I regret it as soon as it's out of my mouth. I could have just said I wrote grant proposals for a company. But I knew start-up sounded fancier.

What the hell am I trying to prove?

"Oh," Rebecca says, and doesn't seem to know what to say next.

A chorus of groans goes through the bleachers around us. The band might be better, but the Oak Falls Chargers, apparently, are not, and they've already lost the ball.

Cody lets out a long-suffering sigh and glances down the row. "Got any plans for the weekend, Mike?"

Michael shrugs. "Mostly prep for school, I guess. Get my classroom set up."

And that leads to Rebecca commiserating about the lesson plans she has to do. And Brendan saying he has to go all the way out to the Home Depot in Monroe to get a new lawn mower because his old one broke.

And now they're basically ignoring me, which is better and worse at the same time. Because maybe I don't know how to talk to them, but now it's obvious they don't know how to talk to me, either. They don't know what to do with any of the pieces of me that aren't the same as the Darby they knew. And it doesn't even have anything to do with being trans.

On top of that, I forgot there would be mosquitoes and didn't put on any bug spray, and now I'm getting eaten alive.

I learn that Rebecca and Cody are engaged and planning a winter wedding. Even weirder, Natalie and Brendan are married. They have a two-year-old, who's currently at Cheryl's house while Natalie and Brendan are at the game.

And through all of it, Michael just sits easily next to me, cheering when something relevant happens on the field. Booing at a bad ref call. The only time I notice a flicker of something that's not quite so comfortable is any time Brendan opens his mouth. Michael's fingers tap on his knee when Brendan talks about what kind of lawn mower he wants to get (a riding kind, with an actual cup holder). Michael chews his lip and stares at his shoes when Brendan talks about how his two-year-old son wanted to play with a Barbie at day care. And when Brendan mentions Fox News—just in passing—I see Amanda reach over and casually put her hand on Michael's knee to stop him jiggling his leg.

I have no idea how I make it to halftime. But when the players finally wander off the field and the marching band troops on, I feel ready to explode. I don't know how to square any of these adults with the people I grew up with, and I don't know how to fit into this evening with any of them. It's not like football was ever my thing, but I feel like I'm stumbling through a role in a play, except I never read the script.

The marching band launches into some familiar pop song that I can't quite place, and Liz stands up. "I'm gonna get a hot dog," she says. "Anybody else want anything?"

I shoot to my feet like someone lit a firecracker under me, desperate for a chance to shake off this feeling that's even weirder than walking into the bookstore and traveling. "Yeah, I'll go with you."

I can feel Michael looking at me, but I don't look back at him. I'm too afraid of what I'll see if I do.

"Grab me a pop?" Amanda says.

Liz gives her a thumbs-up and then jerks her head at me. I hesitate for a second, kind of hoping Michael will stand up and announce he's coming along, but he doesn't move. Just turns and looks back out at the field.

So I follow Liz down the bleachers. My mom is still sitting with her teacher friends in the front row, talking and laughing, Mr. Grumpy flopped at her feet.

The concessions stand is around the far end of the bleachers, manned by two teenagers in Plainview High T-shirts and baseball hats. There's already a line forming.

"So they basically got all the same stuff they've always had," Liz says, as we join the back of the line. "Hot dogs, popcorn, fries . . . Also, sorry Natalie's a jerk."

That catches me off guard. "Um. What?"

Liz just raises an eyebrow at me. "Oh, come on. You looked like you wanted to throttle her."

Shit. "Sorry. I didn't actually mean to."

She snorts. "Oh, I know. Natalie and Brendan are just . . . you know, buy-the-house, mow-the-lawn, have-the-two-point-five-kids people. And Brendan can be a bit of an asshole."

I think back to Michael jiggling his leg. To the younger version of Michael looking at Natalie and Brendan in the bookstore with that vulnerable expression.

"But you guys are all . . . friends?" I ask.

Liz sticks her lip out, thinking. "I mean, we all live here," she says. "We see each other all the time. Rebecca's not bad. And Cody and Natalie and Brendan . . ." She lets her breath out. "We can hang out with them at the game. We don't need to invite them for Thanksgiving. You know?"

"Yeah," I say, but I'm honestly not sure if I do. The bright blast of the marching band, the closeness of the people in line, the salty smell of fries and popcorn . . . it's all a wave of familiarity and strangeness that's drowning me. I should have realized Michael would have other friends to see at this game. He's had years in Oak Falls. He knows everyone here. Michael inviting me to tag along didn't mean we were going to have some lovely evening all to ourselves. It's a *football game.*

I feel like a fool and also like I'm rapidly devolving into my jagged sixteen-year-old self. Like maybe Michael is out in that marching band and I better get back to the bleachers before I miss the whole halftime show.

I hold up one hand and stare at it. The creases in my wrist, the freckle on my thumb, the hair that runs up my arm. *I am not that Darby I saw back in the bookstore.*

So why can't I just go back up to the bleachers and cheer when the Chargers catch a pass? Why can't I sit the way Michael was sitting on the bleachers—legs apart, elbows resting on his knees, a confident kind of masculinity that just . . . exists, fitting in seamlessly with Cody and Brendan and every other guy here?

I should be able to speak this language. I spent plenty of time here. I know how all of this works.

And I still don't fit.

A mosquito lands on my arm. I slap at it, but it gets away. Of course.

Okay, fuck it. I need a break. From the goddamn mosquitoes if nothing else. Why didn't Mom remind me about bug spray?

"Darby."

I look up. Liz is staring at me, eyebrows raised. We've reached the front of the line. The teenager behind the stand is clearly waiting for me to order.

"Uh, actually, I'm good." I jerk a thumb over my shoulder in the direction, vaguely, of not the football game. "I'm gonna get some air for a minute."

Liz gives me a look that clearly says, *We're outside; you're not fooling anyone.* But all she says is "You do you." She turns back to the concessions stand.

And I turn and head for the parking lot. The noise from the marching band turns more diffuse the farther I get from the bleachers. Bouncing into the air, blurry and vague.

On an impulse, I head for the high school, crossing the lawn, which is starting to dry out in the end-of-summer heat. The grass crunches under my shoes. I go up the front steps and tug on one of the doors. It's locked.

Which makes perfect sense. What high school wants random adults wandering in, especially these days?

So I turn around and sink down on the cement steps. Maybe it's for the best that I can't get into the high school. It would probably just make all of this . . . *this* . . . worse.

I'll just sit here and get mauled by mosquitoes. It seems kind of appropriate. I'm perfectly aware I'm feeling sorry for myself and cowardly, and yet I'm still sitting here—feeling sorry for myself and cowardly. I might as well let the mosquitoes drive home how much of a fool I am.

I catch a flicker of movement from the corner of my eye—someone crossing the parking lot toward me, just a shadow against the bright lights from the field. Maybe I'm not alone in being done with the football game.

"Darby?"

It's Michael—he's close enough now that I can see his face as he crunches across the lawn toward me, hands in his pockets.

Terrific. Now I really feel like a loser. "Hey."

He reaches the bottom of the steps and stops. "Liz said you were hiding."

"I'm not hiding." I'm definitely hiding. "I was stretching my legs."

He glances past me to the doors. "Were you trying to get in the school?"

I cringe. "God, you saw me?"

"There are restrooms over by the concessions stand if you need one."

My face feels like it's on fire. "No, I'm fine, I was . . . I was honestly just trying to get away from the mosquitoes." It's not untrue. Even if I'm not sure it's the whole story.

His eyebrows jump. "Oh."

"Yeah, I know. I forgot bug spray."

"Rookie mistake, Madden." It comes out teasing. But not unkind. "Come on, I've got some in my car."

I push myself up and follow him through the parking lot to an old white Toyota pickup truck, sitting in a spot marked with a RESERVED sign. "Wait a minute. This isn't—"

"No." Michael unlocks the truck and shoots me a small grin. "It's not quite *that* old."

It looks almost exactly like the pickup truck that belonged to his dad—the one he learned to drive in, the one he used to pick me up in when it was too cold to bike around Oak Falls. The one he drove Liz to school in, senior year, when we weren't talking anymore.

"You got a clone of your dad's truck?"

The grin turns self-conscious. "It's ten years newer. I swear. It just happened to come in to Davis Toyota when I needed a new car." He slams the door and tosses me a small aerosol spray bottle.

I catch it, which I actually feel mildly cool about, given that the lights from the football field don't do much good out here, and I've never been athletically coordinated. "Thanks." I spray my exposed arms, wrinkling my nose. "This stuff is foul."

"It's the smell of summer," Michael says.

A last finishing flourish from the marching band echoes into the air, followed by a distant cheer.

I glance in the direction of the football field. "I guess we should, uh, go back."

"Football still really isn't your thing, huh?"

I look at him in surprise. And then I feel guilty. "Was it that obvious?"

He holds out his hand, and I toss the bug spray. He catches it easily. "Just now or back in high school?"

Oh. I rub the back of my neck, suddenly too warm, even in the cooling evening. "So I'm basically the worst is what you're saying."

The look he gives me is painfully familiar—forehead wrinkled up, eyes unguarded. It's all concern and caring, and it drills a hole straight through me. "No, sorry, that's not what I . . . I just meant, I knew it wasn't your scene, and you showed up anyway, and that's . . . that meant a lot to me." He hesitates, and then says, quieter, "It means a lot to me."

My breath hitches.

Another cheer from the bleachers, and then the amplified, distorted voice of the announcer cuts through the air. The game is starting again.

Maybe it's all the ping-ponging I've been doing—inside the bookstore and outside of it, then and now. Maybe it's all the tangled, uncomfortable, leftover feelings from high school that got stirred up again the second I saw Natalie Linsmeier sitting on the bleachers. But suddenly I'm saying, "I really miss you, Michael."

Maybe I'm *still* ping-ponging between *now* and *then*, because I don't even know if I meant to say *I miss you* or *I missed you*. I just know I feel cut up and raw inside, and standing here, covered in bug spray next to a truck that looks just like the one he drove in high school . . . I don't care if I'm wandering too close to whatever's off-limits.

He's so still it's like he's turned to stone. His eyes are locked with mine, and I can't read them in the dark. But I don't look away.

And then, so suddenly it's like the ground shifts, he moves toward me, fingertips touching my chin, and kisses me.

It's the last thing I expected and simultaneously feels like everything I wanted without realizing I wanted it. The ache in my chest turns so sharp and desperate that I reach out and grasp his arms, but that just makes it worse—because now that I'm touching him, I only realize how far away he's felt and how much I wanted to touch him, like I needed to prove to myself that he was the same Michael I remembered.

And now, touching him, kissing him, I don't know if he is or if he's someone completely new.

And I don't care.

CHAPTER SEVENTEEN

AUGUST 26

I don't know which of us pulls away first, only that we separate. His fingers leave my chin and I let go of his arms. And now we're staring at each other. He's closer than he's been since I got back—maybe closer than he's ever been. Even in the shadowy parking lot, I could count his eyelashes and the bright pinpricks in his eyes from the distant football lights. I can hear him breathing and my heart hammering. I can feel his warmth.

And then he takes a step back, letting go of me. Something crosses his face that I can't read.

"I should go back," he says.

Wait. What?

But he's already retreating, moving away from the truck, from me.

"Michael," I say.

He turns away, shoulders hunching up to his ears. And he keeps walking, weaving through the cars in the parking lot, heading for the bleachers.

What just happened?

I stare after him, my mind spinning, and I can't decide whether I should yell at him or run after him, but I can't come up with anything to yell and my feet are rooted to the asphalt. How did he go from giving me bug spray to kissing me to abandoning me in the span of five minutes?

But now it's too late, because he's gone. Disappeared around the corner of the bleachers, and I'm alone.

What am I supposed to do now? I can't just go back to the bleachers and climb up and sit next to him again like nothing happened. I can't imagine getting through the rest of the football game, hanging on the edge of the conversation with Natalie and Rebecca and Cody and Brendan, pretending to be fine.

I bite my lip, and it still tastes like him—a little salty, a little like popcorn.

I press my fingers to my eyes under my glasses. And then I pull out my phone. But I don't text Michael. I text my mom.

> I'm sorry, I know the game isn't over yet, but can we go? I'm in the parking lot.

I swallow, blinking, because the corners of my eyes sting. My heart won't slow down.

MOM
> On my way.

MICHAEL DROVE ME to school on the last day of junior year, just like he had all week because his bike needed a new tire. But when he parked, we just sat there, staring at Plainview while a warm, early summer breeze wafted through the open windows of his dad's white pickup. Neither of us wanted to get out of the car.

"First thing you're going to do tomorrow," Michael said.

I blearily rubbed my eyes. "Sleep?"

He glanced at me with an expression somewhere between vague concern and deep judgment. "Did you go to bed in your clothes again?"

I looked down at myself. I was wearing cargo shorts and my *Veronica Mars* T-shirt, and they were both wrinkled. "I changed clothes before I got in bed," I said defensively. "It's not like these are yesterday's clothes. Ten extra minutes is ten extra minutes."

Michael sighed. I'd recently started going to sleep in the clothes I was going to wear to school the next day so I could sleep in a little longer in the morning. Sure, I woke up rumpled, but I didn't care; the extra sleep was worth it.

Of course, the only reason I needed those few minutes of extra sleep was because I was staying up way too late reading fanfiction. Which I hadn't told Michael. And I wasn't going to. It wasn't that I thought Michael would be pretentious about fanfiction or something. I had a feeling that if he knew there was Marvel fanfiction he'd start reading it immediately.

It was more that the fanfiction I was reading was . . . gay.

I'd only discovered fanfiction a few weeks ago, after Michael and I watched the episode of *Buffy* where Willow and Tara kissed for the first time. My heart pounded through the whole scene. They were just . . . kissing. Like it was fine. Normal. Nothing to comment on.

Later that night, I went looking for fan art. I wanted to see that kiss again. I wanted to see it become stylized and beautiful. And, I guess, I wanted proof that other people kept thinking about it too.

I found fan art. And then I found fanfiction.

"What's the first thing you're going to do tomorrow?" I asked Michael.

He chewed his lip, staring through the windshield at the front steps of the high school. People were already climbing them; we'd have to get out of the truck soon or we'd be late.

"Go to the video store," he said. He looked at me. "Want to rent the next *Buffy* DVD? We could do a marathon to kick off summer."

My heart fluttered in my chest. We hadn't watched *Buffy* in weeks—since the episode where Willow and Tara kissed. I was starting to wonder if Michael didn't want to watch anymore. I worried maybe it was the kiss. He hadn't said anything when it happened. Of course, I hadn't, either. It was too much. And anyway, the whole episode was, aside from the kiss, a huge downer, so we kind of quickly moved on.

"What about my mom's rules?" I said.

"Maybe she'd let you watch more than two episodes because it's summer?" Michael wiggled the truck key until it came free of the ignition. It tended to get stuck. "Like, we could say we're celebrating the end of school."

I shifted. It was warm enough that my T-shirt was sticking to my back, trapped against the ripped fabric of the truck's bench seat. "I guess I could try." I checked my watch. "We should go."

"Yeah." Michael kicked open his door, grabbing his backpack from the middle of the bench seat, and climbed down from the truck. "We could hit up the bookstore too. When do you start working again?"

"Next weekend." I slammed the passenger door, shouldering my own backpack. I'd worked occasional weekends for the last few months, but Hank had let me take a few weeks off to get through the end of the school year. "Why?"

Michael gave me a look that I recognized as his *I Want Comics* face. He was very good at puppy-dog eyes and genuinely didn't seem to even realize that's what he was doing. It was unfair.

"Oh, come on, seriously?" I rolled my eyes. "Why is it so hard to ask Hank to get your comics?"

"I *do* ask Hank," Michael said. "But Hank doesn't understand comics. He has to repeat the title back to me five times and then gives me this look like, *What is this drivel?*"

I laughed. "This is the real reason you hang out with me at the store. You just want me to keep working there so you can get your comics without talking to Hank."

Michael pulled open the front door of the high school, holding it while I walked through. But before he could walk through himself, Natalie Linsmeier and Rebecca Voss dashed in ahead of him.

"Thanks," Rebecca said.

Natalie glanced at me, her eyes moving over my wrinkled clothes. She didn't say anything to me. But I still heard her when she said to Rebecca, as they walked away, "God, it's so sad when pretty girls don't get how many more guys would hold the door for them if they just put in some *effort*."

"Yeah," Rebecca said.

Michael walked through the door and we started wandering slowly after them and everyone else, heading for homeroom. I think we were both dragging our feet to let Natalie and Rebecca get farther away.

"I didn't hold the door for Natalie on purpose," Michael said.

I knew that, but somehow the fact that he felt like he had to say it—like I needed reassurance that him holding the door had nothing to do with how pretty Natalie was . . .

It made me feel weird. Like we were both acknowledging that Natalie *was* pretty.

Like we were both acknowledging that guys probably *did* hold doors open for her.

Maybe that was why I asked, "Do you think I'm pretty?"

Michael's shoulders rose to his ears. "Um. What do you mean?"

I stopped. So abruptly that he kept walking a few steps without me. "What do you mean, *What do you mean?* It's just a question."

Michael's eyes skipped to my face and then away. "You mean, like, am I attracted to you?"

I felt embarrassed and disappointed and hurt, and foolish for feeling all of those things. "Never mind."

We were silent for the rest of the walk to homeroom.

ALL MOM SAYS when she meets me at the Jeep, Mr. Grumpy waddling along next to her, is "Ready to go?"

"Yeah." I feel childish that I had to text her and grateful that she showed up in the parking lot in less than five minutes, acting like nothing strange had happened. "Is that okay?"

"Oh, it's getting late." She hands Mr. Grumpy's leash to me and unlocks the Jeep. "Grumpy's ready for bed."

Mr. Grumpy just blinks slowly at me, his ears dragging on the ground. I lean down and heave him into the back seat.

We're quiet on the drive back to the house. The noise of the game fades and the darkness gets, well, darker, as we leave the high school behind. I roll down my window, letting cool air hit my face. A few fireflies wink by the side of the road, and the crickets are so loud that I can hear them even over the breeze buffeting my ears.

Mom pulls the Jeep up next to the rental car in the driveway. The motor sputters to silence, and then she looks at me. "Everything okay?"

"Yeah." I say it automatically, because it's always what I've said. Except for when I called her from New York.

And maybe that should have broken down whatever barrier has prevented us from talking about anything *real*, but I still can't bring myself to tell her what just happened. It's too fragile. Too complicated. And anyway, I've never talked to my mom about anybody I kissed. Not the kissing part anyway. She met my college girlfriend and my grad school boyfriend. She'd ask how they were when we talked on the phone. And it stopped there.

And I don't know how I would explain that this was *Michael*. This *is* Michael.

She runs into Michael at the grocery store. I don't know what to do with that.

Despite saying it was getting late, Mom plunks down on the couch as soon as we get inside. It's barely eight thirty, and she's clearly not actually tired.

"How about *Marble Arch Murders*?" she says, picking up the remote.

"Yeah," I say. "Sure."

I fold up on the other side of the couch while she pulls up the next episode. Mr. Grumpy wanders over, and we lean down together and lift him onto the cushion between us. I dig the fingers of one hand into Mr. Grumpy's short fur and make myself stare at the little old lady on the screen as the quirky music starts playing.

But I keep pressing my lips together, thinking of Michael's mouth against mine, and the closeness of him, and the pull of everything I wanted back.

I keep thinking of Young Darby in the bookstore, excited to go off to boarding school, with only a shrug at the thought of leaving Michael and Oak Falls behind.

I keep thinking of the way Michael said, *You mean am I attracted to you,* that last day of junior year, and the curl of hurt and embarrassment in my stomach.

"Mom?"

She blinks, jerking her attention away from the TV. "Yeah?"

I take a breath, hesitating, because this feels dangerously close to talking about something real. "Do you think it was good that I did that semester at boarding school?"

She glances back at the TV. The little old lady has just arrived in a scenic country village in the English countryside and is wandering around, commenting how it's not like London at all. "What do you mean?"

"I guess . . . sometimes I wonder if I missed something by leaving."

She runs her fingers along one of Mr. Grumpy's long ears. "Like what?"

"I don't know. Something important."

She hesitates. "I don't know if I can answer that for you, Darby." She looks at me again, and now her eyes are almost sad. "You didn't really talk to me very much."

My chest tightens, because of course she's right. And she still came right out to the parking lot when I texted her. She must have known something was up. Just like I'm sure, looking back on it, that she knew something was up all those evenings we watched reruns of *Frasier* together in the basement.

If she asked about school, I said everything was fine.

If she asked how my shift at the bookstore went, I said fine.

If she asked about Michael . . .

Well, she didn't really ask about Michael. Not after those first few weeks. When I first got back, she asked every once in a while if I was going to hang out with him soon. If I wanted to have him over and watch TV in the basement.

I kept saying no. I guess eventually she figured it out.

I wish, in this moment, that she would ask about Michael. Telepathically figure out, somehow, that she should ask. If she did, right now—I might tell her. Maybe I wouldn't tell her he kissed me, and I definitely, absolutely kissed him back. But I might tell her that I didn't get how Michael could just *fit* at that football game while I felt like a jumble of mismatched pieces, just like I did in high school.

Instead, all I say is "Sorry."

Mom reaches over and pats my leg. "You don't have to be sorry. And . . ." She sighs. "I think you wanted to leave, Darby."

My stomach twists. I know what she means. That it doesn't really matter if now, looking back, I wonder what I missed by going. Because when I was sixteen, I wasn't thinking about any of that. If I hadn't gone, I would have spent the whole semester wondering what I was missing by staying.

She means that I couldn't see any other option except to go—and since I couldn't, neither could she.

"Yeah," I say.

She puts her feet up on the coffee table, and I lean my elbow on the arm of the couch and set my chin in my hand. We watch the rest of the episode, letting it fill the room while Mr. Grumpy snores. I try to focus on all the ways this is new and different—the two of us surrounded by boxes, in the living room instead of the basement, on the couch instead of an old futon—instead of all the ways this feels familiar, and I feel just as empty.

CHAPTER EIGHTEEN

AUGUST 27

Michael hasn't called or texted by the next morning. I stand over the coffee maker while NPR blasts, trying to compose a text to him that isn't incredibly awkward.

Hey, Michael, it was great to see you last night, could we talk?

Sorry to text, do you have time for a chat?

So about last night . . .

I delete everything I type. I don't even know what I would say if I *did* talk to Michael. The only things I know are that I wasn't lying when I said I miss him, and I have no idea what that kiss meant, and I also don't regret it at all.

The back door opens and Mom comes in, nudging Mr. Grumpy in front of her. "How about a trip to the thrift store?" she says, her voice raised over the radio.

I set my phone down on the counter. "Um. Now?"

"After you have coffee. Grumpy wouldn't stop eating grass, so now we need to wait and see if he's going to barf." Mom glowers down at the basset hound at her feet, who's watching us placidly. "I need to buy more packing tape and Bubble Wrap anyway, so I figured we could run over to Main Street and you could help me unload everything at the thrift store."

My pulse speeds up. Going to Main Street means an easy excuse to stop at In Between Books. And I need to get back there. I need to talk to my younger self. I still don't know how, or what on earth to say, but if the present-day version of Michael won't talk to me . . .

Well, talking to Young Darby seems like the next best thing.

"Yeah. Sure." The coffee maker beeps and I pick up one of the birthday mugs—this one features a pink-haired stick person named Bob. A masterpiece by Darby, age seven. "Give me an hour to get caffeinated and take a shower."

OAK FALLS'S SINGLE thrift store is in the basement of First Church, the Presbyterian church at one end of Main Street, which has a plaque out front proudly proclaiming it as the oldest church in Oak Falls—in case *First* didn't make that obvious enough. It's an old brick building with a tall white steeple that has a big clockface on one side and a bell tower that still chimes on the hour.

The thrift store in the basement is basically like any other thrift store: random pieces of mismatched furniture, shelves of knickknacks, and racks of clothes that aren't remotely sorted, all under a low ceiling and ugly fluorescent lights. The old lady staffing the store just nods when we show her everything in the trunk of the Jeep and waves me and Mom to a back room to unload everything. It takes several trips, and by the end, my arms feel like wet noodles.

But Mom still lets out a contented sigh when we leave the thrift store and go back to the Jeep, where Mr. Grumpy is waiting. "Finally rid of those skis!" she says. "Now I can actually start running things over to the condo."

"You've got movers coming," I say, opening the passenger door and wiggling my way under Mr. Grumpy, who doesn't seem inclined to give up the seat.

"Yes, yes, but I'm not trusting them with everything. Some things are too precious." She turns the key and the Jeep rumbles to life. "Anyway, I've got to pick up the keys from Cheryl, so I might as well use it as an excuse to take a few things over there."

We leave the church parking lot and go all of twenty feet to a free spot on Main Street, so Mom can go to Floyd's in search of packing supplies. Noon on a Saturday is the busiest I've seen Main Street so far. Every table outside Magic Beans is full, and there are actually people waiting in front of the Oak Café.

"See?" Mom waves a hand at the cars that rumble past us on their way up Main Street. "Traffic!"

"Yeah. Sure." But I'm not paying attention. My eyes have gone, without me even thinking about it, to the frosted window of In Between Books just a few storefronts away.

Mom follows my gaze. "We should go in!"

I jerk. "What?"

"The bookstore!" Mom clips Mr. Grumpy's leash to his collar. "Let's see if Hank is there and you can say hi. You haven't seen him yet, right?"

I stare at her. But I'm not thinking about Hank. I'm thinking about something else.

Every time I've walked into the bookstore, I've been alone. No one's come with me—not since I've been back in Oak Falls.

What would happen if I walked in with my mom? Would she travel with me?

My heart slams against my ribs. Forget trying to take a picture with my phone; if I could take my mom with me and she could see everything for herself . . .

Well, I suppose her head might explode at seeing me and Young Darby at the same time. Maybe Young Darby's head would explode at seeing Mom, because there's no way the younger version of me wouldn't recognize *her*, even if she's older and grayer than she was in 2009.

I don't care. I want her to come with me. Because if she could, then I wouldn't be alone, trying to figure out *why* this is happening or what's going to happen between Young Darby and Michael or any of it.

And in this moment, I desperately want to not be alone.

"Yeah." My voice cracks. My throat feels like sandpaper. "Let's go in."

Mom hands Mr. Grumpy's leash to me, and I lift him down to the sidewalk.

"I hope Hank's here," Mom says as we walk up to the door. "He's not in the store much anymore. The latest I heard is that his daughter's taking over. You wouldn't have met her, I think. She grew up with her mom over in Monroe . . ."

I can hear my pulse in my ears. "Should we leave Grumpy outside?"

"Oh, they don't mind Grumpy." Mom reaches out and grasps the doorknob. "Did I tell you there are book clubs now? The daughter—her name is Ann—she's made a lot of nice changes, I think . . ."

The door opens. The bell jingles. We walk in.

And it's wrong.

It smells different. The musty, comforting smell of books and boxes and dust is gone. The air smells flowery. A fake kind of flowery, like scented candles or room spray. The table of new releases is in the same place, but the sign is different—it's a typed sign instead of the literal sheet of plain paper with Hank's handwriting in Sharpie that used to be taped to the table. The handwritten signs on the shelves are gone too, replaced by printed labels. And instead of the magazine stand, there's a big flat table piled with pretty journals, notecards, mugs, and candles.

I guess that probably explains the flowery smell.

The store is more crowded than I've ever seen it. It's still not exactly full, but there are people. People looking at the pretty journals. People browsing the shelves. People picking up books from the table of new releases and flipping through them.

I can't breathe. This isn't 2009. I know it isn't, but I pull out my phone anyway. Just to make sure.

It wakes up, battery at 67 percent.

"Hank isn't around today, is he?"

I look up. My mom has wandered up to the counter, Mr. Grumpy plodding along behind her.

The woman behind the counter shakes her head. She's tall, with light-brown skin and dark wavy hair—in her early thirties, probably. "Sorry," she says. "He hasn't been in for a couple weeks."

"Oh, that's too bad." Mom sighs. "Knee still giving him problems?"

I force myself to move, to walk up to the table of new releases. I already know what I'm going to find, but I flip back one of the book covers anyway.

The publication date is this year. An actual new release.

I didn't travel.

"Darby!" Mom turns around, eyes searching until she finds me. She beckons.

I go up to the counter, but I feel like I'm on autopilot.

Why didn't I travel?

"This is Ann," Mom says, gesturing to the woman behind the counter. "This is my son, Darby. He used to work here with your dad back in high school."

"Oh, how cool." Ann gives me a friendly smile.

I mirror it, my mouth stretching while my mind feels a million miles away.

"Isn't the store nice now?" Mom raises her eyebrows, prompting me. *Say something nice, Darby.*

"Yeah. It looks . . ."

Different. Strange. Cute and Instagrammable.

"It looks nice," I say.

Mom shoots me a frown, but Ann just smiles again. "Thanks," she says. "It's been great to pull more people in from the town. We have book clubs." She reaches to a neat stack of bookmarks on the counter and holds one out to me. A list of book clubs and their meeting dates, all against a soft purple background dotted with flowers. "If you're around, come by and check one out. The next one is the murder mystery club, Labor Day weekend."

"That one's very good," my mom tells me. "Jeannie and I went last month and read an Agatha Christie book."

I nod, looking at the bookmark, but I'm barely seeing it.

Is everything just *over* now? Am I done traveling?

My insides clench. I don't want this to be over—not yet. I can't believe the only reason I traveled for four days straight was just so the universe could remind me that I was confused and lost and kind of a moron as a teenager.

Maybe it's my mom. Maybe something about her presence messed up the wormhole or the singularity or the freaking *portal* or whatever it is that I traveled through. Maybe there was a reason I only ever traveled alone—maybe that's how it works.

I need to get us out of here. I need us to leave so I can come back alone.

"I'll definitely check this out." I wave the bookmark vaguely, forcing as friendly a grin as I can manage. "Mom, should we . . . ?" I jerk my head toward the door.

She looks surprised. "You sure? We can look around more."

"Let's go get the packing supplies."

She shrugs. "Okay, then. Nice to see you," she says to Ann. "Tell your dad we came by. Come on, Grumps."

As soon as we're back outside, Mom shoots me a judgmental look.

"You could have talked to Ann more. I thought you might like to hear how the bookstore's doing these days!"

"I stopped in before," I say defensively, and then pause. I shouldn't argue; this is the perfect excuse. "Actually, you're right. It might be nice to look around the store and hear about these book clubs." I wave the bookmark. "You could run over to Floyd's and I'll come meet you in a few minutes?"

"Well . . ." Mom hesitates. "You sure you don't want company?"

I feel slightly guilty. She wants to go with me—of course she does. She wants me to get on board with the new bookstore just like she wanted me to get on board with the condo.

God, does Mom think I hate Oak Falls too?

I push that thought out of my head. "I'm good. I'll meet up with you in a bit."

She looks a little deflated. "Okay. If you're sure. Come on, Grumps."

I wait until she's gone far enough in the direction of Floyd's five-and-dime that I'm pretty sure she's not going to change her mind and turn around. And then I check my phone one more time (still nothing from Michael), turn for the door of In Between, and pull it open.

Musty smell. Magazine stand. Handwritten signs. And the store is empty—all the people who were browsing a minute ago have vanished.

Oh, thank god.

"Hey."

I turn to the counter. Young Darby is sitting behind it, holding a book and looking at me.

Maybe it's relief that my younger self is still here. Maybe it's everything that happened last night and the deafening silence from Michael. Maybe it's frustration at myself, that I still don't know why this is happening, and now I only have three more days until Michael and I fall out and set everything in motion that'll lead us here, to a kiss I don't understand and this deafening silence . . .

But I snap. I'm too tired of not having answers, and I'm too worn out to pretend that I care about whether I seem like a creeper or not.

"Why are you so eager to get out of here?" I say.

Young Darby's eyebrows jump in surprise. "What?"

"The other day, when we were talking about boarding school, when you were talking to Michael . . . it's like you can't get out of here fast enough. What's so bad about Oak Falls?"

Young Darby shifts awkwardly, shoulders hunching forward, chest caving. "Nothing."

Well, that's an obvious lie. "Then why do you want to leave?"

"Because it's a good academic program. And it's just for a semester." Young Darby sounds defensive. And also like these are lines my younger self has said a million times—justifying it, even though I can't remember who I was justifying it to. Michael? My mom? Myself?

"Yeah," I say, and I can't stop the hint of bitterness creeping into my voice, "that's not an answer."

Now Young Darby shoots me a glower. "Why do you care? You don't know me."

Heat rushes through me. Because in this moment, I feel like I don't. I don't know this kid in front of me at all. "Maybe not. But I know what it's like to fuck things up with a friend and I feel like that's where you're heading."

Young Darby stares at me, looking genuinely confused. "What are you talking about? Michael and I are fine."

It's the clearest answer I've gotten so far, but it doesn't make me feel any better. It just makes me more frustrated. Because if Young Darby can't tell me why everything is about to fall apart with Michael, then nobody can, and then why am I traveling anyway? What's the point of all this?

What am I doing here?

"You're not fine," I say, and I don't even know who I'm really talking about. "Michael doesn't seem to hate Oak Falls. And clearly you do, and all you want to do is run away from it."

"Michael's not a broken, messed-up weirdo like I am!" Young Darby shouts.

It bursts out, like something my younger self has been holding in for a long time, and it hits me with the force of a gut punch, the words curling in like claws.

"You're not a messed-up weirdo," I say, but it's flat in my ears. An automatic response that I'm not even sure I believe.

"Thanks." Young Darby's voice comes out sour. "But you have no idea."

"How would you know?" I sound petty and challenging, but I don't care. "You don't know anything about me, either."

"Yeah, well, nobody else seems to feel like this," Young Darby says, as bitter as I sounded a minute ago. "Everyone else here seems to exist just fine—except me. So I think I know."

I have a sudden, very unhealthy urge to strangle myself. "You don't have any way to know what anyone else is feeling."

"And you don't know what I'm feeling, and you don't know me," Young Darby shoots back.

"Fine." This is going nowhere. I don't know what to say to convince my younger self that I get it, that I *do* know, without just telling this version of me that I'm trans. That *we're* trans.

But I can't do that. Why would Young Darby even believe me? What if I make it worse because Young Darby isn't ready and can't hear it? The last thing I need is to send my younger self into an even worse state of denial.

I rub my eyes. How did I realize I was trans anyway? How did I *really* figure it out?

I can't remember.

I think it crept up on me. And then it was just there. But I can't remember some singular moment everything shifted or what pushed me over the edge. I remember when I came out to Olivia. I remember when I told Ian.

But I don't remember the moment I admitted it to myself. The moment I understood anything clearer than *broken, messed-up weirdo*.

This isn't helping. None of this is helping. And I need to go catch up with my mom, before she comes back to the bookstore looking for me.

I don't know how to fix this, and I'm suddenly too overwhelmed and angry to try.

"Fine," I say again, like that settles anything. And then I turn around and storm out of the bookstore, leaving Young Darby behind.

CHAPTER NINETEEN

AUGUST 27

I pull my phone out of my pocket as soon as I'm outside to check if there's anything from Michael—but it's dead. Obviously. And that just makes me more frustrated. Frustrated that I forgot my phone would be dead, frustrated that now I have no idea if Michael's texted or tried to call me, frustrated that I basically just got in a fight with a younger version of myself and I didn't even win.

I catch up with my mom as she's stepping out of Floyd's with Mr. Grumpy, a roll of Bubble Wrap under one arm.

"Perfect timing!" she says. And then she frowns. "What's wrong?"

"Nothing." I shrug, restlessly tapping my fingers against my thumb. "Um . . . remember those books you wanted to give to Michael?"

Mom sighs. "Yes, yes, that's still on my list."

"What if I run them over now?"

She looks confused. "They're back at the house."

"Yeah, I know. I was thinking we could go back to the house and then I could take the books over to Michael's in the Jeep."

Her face lights up. "Oh! That would be very helpful of you, Darby. Then I could finally check that off."

I'm fidgety the whole ride back to the house. Mom doesn't pull the Jeep into the garage, just leaves it in the driveway, and I practically shoot out of the car and into the house to get the boxes of books for Michael. There's only two—banker boxes with handles, which at least makes them slightly less awkward to wrestle into the trunk of the Jeep despite my tired arms.

"You told Michael about these, right?" I ask, as Mom helps me shove the last one in.

"Oh, I haven't told him a thing," she says.

Is she joking? "Why not?"

"Well, I was going to, but then I figured why give him the chance to say no? Just show up. He'll be polite and take them." She beams. "And then they won't be my problem anymore."

I can't tell if my mom is incredibly conflict avoidant or actually a mastermind at manipulating the laws of Midwest Nice. But I don't care. If the books give me an excuse to go over to Michael's, that's all that really matters.

It's just after noon when I turn the Jeep into Michael's long driveway, pulling up behind his old pickup truck, which glints so brightly in the sun that I have to squint. Summer seems determined to make the most of the last few days of August, and it's hot and humid. The muggy air presses on me like a wet towel.

I open the trunk of the Jeep and realize there's no way for me to carry both boxes by myself, so I just grab one, leave the trunk open, and head for the house. A lone cicada picks up somewhere in the distance as I climb the porch steps. The lawn chairs are still there; there's a pair of flip-flops cast off under one of them and an abandoned soda can on the arm of another.

I hit the doorbell with my elbow. I hear it echo in the house, a mournful *ping-pong*. And then silence.

Great. Maybe nobody's home. What do I do if Michael's not even here? Leave the books? If I leave the books, that kind of gets rid of my whole excuse for trying to talk to him . . .

The front door creaks opens and there, on the other side of the screen, is Michael. His hair looks very uncombed and he's wearing his glasses and a stretched-out T-shirt and shorts.

He stares at me like I'm the last person he expected to find on his porch. "Hi."

His expression just makes me more annoyed. "Hi. I have books."

"Books?"

"Yeah, my mom thought you might want these books she used to have in her classroom." I look down at the box I'm carrying, mostly so I don't have to look at Michael. "She's trying to get rid of some stuff before the move, so . . ."

"Um. Right. Come on in." Michael opens the screen door.

So I step over the threshold and set the box down in the entryway next to a pile of shoes. "There's another one in the Jeep."

"Oh," Michael says.

I wait for him to say something else, but he doesn't, so I turn and dodge past him, back out onto the porch. I grab the other box from the Jeep, somehow wrangling the trunk closed, and when I climb the porch steps again, Michael has stepped outside to hold the screen door open more easily and leave me more room to walk past him.

And that makes me annoyed too. Like it means he doesn't want me too close.

I set the second box down next to the first. Michael steps back into the house, the screen door creaking closed behind him. And now it's just us, standing awkwardly and staring at each other while another cicada buzzes outside.

"So, will you take the books?" I ask.

He glances at the boxes. "Yeah, of course. Tell your mom thanks. I'm sure I can use them in my classroom . . . or another teacher can."

I let my breath out. I wanted him to put up a fight. To say he didn't need the books or didn't want them, just so I could argue with him about something that wasn't as raw as everything I actually want to say.

His eyes skip back to my face. "You, um . . . you just came to drop off the books?"

Does he really want me to leave that badly? "Fine. Point taken. I'm going."

I start for the door, but he moves in front of it. "No. I'm sorry, that's not what I meant. I just . . . I thought you were here because . . ." He stuffs in his hands in the pockets of his shorts, shoulders creeping toward his ears. "Last night."

I stare at him. I can't decide whether to feel relieved or annoyed all over again. "So you didn't just magically forget about that."

It comes out a bit sour and not at all like a question. He shrinks back, ducking his head. "No." His voice is quiet. "I didn't."

"So . . . were you going to talk to me at some point? Or just ignore me all over again?"

Michael glances up, and his eyes look just as bare and vulnerable as they did in the bookstore, thirteen years ago when he looked at Natalie and Brendan as they disappeared into the rows of shelves. "I didn't mean to kiss you. Or . . . I didn't know I was going to before I did, and then I . . . I guess I kind of freaked out. I thought maybe I overstepped and you were just . . ." He lets his breath out, running a hand over his face. He looks frustrated now too. "You had just gotten back, and I wouldn't normally do something like that at school, at a football game, and we're complicated. The last thing I wanted to do was make all of this more complicated . . ."

It takes everything I have not to shout, *Why are we complicated?* "So your great plan after kissing me was to hightail it out of there and hope I forgot by the next day?"

His face flushes. "No, that's not—"

"Do you wish you hadn't kissed me?"

His eyes meet mine. He hesitates, and then he says, "No."

My heart rises in my chest, and all my frustration evaporates. "Could we just . . . stop being complicated, at least for now?" My voice comes out rough. Cracking. "I know I'm a mess and I have no idea what I'm doing or even what I want, but I wanted that. When you kissed me. I wanted that."

Michael looks at me for a long time. I can hear my heart pounding through the seconds, so loud I'm half convinced he can hear it too.

And then he takes a step forward, tentatively, like he's giving me a chance to change my mind. His fingers run along my jaw and he leans down and he kisses me again. I reach up and wrap my fingers around the back of his neck. I feel weightless and like I'm careening over a cliff at the same time.

He pulls away and I let him go. I wait, holding my breath.

For a second, it seems like he's holding his too. Then the corner of his mouth turns up. "We can stop being complicated for now," he says.

I smile back, but there's a lump in my throat I can't manage to swallow. *It's not as easy as that, is it?*

Because there's still something he's not telling me. I can feel it there, hovering around us like a shadow. And I'm sure it's connected to every-thing Young Darby is missing in the bookstore. I'm sure it's connected to that version of me feeling like a broken, messed-up weirdo, and to what-ever is going to drive Michael and I apart at my birthday party.

But, god, I want it to be this easy.

Michael takes a breath. "I'm working on lesson plans and school stuff today, but . . . are you free tomorrow? Maybe we could do something. Get coffee or go to Krape Park or—"

"Yeah." Something sparks in my chest. "I'm free."

A smile tugs at his mouth. "Okay. Krape Park? Four o'clock?"

"Sure."

He leans down, and I turn my face up and kiss him again, just briefly. It sends a tingle down my back, the feel of his mouth against mine. This person who was my best friend and seems like a stranger at the same time.

"I'll see you tomorrow," he says again, and opens the screen door.

I step back out onto the porch, that warm spark spreading through me at how familiar those words sound. "Yeah," I say. "See you tomorrow."

CHAPTER TWENTY

I take a last sip of my coffee from Magic Beans, staring at the frosted window of In Between Books. I've been standing in front of the bookstore for the past five minutes, finishing my coffee and working up to walking in.

I spent the rest of yesterday going through my room in an attempt to distract myself from thoughts of Michael and his front porch and what might happen at Krape Park today. My mom offered to help, but I turned her down. I had a feeling if she was there when I unearthed remnants of my childhood that I'd forgotten about, the whole thing would take three times as long because she'd have to reminisce about everything, and I wasn't sure, in that moment, that I could handle it. The warmth I brought with me from Michael's was fading, everything Young Darby and I had snapped at each other welling up in its place. If Mom was there while I pulled stuffed animals out of my closet and tried to decide whether to keep them or not . . .

I was worried I'd snap the same things at her that Young Darby had snapped at me. I was worried she'd want to remember some sweet little kid with a sweet childhood, and sooner or later, I'd end up sniping that I didn't know who she was talking about, because the only Darby I remembered was the broken, messed-up one—and honestly, I was wondering if I wasn't *still* broken and messed up.

So I sorted through stuffed animals alone, picking out a few that I remembered the most for Mom to keep, because I knew she'd want to keep some. I bundled the random articles of leftover girl clothes that were still floating around my closet into a bag, wondering why I hadn't done all this *before* we went to the thrift store. I threw out some hideous clay people I seem to have sculpted at some point, smuggling them past my mom, who was carefully taking art off the walls, so she couldn't declare they deserved to be kept just like the birthday mugs.

And then I went to bed and drifted in and out of more strange dreams. Dreams where I couldn't find Michael after a football game. Dreams where my hair was long again—like it was back in middle school—and everyone commented how pretty it was and didn't seem to believe me that it was wrong.

I don't even remember what all the dreams were about, but when I woke up, I felt like I had a dysphoria hangover. And I barely ever feel dysphoric anymore. I had to go stare into the bathroom mirror, just to remind myself that nobody had misgendered me in years. I definitely felt like some horrible cliché of a trans person, standing there studying my face—the shape of my nose, the thickness of my eyebrows, the sparse stubble that I'd never tried growing out because it was clear it would never become a respectable beard.

And that's when it hit me.

Maybe I was wrong about why I was traveling. This whole time, I'd been thinking that traveling was just—I don't know—random but kind of convenient. That if there was any reason for it at all, it was so I could talk to my younger self and try to figure out why Michael and I fell apart so spectacularly.

But what if it's something else?

What if the bookstore keeps bringing me back to that week on purpose, because I have a chance to do something differently?

What if the whole point is that I'm supposed to change something?

So this morning, I helped my mom wrap up framed pictures and the art from the walls, going over in my head what I wanted to say to my younger self. And then I took the girl clothes and the stuffed animals to the thrift store. I picked up coffee. And I drank the coffee, standing in front of the bookstore, trying to convince myself that what I'm about to do won't cause some sort of Darby-turns-see-through-and-starts-fading-away catastrophe like I'm in *Back to the Future*.

I close my eyes. I'm not really going to alter anything huge. I'm not

going to give my younger self any answers I won't get to on my own—
eventually.

I toss the coffee cup into a trash can at the edge of the sidewalk and
walk into the bookstore.

Today, Young Darby is sitting at the counter, chin cupped in one
hand, staring at the bulky computer monitor. Young Darby's hair looks
particularly scruffy—I need a haircut—and my shoulders are hunched
forward, hiding my chest under my oversize T-shirt. My oval glasses are
slipping down my nose.

The store is empty. Nobody else is here, and still—my younger self isn't
comfortable. I can't even exist without anxiety in an empty bookstore.

I clear my throat. "Hey."

Young Darby keeps staring at the computer monitor. "Hey."

I take a few steps toward the counter. "Listen, I know you don't know
me and I don't know you, and I barged in here and said a bunch of shit
yesterday, but . . ." I take a breath. Here goes. "I think we have some
things in common. More than you might think. I'm sorry that I got a
bit . . . intense about it."

Young Darby shoots me a suspicious look. "What things do we have
in common?"

I chew my lip, choosing my words carefully. *God, I hope this isn't about to
fuck everything up.* "Well, we both have a friend who likes Marvel comics."

Young Darby frowns. "We do?"

"And . . . I grew up here too."

Young Darby looks at me a little more closely. "You grew up in Oak
Falls? I didn't . . . you don't look familiar."

Well, I knew my younger self didn't recognize me, but if I don't even
look remotely familiar . . . apparently I was less observant in high school
than I thought. "I moved away for a while. Because I didn't feel like I
belonged here."

Young Darby pulls away, chest caving even more.

"Remember when you helped me find the first Percy Jackson book?
You told me you and your friend Michael spent a week calling each other
Percy and Grover."

Now Young Darby turns pink and scrapes a fingernail over the surface
of the counter, staring at it. "Yeah, I know, it was silly and—"

"I did the same thing with a friend of mine once."

Young Darby's gaze jerks up. "Um. With Percy and Grover?"

I open my mouth and hesitate. "Uh . . . no, with . . . with some other characters. It doesn't matter. It was before high school—a long time ago—but . . . but I got really into it. It was kind of . . . ridiculous. How into it I was. But it was like, when my friend called me by this character's name, when I was kind of pretending to be that character . . . I felt more like me than I ever had before."

Young Darby stares at me—a vulnerable, naked look, as though I've just spoken my younger self's most intimate secret out loud.

Which, honestly, I have.

Because this has to be the point. This has to be why the bookstore is bringing me here: so Young Darby has a way out of feeling like a broken, messed-up weirdo. So maybe I can find that way out, before I leave, before I ruin everything with Michael.

Because maybe if I do . . .

Well, I don't know, but I can't help hoping that if Young Darby can get a few things figured out just a little bit sooner, maybe I might feel a little less broken and messed up too. Maybe my younger self can change my present for the better.

Young Darby swallows, still staring at me. And then says, "I kind of wished I was Percy. Like . . . for real."

I nod slowly. "I mean, being the son of Poseidon would be pretty cool."

A smile slips across Young Darby's face. "Yeah." The smile fades. "The character you pretended to be . . ." My younger self looks away, hesitating. "Was that character, um . . . a guy, like you?"

I bite back a grin. Young Darby has no idea how complicated that question is, even if it's also, at the same time, very simple. Yes, Percy was a guy, just like me. I just didn't know it at the time. "If you're asking if that character was the same gender I thought I was . . . no."

Young Darby frowns at me. I can practically see the gears turning in my head while I work this out. Or try to work this out. Catching on *gender* and *thought I was* . . .

The frown disappears. "Oh," Young Darby says, very quietly.

Part of me wants to push. Wants to ask if Young Darby really gets what I mean. If any light bulb has gone off.

Instead, I say, "You can order books, right?"

Young Darby looks blank. And then jerks, reaching out toward the computer keyboard. "Yeah, we can get things pretty fast usually. If we don't have it in the store."

This book definitely will not be in the store. Not in a place like Oak Falls. Not in 2009. "There's a book called *Transgender History*," I say. "Could you order it for me? And actually . . ." I say it as casually as I can, like it's an afterthought. "You might find it interesting. You could look at it, if you want, before I pick it up."

Young Darby types on the clunky keyboard and reads off the computer screen. "*Transgender History* by Susan Stryker?"

"That's the one."

"Do you want to leave a phone number? Then we can call you when it comes in."

I shake my head. "That's okay. I'll just stop by. I don't mind a trip to the bookstore."

Young Darby looks doubtful. "Okay. If you're sure. It's easy to call . . ."

"I'm sure."

Young Darby hesitates, glancing between me and the computer screen.

Behind me, the bell over the door jingles. Young Darby's eyes jerk toward the sound, face lighting up and closing off at the same time. "Hey!"

"Hey, Darby." It's Michael's voice.

I turn. The younger version of Michael is in the store again, the door swinging closed behind him. This time he's wearing a Pokémon T-shirt that's eerily familiar. His glasses are sitting slightly crooked on his nose.

I turn away quickly, picking up a random book from the table of new releases and paging through it.

"You want a ride tonight?" Michael goes up to the counter and leans his elbows on it.

I glance sideways, just in time to see Young Darby turn the computer monitor just slightly so there's no chance Michael will be able to see what's on it.

My heart sinks. *Transgender History* is probably still there, since my younger self hasn't actually put the order through.

"How early do you have to be there?" Young Darby asks.

"Like an hour before game time. We're supposed to warm up in the band room."

Right. It's Friday here. I glance toward the big picture window and the banner still strung up over the video store. Football season opener. Young Darby is going to watch Michael in the band.

"Um . . ." Young Darby fidgets, scratching a fingernail on the counter again. "I'll just meet you there."

Michael's face falls. "I could come get you on my bike," he says. He sounds hopeful.

Young Darby shrugs a shoulder. "I don't know. I gotta go eat dinner and stuff after I get off here, so . . ."

My heart sinks even lower. Young Darby doesn't sound excited at all. I honestly sound like I'd rather be anywhere else. Dinner has nothing to do with it—I don't want to go with Michael because it means more time sitting around on the bleachers by myself, feeling weird and out of place.

"Okay," Michael says. "If you're sure."

"Yeah. I'll meet you there."

Michael nods, but he's not looking at Young Darby. He's looking down at the counter, foot tapping against the ground, like he's waiting, hoping Young Darby will say something else.

But Young Darby is silent, still scratching at the counter. Like my younger self is waiting for Michael to leave.

"Okay," Michael says again. "I guess I'll see you later then."

"Yeah." But Young Darby barely glances at him. "I gotta go sort through some stuff in storage anyway, so . . ."

That sounds like a lie, and it's clear they both know it.

"Sure." Michael nods.

Young Darby tries for a grin—it's tense and small—and then turns and disappears into the back room.

And Michael heads for the door.

I look after him.

Fuck this.

He's right here. I have to try. I have to say something, ask him something. Young Darby clearly thinks everything is fine with Michael. Young Darby has no idea there's a fight coming . . . but maybe Michael does.

Maybe the bookstore is bringing me back here to help my younger self feel less broken, but if Michael's right here, right now . . .

I close the book I'm holding, glancing at it just long enough to set it back where it belongs on the table of new releases. And then I turn for the door.

Michael's gone. Like he vanished into thin air.

But I didn't hear the bell. I didn't hear the door open. He's just gone, like he was never there to begin with.

A faint flowery smell hits my nose. I blink—through the glass in the door, the sidewalk beyond is bright and sunny. It should be cloudy. It *was* cloudy a second ago, wasn't it?

I hear voices. A faint murmur of conversation. I turn toward the sound, and my insides lurch so hard I feel sick.

There are people standing in an aisle, pointing to picture books and talking to each other. And the sign labeling the shelf of children's books is printed. The books on the table of new releases in front of me are all wrong. The magazine stand is gone, replaced by a table of journals and note cards . . .

I'm in the present. I'm in the bookstore that belongs to my present.

I glance at the counter, just to make sure, and Ann is behind it, typing on the much sleeker computer.

What happened?

I cross the store, all the way to the farthest row of shelves, peering down every aisle like I'll somehow find the old bookstore hiding somewhere.

This isn't how it's supposed to work. I walk into the bookstore, and as long as I'm alone, I travel. It's the past. When I leave, it's the present.

What did I do to end up here? Maybe I did something, triggered something, without realizing it.

I go back to the table of new releases. Pick up a book, set it down, and turn toward the door—just like I did when I was going to talk to Michael.

But nothing happens. I'm still in the present, staring through the door at the coffee shop tables across the street.

My heart thuds. This doesn't make any sense. I've picked up books in the past. I bought *The Lightning Thief* and walked out with it. That didn't pull me out of the past and plop me into the present version of the bookstore.

I need to get out of here. I need to get back to the old In Between, where I'm supposed to be. I head for the door, pulse racing, skin tingling, and push it open, stepping out onto the sidewalk. As soon as the door closes behind me, I turn around, open it again, and walk back inside.

Young Darby is just coming out of the back room, carrying a few books. The magazine stand is back. The flowery smell is gone. This is the store I was in a minute ago.

Except . . .

"Did Michael leave?"

Young Darby looks up. "Um, yeah? I mean, he said he was heading out . . ." My younger self slides the books onto the counter, raising an eyebrow at me. "Did you . . . need him for something?"

"No," I say quickly. "It's nothing." My eyes stray to the book clock above Young Darby's head. It's almost four. I'm supposed to meet the Michael I know—the present version of Michael. And now that my phone's very definitely dead, I can't text him to say where I am if I'm running late.

Which means I should go.

I waver, heart still going too fast. And then I turn for the door again.

"You sure you don't want to leave a phone number for that order?" Young Darby asks.

I glance once more at my younger self, watching me with raised eyebrows, still holding the books. "Yeah, I'll just . . . I'll come back. Thanks." And I leave the bookstore before I can second-guess it. The door jingles and creaks behind me.

A fluke. That's all it was. Some weird fluke, because this whole thing is impossible, and I have no idea how it works, so why wouldn't there be a weird fluke?

But I feel unsettled. Like there's an itch under my skin. I turn back once more, pull open the door, and just stick my head in.

The magazine stand is still there. Young Darby is just disappearing down a row of shelves with the armful of books.

I let go of the knob and the door swings gently closed.

It's still there. The bookstore is still there. I can still get to it.

That was just a fluke.

CHAPTER TWENTY-ONE

AUGUST 28

Michael is waiting for me near the ticket booth for the carousel in Krape Park, turning his phone over in his hands. He's wearing a short-sleeve button-down and trim khaki shorts, and he looks very attractive and very grown-up.

I didn't even put on a polo shirt. I'm wearing a boring T-shirt and jeans that are rolled up past my ankles. And sandals.

God, Michael's dressed like this is a date and I'm dressed like . . . like I've been preoccupied all day trying to gently suggest to my younger self that I might be trans and not just a major fuckup.

He smiles when he sees me and holds up his hand, like I might not see him if he doesn't wave, despite the fact that he's the only person standing near the carousel who doesn't have a small child attached to them.

"Hey," he says, when I reach him. "Glad you got my text."

I look at him blankly. "What text?"

"I texted you to tell you I was by the carousel."

"Oh. Sorry. Um . . . my phone died. I forgot to charge it. I just saw you from the parking lot." I flap a hand in the direction of the parking lot where I left the Jeep.

"Well . . . you found me. That's what counts. So." He jerks his head toward the carousel and raises his eyebrows. "You ready?"

I look between him and the antique carousel. Even though it's not dark yet, the carousel lights are already on, twinkling along the edge of its pointed roof like a crown of stars. They send a warm golden glow over the brightly painted horses on their brass poles. "Are you serious?"

He grins and fishes a few quarters out of his pocket. "We're here."

"You're ridiculous."

He just laughs and flips the quarters at me, which I somehow manage to catch.

We both stick out like sore thumbs as we go through the line, trading the quarters for old-fashioned paper tickets. All the other riders are under the age of ten. I feel oddly tall as I climb up on a white horse with a gaudy gold saddle and a black mane.

"I don't think I've been on this thing in twenty years," I say, as the tinkling music starts up.

Michael climbs onto a bright-yellow horse with a red saddle. "Oh, I ride it every week," he says, with a perfectly straight face.

"You do not."

"It keeps me young."

The carousel creaks into motion, gradually picking up speed. The faster it turns, the more the scratchiness under my skin fades. The music and lights and Michael's crooked grin are like an anchor, tying me here, to the present, while the world whirls by around us. By the time the ride ends, I've managed to push the bookstore away completely.

From the carousel, Michael takes me to the old antique fire truck, which is deserted, so we sit on its wide, flat bench seat, me behind the steering wheel.

"I definitely remember this being bigger," I say.

"Yeah, it's kind of disappointing how everything gets normal size when you're an adult," Michael says. He glances around. "Well . . . a lot of stuff is probably still kind of big for you."

I elbow him. "Yeah, thanks, you're hilarious."

From the fire truck, we wander past the playground, past the big gazebo and the picnic tables and the band shell. And we talk about nothing. The last time Michael played in the band shell. Who came to that birthday he had at the gazebo. He asks if New York has any carousels, and I shrug and change the subject—because I don't want to talk about New York.

I tell myself that's because I'm here to get away from New York. And not because the second he asked about New York, I felt a strange little tug behind my ribs and suddenly caught myself wondering what Olivia was doing right now. Whether she was with Joan. Or Ian. Whether they were all hanging out together without me.

We walk around the trails of Krape Park until the mosquitoes come out and the sun starts to sink in the sky. And then we turn around and go back to the parking lot, because I forgot to put on bug spray (again) and I'm getting eaten alive, which Michael teases me about.

He walks me to the Jeep in the parking lot.

I reach out and grasp his hand. "This was fun."

"Yeah." He smiles, but he gently pulls his hand away. "Listen, I have to be at school tomorrow for a meeting, but . . . do you want to come by for dinner? I mean, nothing special, just me and Liz and Amanda, but you're welcome. If you want."

I tuck my hand in my back pocket. I don't know what else to do with it. I don't know why he pulled away. "Yeah. Sure."

"Great."

I lean up, rising up on my toes, but he makes no move to kiss me. Just gives me another crooked grin and turns away, heading for his pickup truck.

I PLUG MY phone in as I climb into bed, trying to keep the bookstore from creeping back into my mind. Trying not to think, over and over, about Michael pulling his hand away.

What was that about?

After a minute, my phone wakes up. Two notifications pop up on the screen.

The first is a text from Michael—the one he sent earlier that I didn't see, saying he was at the carousel.

The second is from Ian.

IAN ROBB

Hey Darb I know you've got a lot going on, but Ollie really misses you. Shoot her a text sometime?

xx

CHAPTER TWENTY-TWO

AUGUST 29

I take the Main Street route to Michael's for dinner the next day so I can stop by the bookstore first. Now that the weekend is over, Main Street is quieter again. There are plenty of free parking spots, and only one family lingering over ice cream outside Ethel May's.

There's no sign of the younger version of Michael when I walk into the bookstore. It's Saturday here, but the store is empty. Young Darby looks kind of at loose ends, sitting behind the counter, staring out the window.

"Have you got a book for me?" I ask as the door creaks closed behind me.

Young Darby's gaze jerks away from the window. "Oh, hey. Sorry, it's not here yet. We usually get things fast, but . . . not that fast."

"No problem." I wasn't really expecting the book to be here. Twenty-four hours would be fast even for Amazon. It just seemed like the easiest excuse to give for why I'm here—I couldn't exactly say, *So. Any massive gender revelations yet?* "I just thought I'd check. I was in the area."

Young Darby nods.

I wait, but Young Darby doesn't seem inclined to say anything else.

Right. My turn, I guess. "So, um . . . must be weird, not going back to school here."

"Yeah."

What's going on? I thought Young Darby would be . . . I don't know, excited? Or at least a little less miserable? I mean, I just gave myself language and a book that I know I didn't have when I was sixteen. Didn't Young Darby at least go home and google?

"How was the football game?" I ask.

Young Darby's shoulders hunch forward, chest caving. "It was good."

Well, that sounds like a lie. "Uh, listen . . . that book I told you about . . ."

"Yeah?"

"Did you look anything up about it?"

Young Darby's fingers tap against one thumb. "I put the order through."

"No, I mean . . . did you google anything? Or . . . I don't know, I just thought it might interest you, so I wondered if you looked into it any more."

Young Darby shifts, and the stool rocks a little. "I found something on YouTube . . ."

I blink. That's not what I was expecting. "YouTube?"

"Yeah, um . . . this guy, or . . . this person who was—is—transgender." Young Darby stumbles quickly over the word. "He was . . . talking about what it meant. And his life and stuff."

I never found anything on YouTube. I never even thought of looking there. The hair stands up on my arms. *I changed something.*

I desperately want to ask, *Did you see yourself?*

Did you understand anything?

But all I say is "That's cool."

Young Darby nods . . . but not with any enthusiasm. "He lives in Boston."

Oh.

My younger self goes back to staring out the window, and I think I get it now. Boston is a city. Boston is on the East Coast.

Boston isn't Oak Falls, Illinois.

"That doesn't mean anything." My voice sounds desperate in my own ears. "People can be . . . anywhere."

"Yeah." Young Darby doesn't sound convinced.

Shit. This isn't helping the way I wanted it to.

Maybe my younger self just needs more time. Maybe once the book gets here, and Young Darby has a chance to look through it, my younger self will realize that just because it's not *obvious* there are queer people around doesn't mean we don't exist . . .

My thoughts skid to a stop. I could swear I'm hearing music. Some low-key, easy-listening thing floating in from somewhere far away, muffled like it's on the other side of a wall . . .

"What is that?" I say.

Young Darby's eyebrows go up. "What's what?"

"That music. Where's it coming from?"

Young Darby leans over to look out the window. "I don't hear anything . . ."

I turn for the door. Maybe it's a car outside with a radio . . .

Everything around me shifts. The music is suddenly louder, suddenly *here*. It's filtering over speakers in the store. A gentle, jazzy saxophone . . .

The air smells like flowers. The magazine stand is gone.

No, no, no . . .

"Hey," someone says.

I turn toward the counter and feel dizzy.

"Darby, right?" Ann says. "I didn't see you come in."

I'm back in the present. Like I fell right out of the past into the new version of the bookstore. Again.

What is going on?

"Hi," I say weakly. But I can't come up with anything else, and I can't return Ann's smile. My heart is pounding so hard, it hurts. My vision swims. I turn and push my way through the door, the bell jingling overhead.

I hit the sidewalk. Squeeze my eyes shut. Force myself to count to five. And then I go back inside.

"Forget something?" Ann asks.

Fuck. *What the fuck is happening?* I didn't travel. I still didn't travel. Young Darby is gone.

"No," I say. "I'm good."

And I leave again.

I DON'T KNOW how I get through dinner. My heart won't slow down. I push the vegetarian casserole Liz made around on my plate, too unsettled to eat anything. We sit around the dining table in the kitchen—Michael, Liz, Amanda, and me—and all three of them talk and laugh, but I can barely follow any bits of conversation.

Something's wrong.

Something's happening to the bookstore, to whatever allows me to travel. I still don't know what's going to cause Young Darby to fight with

Michael, and giving my younger self new language for my identity isn't the magic solution I thought it would be.

I'm supposed to have two more days. Two more days to fix things or figure things out or whatever the hell the *point* of all this is. And now I'm not even sure I'll be able to reach Young Darby again.

We finish dinner and clear away the dishes, and before I'm even really aware of what I'm doing, I say, "I should go."

Liz and Amanda glance at each other.

Michael says, "You don't have to."

I look up at him. He's wearing his glasses. I didn't even notice until now. "Sorry," I say. "I'm just really wiped. All the packing."

A frown crosses his face, but he nods. "Um . . . sure. I get it."

We walk together down the hall to the front door, leaving Liz and Amanda in the kitchen behind us. I realize, guiltily, that I didn't even ask him how his day was. How school prep was going. What he would teach. If he'd figured out what to do with the books.

But now it feels like too much. Too awkward. I can't even figure out how to form a question.

Michael opens the screen door, and we step out onto the porch. Twilight is already deepening in the front yard. I can practically feel the days getting shorter now.

"Well, um . . . thanks for coming over." He reaches out and grasps my hand, and the motion trips something in my brain.

I pull my hand away. "You didn't like me holding your hand yesterday."

He leans back a little, surprised. "What do you mean?"

"At the park. I took your hand and I thought you were going to kiss me, but you pulled away. What was that about?"

He shifts, glancing away, and stuffs his hands into his pockets. "I just . . . I'm not big into PDA."

"Seriously?"

"I told you," he says, a little defensively, "I don't usually kiss people in the school parking lot."

"Well, yeah, but I guess I figured that was more because you . . . hadn't had the opportunity." Something prickly settles in my gut. "Hang on. Is this because you're gay? Because we look . . . gay?"

His eyes come back to me, suddenly guarded. "What are you talking about?"

I let my breath out. Sharp and annoyed. "It's not PDA. You're fine being gay in Oak Falls as long as nobody has to deal with the fact that you're gay. That's why you go to football games and you manspread and that's why you wanted me to come over here for dinner. Because nobody's watching here. You can kiss me and not be worried somebody might notice you're not a heterosexual man."

Michael takes a step back. "That's not true."

But I can't deal with this anymore. I keep hearing Young Darby in the bookstore saying, *He lives in Boston.* I keep hearing Olivia asking why the hell I'd want to go back to *bumfuck nowhere.* I keep thinking about Ian's text, unreplied to on my now-dead phone.

"I have to go," I say, and I turn and head for the Jeep before Michael can stop me.

CHAPTER TWENTY-THREE

AUGUST 30

"I'm going to throw you a birthday party," Mom says, as soon as I walk into the kitchen the next morning. "It's your thirtieth. You should have one."

I rub my eyes. I feel like I barely spent any time asleep last night, and I'm definitely not awake enough for announcements like this. "When? My birthday is in two days."

"Tomorrow!" Mom beams at me. "I already reserved the rooftop deck at the condo. I thought maybe I'd have it be a surprise, but that just seemed too logistically complicated, and anyway, I want you to help pick out a cake."

I let my breath out. "I don't need a birthday party."

"Oh, hush. You're here. It's the perfect opportunity. I haven't gotten to throw you a birthday party in years! Anyway, I've already invited people."

"Who?"

"Michael. His roommates. I don't really know who all you were hanging out with at that party at his house or the football game, so I just told him to invite whoever he wanted."

Oh, god. After last night, I'm not sure Michael will even show up. "Mom, I really don't . . . I don't need a birthday party. I mean, it's nice of you, but . . ."

"Well, it's not just for you." She looks slightly self-conscious. "Plenty of my friends will be there too. I thought it could be a joint party. Birthday party for you, moving party for me! I've been wanting to try out the rooftop deck. We'll have to be done by nine o'clock for quiet hours, but that's my bedtime anyway."

Oh. So that's it. Mom wants a party—something special to mark her move to the condo—but she can't just throw a party for herself. That would be selfish. The second cardinal sin of the Midwest, right behind accepting an invitation you were clearly supposed to turn down.

My birthday gives her the perfect cover.

I can live with that. "Okay. When do we need to pick out a cake?"

"As soon as you've had breakfast." She picks up a pad of paper and a pen. "I'll start a list right now. We'll need snacks and pop and paper cups and plates . . ."

My phone buzzes in my pocket, and my heart leaps straight up my throat. It's Michael, texting to tell me he's absolutely not attending this party. Or maybe it's Ian, wondering why the hell I'm ignoring him.

But it's neither of them.

OLIVIA HENRY
Happy birthday week

My breath sticks in my lungs.

Happy birthday week is something Olivia started once we were all out of school. In college, Olivia and Ian and I always celebrated one another's birthdays on our actual birthdays. But once we were out of college, life happened and jobs happened, and sometimes I had evening classes in my master's program, and Olivia was fitting in stand-up, and Joan has weeks where she's working all the time . . .

So Olivia invented Birthday Week. Parties and gifts could happen anywhere in the week and it all counted.

My Birthday Week technically started yesterday, on Monday. But I don't care. She texted. It doesn't have five million exclamation points the way most of her texts do, but she texted.

And suddenly my mind isn't on cake. It's on sexy fries. And sexier fries. And beer. And Olivia and Joan and Ian all crammed into a booth at some weird bar that Olivia picked for me, because I don't know the first thing about bars and I'll never be cool enough to find the ones without signs. I'm picturing Olivia passing off her plastic-bling tiara like she's passing off a royal crown. I'm picturing Ian giving me a free download of some game he designed, because that's what he does for everyone as a present, every year. I never play them, because I don't have the gear you need to play them, but it doesn't matter, because we always end up at Ian's apartment sooner or later and play the games there . . .

"You okay?"

I jerk out of my thoughts and look up from my phone. My mom is looking at me over her round red glasses, a slight frown on her face.

"Yeah. Fine." I turn back to the coffee maker and stuff my phone in my pocket, trying to ignore the strange hollowness opening up in my chest.

MOM INSISTS I go to Floyd's with her to get party supplies. I almost try to come up with an excuse to go over to the bookstore. It's right there. I could walk in and see if the book I ordered has arrived, if it seems like anything's changing for the better . . .

But I'm too scared. Too scared of walking in only to find it's still the bookstore of the present.

And anyway, I don't feel any different. Nothing seems better in my present, either—so maybe that means Young Darby still feels like a broken, messed-up weirdo.

So I just follow my mom around through the aisles of Floyd's, holding the basket and offering an opinion when she insists I give her one. We buy plates and cups and napkins and a paper tablecloth printed with party hats, and then we head to the grocery store to pick out snacks. (Mom decides she'll leave the cake until tomorrow so it doesn't get stale.)

And somehow the whole day goes by. I feel like I'm in a daze. I think about texting Michael, and I don't. I think about texting Olivia, and I can't figure out what to say.

After dinner, I end up in my room, trying to pack things up in my suitcase, because the movers are coming the day after tomorrow and my clothes are everywhere.

God, I don't even know what I'm doing. I have to return the rental car in a few days. And if I'm not returning it in New York, then I have to find a rental location here to return it. I've still got these boxes and trash bags—all this stuff I brought from New York, and I haven't even really thought about whether the movers will be loading that up too. Whether all of this is going to end up in the second bedroom of my mom's condo in two days *because I still haven't figured out what I'm doing.*

I give up. Finally, sitting in the middle of this mess, surrounded by clothes, I do the thing that's been poking at the back of my mind all day. I open a browser window on my phone and google time travel again.

All the same hits as last time. I scan them, looking for anything about portals and singularities. Looking for some answer about why time travel might break down. But there's nothing, because time travel, especially backward, is impossible.

I try a different search. *Wormhole breaking down.*

This just gets me a bunch of hits explaining what wormholes are. Not helpful.

Singularity breaking down.

Stuff about black holes and Stephen Hawking.

Time travel portal breaking down.

Pseudo-science websites and tabloid articles.

I drop my phone on the floor and pull off my glasses, pressing my fists into my eyes. *Fuck.*

I'm losing my mind. Maybe that's really the answer. My first thought, from that first day I walked into the bookstore, was right after all. I'm having some sort of massive existential crisis that tipped me right over into the deep end and now I'm losing my grip on reality and googling singularities like I even know what that word means.

No. I can't quite believe that. It's too real—it's all been too real.

I put my glasses back on and grab up my phone. It's 7:45.

Shit.

The bookstore closes at 8:00.

Some tiny part of my brain tries to suggest that I could wait until tomorrow morning. That there's no way I can really get there before the store closes.

But every other part of me insists I have to go *now.* I have to go and make sure I'm not losing my mind, that it's real, that it's not gone and I can still reach my younger self.

I push myself up, tripping over a pile of shirts, and head for the hall. "Mom?"

"Yeah, Darby?" She's in the kitchen, packing away the few remaining pots and pans, the toaster, cooking utensils.

"I'm, uh . . . I'm going over to Michael's," I say.

Her eyebrows go up. "Oh. I was going to pack some more stuff into the Jeep to take over to the condo tomorrow—"

"I'll take my rental car."

"Okay." She frowns at me. "Everything all right?"

"Yeah. I, um . . . I just need a break." I don't even wait for her response. Just go back to my room, unearth the rental car keys from the pile of crap on the bedside table, and leave the house.

The rental car dings pleasantly when I start it up. I've gotten so used to the old Jeep that the lights on the dashboard seem too shiny and bright and the driver's seat feels awkwardly stiff and bouncy.

It's 7:58 when I park the car on Main Street. I don't even bother locking it, just slam the door and run for In Between Books . . .

The sign on the door is flipped to CLOSED. Inside, the store is dark.

But when I worked at the bookstore, I stayed late all the time if I was on the last shift. Even after the store was technically closed, I was unpacking books or cleaning up in that half-light I liked so much. I never locked the door until I actually left. So maybe I can still get in. Maybe if the door hasn't been locked in 2009 . . .

I grab the knob and pull, but the door won't open. I rattle the knob. I pull again, with everything I've got, but the door doesn't budge.

"Come on, come on, come on . . ." I'm muttering under my breath, shallow, shaky panic-whispers while my heart pounds against my ribs. I rattle the knob again and again, but it's useless. It won't turn.

I can't get in.

My eyes sting. I lean my forehead against the door.

I can't get in.

A car engine rumbles down the street behind me and brakes squeak. "Darby?"

I jerk, letting go of the doorknob and whirling around like I've been caught stealing.

A white pickup truck is pulled up to the curb, passenger window rolled down. Leaning down to look at me from the driver's seat is Michael.

Everything inside me crumbles. I'm relieved to see him and embarrassed at the same time. Embarrassed that I'm here, trying to get into a
closed bookstore. Embarrassed by everything I hurled at him last night.
Too aware, suddenly, of my shirt sticking to my back and my hair sticking to my forehead and the raw and ragged feeling in my throat.

"Hi," I say.

He glances past me to the bookstore. "What are you doing?"

Falling apart. Coming undone. Losing my mind.

"Nothing. I just . . ." My eyes burn. I pull off my glasses so I can rub
them. My hands are shaking. "I don't know."

"Can I give you a ride home?"

I point, half-heartedly, up the street to the white hatchback. "My car's
right there."

He turns, glancing at it through his back windshield. Then he chews
his lip and looks back at me. "Want to come to my place for a bit?"

I take a shuddering breath, perilously close to folding up right there on
the sidewalk and starting to cry. "Sure."

He leans over and opens the door for me. I climb into the passenger
seat of his truck, and we rumble away down Main Street, leaving the
bookstore and the rental car behind. The breeze streaming through
the window is almost chilly. It cools my face until I don't feel quite so
hot and puffy and panicked. And eventually, I realize something in
the truck smells salty and spicy and amazing. I glance down—there's
a white plastic bag on the bench between us that says CANNOVA'S. The
Italian restaurant on Main Street.

Michael notices me looking at it. "Takeout," he says self-consciously.
"Amanda and Liz are out on a date night and I couldn't get it together to
cook, so . . . takeout."

I nod. I can't seem to focus on anything, and I can't think of anything
to say, so I go back to staring out the window.

Michael turns the truck into his long driveway. I follow him up the
porch steps and into the house.

"We could go upstairs," he says. "Hang out in my room and watch
something, or . . ."

He sounds tentative. Like he did in the bookstore—like his younger self did, asking if Young Darby wanted to rent a *Buffy* DVD from the video store. A little hopeful. A little like he thinks I might bite.

"I'm sorry," I say. "I shouldn't have said all of that, last night. I got in my own head."

He shifts. Uncomfortably. "You want some takeout?"

He doesn't want to talk about it. Just like he doesn't want to talk about why we fell apart.

The corners of my eyes prickle. "Yeah. Sure."

He turns and climbs the stairs to the second floor, so I follow him, dimly realizing I've never been up here. I had no reason to come up here when it was Michael's grandma's house.

There's a small landing. A bathroom. A set of sliding doors that looks like a closet. At one end of the hall is a bedroom, the door partly open. I see a bed with a striped comforter and a whole bunch of throw pillows.

Michael heads for the bedroom at the other end of the hall. His bedroom. It's strange and intimate to see it. A neatly made bed with a plain blue comforter. A desk covered in textbooks and notebooks, a laptop balanced precariously on top of the mess. An old, worn dresser against another wall, with a familiar Pikachu plushie sitting on top of it. The plushie I gave him. A remnant of the old Michael, and the old Darby.

Michael sets the takeout bag and the forks down on the nightstand, and opens up his laptop on the desk. "We could watch a movie?"

"Sure."

He glances back at me. "Any suggestions?"

I literally could not care less. I'm a mess of exhaustion and anxiety and a creeping sense of dread, and I can't figure out how to have an opinion about anything. "Whatever you want."

He looks at me a moment longer and then goes back to his computer. He hunts around various streaming services for a couple minutes, and then he starts playing *Singin' in the Rain*.

We sit on his bed, pillows behind our backs. He opens the takeout containers and hands me a fork. I could swear I'm not hungry, but I end up eating anyway—stabbing bites of spaghetti and twisting them around the fork. It's good.

Eventually, we're done with the takeout and the containers end up back on the nightstand. Sometime while Debbie Reynolds is singing "Good Morning," his arm goes around my shoulders, and I tuck myself against him. He's warm and solid and grounding and comforting and *here*. And I desperately want to be here. I desperately want to be comforted. I desperately want to convince myself everything is okay.

I turn my face up, and he looks at me, and I'm not sure which of us moves first, but our lips meet, and I'm kissing him. Or he's kissing me. The kiss is happening anyway, and then it's turning deeper, his arm tightening around me, my hand venturing up to cup his face.

And maybe it's desperation or anxiety or panic or all three, but I feel like someone lit a match in my chest, a spark into a flame. I turn toward him, my hand leaving his face and moving down his neck, over his chest. Before I think about it, I'm climbing onto him, running my fingers through his rumpled hair. He finds the edge of my T-shirt and his hand slips underneath, fingertips grazing my top surgery scars. And now my shirt just seems like it's in the way, so I pull it off over my head. And then that doesn't seem fair, so I tug frustratedly on his T-shirt, and he pulls it off. I run my hands over his chest and kiss him again, and then that's not enough, so I unbutton his jeans.

He pulls away. "Darby . . ."

I stop, leaning back, fear rising up my throat. "Sorry. I'm . . . I can stop."

He shakes his head. "No, I . . . I'm good. I just . . . are you?"

I manage a tiny shaky nod, suddenly too breathless to speak. My hands go back to his jeans, and he says, "Wait."

I pull back again.

"Pants off?" he says.

I'm catching on fire. "Yeah."

I climb off his lap and he sort of scoots his way out of his jeans, because there's honestly no sexy way to take off pants. The jeans drop on the floor and I'm about to slide back onto his lap when his hands come up, catching my hips, and he tugs on my belt loop.

I swallow, the rawness back in my throat. But I shimmy my way out of my jeans too. My heart thuds, and I want, and I need, and I'm terrified. "I, um . . ." My voice is raspy. "Have you . . . ? I mean, with a trans guy? Because I'm . . ."

Michael's face is already flushed, but he turns even pinker. "I have, actually. Once."

That wasn't what I was expecting. "Really?"

"In college." He swallows, and I see his Adam's apple move up and down.

The wanting rushes back. I kiss him, and he pulls me back onto him. At some point, even boxer briefs feel like too much between us, and we get rid of those too. And then his hands are exploring me, and mine are exploring him, and it's really a good thing Amanda and Liz are out because I'm starting to make *sounds* . . .

We pause again, just long enough for him to unwrap a condom and me to slam the laptop shut and set my glasses on the bedside table and turn off the light. And then his hands find me, and we're both on the bed, and I let myself turn desperate until everything is just us shutting out the world. Until my mind really is white noise, and I'm not just catching on fire, I'm burning.

CHAPTER TWENTY-FOUR

AUGUST 31

I wake up to the sharp smell of coffee. My eyelids feel sticky; it takes me a few blinks to actually open my eyes.

I'm staring at an unfamiliar popcorn ceiling with a single light fixture in the center. What Olivia likes to call a boob light. She has a whole stand-up routine about it.

Wait a minute. Am I back in New York?

I blink again and yesterday comes back to me in fractured bits and pieces. The locked door of the bookstore. Michael and his truck. Michael's house and then Michael's mouth and hands and . . .

I push myself up onto my elbows, blinking the rest of the room into focus. Sunlight floods through the window over Michael's desk.

"Shit." I scramble around, tangled up in Michael's pin-striped sheets, looking for my phone. "Shit, shit, shit."

Next to me, still face-planted in his pillow, Michael groans. "What?"

"I slept here." *Where is my phone?* "Shit."

Michael rolls over and squints at me blearily. "So?"

"I didn't mean to fall asleep. I told my mom I was coming over here, but . . ." I lean over the edge of the bed. My phone is on the floor. I grab it, fumbling for my glasses on the bedside table. I don't have any voicemails. Or text messages. I guess that's a good sign.

"She probably assumes you spent the night," Michael says, sitting up. He's shirtless, leaning back on his hands.

Oh, god.

I never even told Mom Michael had kissed me, but . . . how much has she figured out?

I rub my eyes. "I should go."

Michael reaches out, but he stops just short of touching me. "Yeah. I mean, sure."

I take a big gulp of air, but I feel like there's a rubber band tight around my lungs.

"Are you okay?" Michael asks.

"Yeah." I push back the sheets, swinging my legs over the side of the bed. I seem to be wearing underwear. I honestly don't even remember putting my underwear back on. "Why wouldn't I be?"

"Never mind."

I glance at Michael, but he isn't looking at me. He's reaching for a T-shirt. Pulling it over his head.

So I grab my clothes, pulling on my pants and my T-shirt. There's a weird nervous pain in my chest, a scratching under my solar plexus. My birthday party is tonight. Young Darby's birthday party is tonight.

I'm out of time.

Tomorrow, even if the bookstore is still there—even if I can still travel—Young Darby will be gone.

"I'm just gonna run to the bathroom," I say.

I'm terrified, as soon as I leave the room, that I'll run into Liz or Amanda, but I hear the murmur of their voices coming from downstairs. The coffee smell is stronger out here, and it nudges me awake as I go into the bathroom. I close the door behind me, leaning against it. It's not a very big bathroom, and the vanity is crowded with toothbrushes and contact lens cases and mouthwash and toothpaste and somebody's hair straightener.

I stare at the jumble, trying to make myself hang on to that *wanting* feeling of last night with Michael. But I can't find it. All I feel is anxious.

I splash water on my face, but that doesn't make anything clearer. And then I realize none of these towels belong to me, and I'm not sure what I should use to dry my face, so I end up just sort of patting it with my hands, like that'll help.

The scratchiness won't leave my solar plexus.

When I go back to Michael's bedroom, he's gotten out of bed, and he's dressed, in the middle of running a hand through his rumpled hair.

"Hey," I say.

He picks up his glasses from the desk, but he doesn't look at me. "Hey."

I lean over, picking up my socks. "I should go get my car."

"Yeah. Sure."

"Michael—"

He looks at me. Finally.

"I really just feel like I should go," I say. "This isn't about last night."

He hesitates. "You sure?"

"Yeah." And I am. And I'm not.

He nods. I can tell he's deciding to believe me, and I don't know if that makes me feel better or worse. "Do you want any coffee? Or breakfast?"

No. I want to go back to the rental car immediately. I want to try to get back into the bookstore again.

I glance at my phone. It's barely nine. The bookstore isn't open yet.

The scratchiness turns painful.

"Sure," I say. "Breakfast sounds good."

It's almost ten thirty when Michael drops me off on Main Street. I somehow managed to drink coffee and eat a piece of toast, and be with Michael and Liz and Amanda as they moved around the kitchen, going through their morning routines. I watched the way Michael relaxed around them. The way they talked and laughed with one another. Neither Liz nor Amanda seemed that surprised or thrown by the fact that I was there in the morning with no explanation.

It was all just . . . normal. Normal, comfortable, easy. And I felt like I was watching it from far away.

"So I guess I'll see you tonight?" Michael asks, as I climb out of the truck. "At the party?"

"Yeah. See you tonight."

He drives away, and I turn for the bookstore, stomach churning. I grasp the doorknob, tugging open the door, walking through . . .

And it's still here. The musty smell, the new releases that aren't new, the magazine stand. I'm in 2009. I made it.

My breath rushes out. The scratchiness in my chest fades. I turn to the counter, and there's my younger self, just coming out of the back room, holding a book.

"Wow, perfect timing," Young Darby says. "Your book just got here." And my younger self holds up the book—*Transgender History*. I recognize the cover immediately.

I glance quickly at Young Darby's face. My pulse speeds up. "Um . . . that's great. Did you . . . have you read it at all?"

Young Darby glances down at the book. "I was just starting to look through it."

Something catches my eye behind the counter—a blurry shape, like a moving shadow. But when I look again, it's gone.

I try to focus on Young Darby. "What do you think? I mean, about the book?"

"Um . . . it's . . ." Young Darby glances at me, and then quickly away, shrugging one shoulder. "I'd like to read it."

God, am I hearing music again? It's faint, slightly distorted, almost like it's underwater.

Another flicker at the corner of my eye. The magazine stand is flashing—like it's there one minute and gone the next.

Young Darby doesn't seem to notice.

"You can keep the book if you want," I say, but my voice sounds a mile away. Like I have cotton in my ears.

Young Darby frowns, looking down at the book again. "Keep it?"

"For now." I squeeze my eyes shut, trying to ignore the distant music, like maybe if I do, it'll go away. "I mean . . . why don't you read it? I'll come back later."

"I guess," Young Darby says. "If you're sure, then—"

But I don't find out *then what*, because I open my eyes, and Young Darby is gone. I'm standing in the other bookstore, the present bookstore. Journals. Mugs. Soft music playing over the speakers. Someone I don't recognize is behind the counter, talking to someone else who's in the middle of buying a book.

Fuck.

I head for the door, pushing my way out onto the sidewalk.

I don't turn around and try to go back in. I don't even know what good it would do. I don't know what I would say to my younger self.

It's too late. *I'm* too late.

I walk toward the rental car, barely seeing anything except the sidewalk in front of me.

Maybe this was all just random—the universe being strange and unknowable, and I just wanted there to be a purpose to it because I'm a human and that's what humans want. Maybe I was never going to be able to change anything for the better. Maybe I was never going to be able to change anything at all.

I climb into the rental car, and I sit for a while, resting my head on the steering wheel.

But I can't even summon the energy to cry.

CHAPTER TWENTY-FIVE

AUGUST 31

The roof deck of the condo is crisscrossed by patio string lights sending a warm glow over the deck chairs and tables. There's an honest-to-god fire roaring away in the firepit, and a folding table draped in the paper tablecloth from Floyd's. On the table is a sheet cake and stacks of paper plates and plastic cups.

And in the middle of it all, currently unwrapping a package of napkins, is my mom.

I dropped her off here (along with Mr. Grumpy) almost an hour ago so she could start setting up, while I went hunting for plastic silverware that we'd forgotten to get. I couldn't bring myself to go back to Floyd's, because that meant going back to Main Street, so I drove all the way out to County Market.

"Darby!" Mom drops the bag on the table and hurries over, careening into me so hard that I let out an actual *oof.* "It's my birthday boy!" She wraps her arms around me and gives me a squeeze. "Happy thirtieth, sweetheart."

"Thanks, Mom." It comes out a bit strangled. "My birthday's, um . . . tomorrow."

She lets me go and waves a hand. "Yes, I know that, but today's the party. It still counts. Did you get the silverware?"

I hold up the plastic bag. "Yeah. Just forks, right?"

"Yes, yes." She takes the plastic bag and pulls me over to the folding table. "You haven't seen the cake yet! What do you think?"

The sheet cake is peak grocery-store cake—perfect white frosting, a few blobby flowers around the edges, and a scattering of sprinkles. HAPPY NEW ADVENTURES DARBY & PHYLLIS! is written across the surface in loopy blue frosting that reminds me vaguely of toothpaste.

I squint at it. "It kind of sounds like we're a couple, Mom."

"What?" She looks at the cake. "No, it doesn't! It's just wishing us both new adventures! There wasn't room to say happy birthday *and* happy condo-warming or whatever."

"Okay."

"Get your brain out of the gutter." She slaps the back of my head lightly and looks down at Mr. Grumpy, standing next to the table and watching us placidly. "I'd better take Grumpy outside to go potty before the party starts. Finish with the silverware, would you?"

And she pulls the basset hound toward the door, her flip-flops slapping against her heels. Leaving me staring at the cake.

Happy new adventures.

The shaky, panicked feeling boils back up in my stomach. I pull my phone out of my pocket, glancing at the time. 6:33.

An hour and a half until the bookstore closes.

Two hours until my party starts back in 2009.

I swallow, feeling vaguely sick, and lean my head back, staring past the string lights to the sky, turning darker blue, fading to purple at the edges. The first bright star is twinkling—probably actually a planet, I guess, if I can see it already, although I have no idea which one.

I decided this was random. I decided there was no explanation. So I have to let this go. Maybe the only reason I traveled was to remind me I have no fucking control over anything. Life just keeps moving, and I get swept along, and suddenly I'm standing on the roof deck of my mom's new condo, about to turn thirty with no idea how I got here.

I need a drink. Lightweightness be damned.

Behind me, a door creaks. "Wow. This is amazing."

I turn. Michael's standing on the roof deck, holding a cooler, which makes the sinewy muscles of his arms stand out. He's looking up at the lights strung overhead. "Your mom do all this?"

"I think the string lights are just here, actually." I wander toward him. "Want help with that?"

"Yeah, thanks."

We carry the cooler across the roof deck, setting it down next to the table. Michael eyes the cake.

I wince. "I know."

"It's nice," he says.

"It's weird."

He grins. "It's a little weird."

I take a slow breath, trying to swallow the acid rising up my throat. "Please tell me you're not the only one coming."

"Liz and Amanda are right behind me with more ice," he says. He loops an arm around my shoulders and pulls me into a sideways hug. "Happy birthday."

It sounds like he means it, but the hug just feels awkward, and I can't tell if it's him or me. That rubber band is back around my lungs. The party hasn't even started yet and I already want to leave. "Thanks." I pull away and pick up the bag of plastic silverware, emptying the rest of it onto the table.

"What's wrong?" he asks quietly.

I glance at him. He's standing with his hands in his pockets, watching me with a slight frown. "Nothing." I turn back to the plasticware. "Do you think you could find a trash can? We're gonna need one."

He stands there a moment longer, and then he says, "Sure." I hear him walking away, back toward the roof deck entrance. The door creaks open and then closed.

I pull out my phone again.

6:37.

DESPITE ALL MY anxiety that the party would be a bust, people show up. Jeannie Young. A bunch of Mom's old teacher friends. Mrs. Siriani. Rebecca Voss. John and Lucas. Cheryl Linsmeier, although not Natalie or Brendan, thankfully. And, of course, Liz and Amanda and Michael. The roof deck fills up with talking and laughing and people balancing plates of sheet cake and paper cups, while the sun sinks and the leaping flames in the firepit throw flickering shadows.

And all of this feels wrong.

I feel like I'm in the middle of my own party and watching from the sidelines all at once. Like I can see a path unfolding from here—moving into the second bedroom in my mom's condo and maybe eventually into Michael's house, learning to be okay with driving to Chicago for hormones or a doctor who knows things without me having to fill in the gaps. Learning to live in the same town as my mom, learning to spend an hour at the grocery store because I keep running into people I know, learning to be queer in the way Michael and Liz and Amanda are queer.

Learning to be okay if Michael never holds my hand outside, when there's a chance anyone else would notice.

I could buy a car, because I'll have to drive everywhere, especially in the winter.

I could get used to going back to my high school, on Friday nights for football, or because I'm bringing Michael a lunch he forgot, or because it's raining and he doesn't want to bike home.

I could text Olivia and Ian and Joan. I could FaceTime them. I could plan a trip a year to see them, if I could afford it. I could learn to be okay if they never came to see me.

I could learn to be okay if they did, and didn't understand any of this.

But maybe that's the really terrifying part. *I could learn to be okay*.

I could exist.

And I'd have Michael. I want that, don't I?

He brings me a piece of cake and then a drink. We stand around the firepit with Liz and Amanda and John and Lucas. I try to be part of the conversation, but I keep losing track of it. I keep pulling out my phone and checking the time, like a nervous tic, like something I can't control.

7:25.

7:35.

My phone buzzes in my hand, just as I'm about to stick it back in my pocket, right as the time clicks over to 7:36.

OLIVIA HENRY

Happy birthday eve

I feel like someone reached into my chest and squeezed my heart.

A few people brought condo-warming presents for my mom, even though (according to the invitations she emailed) they weren't supposed to.

We watch her unwrap a bottle of wine, a gift certificate for Magic Beans, and an embroidered dish towel. Jeannie Young insists that Mom open her present last—a fuzzy throw blanket with a giant penguin on it. Liz covers her mouth to keep from laughing. My mom shoots me A Look, but manages to paste on a smile and thank Jeannie for the gift.

And the whole time, Michael is right there next to me. Close enough for our arms to touch. I can practically feel his voice and his laugh vibrating in my chest.

But I'm a million miles away. None of this feels like home. It's like some alternate reality—like I walked through another doorway and traveled, and I've arrived in some different version of my life.

I finally can't take it anymore, and while everyone is laughing at my mom giving Mr. Grumpy a tiny piece of cake, I slip away to the other side of the roof deck. Take another deep breath, trying to break the rubber band around my chest. Take a gulp of my drink—too big a gulp. The alcohol burns down my throat.

I pull out my phone.

7:53.

"Hey."

I jump, quickly lowering my phone. It's Michael. I didn't even hear him come up behind me. But he's standing here now, hands in the pockets of his worn jeans, shoulders hunched up, eyes searching my face.

"Hi," I say.

He takes a few slow steps forward until he's standing next to me and leans his hands on the railing of the roof deck, looking out over the treetops of Krape Park.

"Darby," he says quietly, "what's going on?"

"Nothing." He's not looking at me, but I try to smile anyway. My face feels too tight. I can't seem to make my mouth stretch.

He lets his breath out. A frustrated sound. "Is this . . . is this about last night?"

I rub my temples. My head aches. "No. It's not. I promise it's not."

His eyes search mine again, and he seems to find the answer he needs. He swallows. Nods. "Okay. Then . . . what?"

I run a hand through my hair, staring out at the park. At the darkening sky above it. Twilight slipping into night. I open my mouth, but I don't know what to say. Time feels like it's getting away from me and I can't figure out how to catch up.

"I'm fine," I say, but it's not convincing at all.

He runs a hand over his face. "I don't think you are."

The rubber band around my lungs snaps, sharp and sudden. "Fine," I say. "I'm not. But I don't want to talk about this. It's not something you can understand, okay?"

A crease deepens between his eyebrows. "What's that supposed to mean?"

I fumble for words, but I can't find any. "I don't know, Michael. It means what it means."

He leans away from me. "Right. This is starting to feel familiar."

"What?"

"I get that you have a lot going on." Michael's voice is rough. "It's your birthday and your mom's moving and you're trying to figure things out, but . . . I'm right here, and it kind of seems like every time I'm here, you just push me away. Like I'm not worth trusting."

I stare at him. "What are you talking about?"

A spasm of hurt crosses his face. "This feels a lot like what happened the last time we celebrated your birthday, Darby."

We're too far away to hear the Falls—way too far away—but I could swear there's something roaring in my ears. A rushing sound just like water plunging down a cliff.

He's talking about my seventeenth birthday party.

He's talking about *back then*.

"That was . . . that was years ago," I say.

"Yeah, and yet somehow this feels like history repeating itself," he says flatly.

I feel like the ground I'm standing on is turning to water. "I don't know what you think is repeating itself, Michael. You got upset with *me*. I don't even know why we started fighting—that's why I *asked* you what happened. You didn't want to talk about it."

He shakes his head. His eyes look too bright. "Was it really that forgettable for you?"

"Forgettable?" All the panic churning in my stomach rises up my throat. "You were my *best friend*. And suddenly you were more upset than I'd ever seen you, over some little thing I said that I don't even remember, that wasn't even a big deal, and suddenly we were yelling at each other. You cut *me* out, Michael. You didn't say goodbye when I left, and when I came back, I was apparently dead to you."

He shakes his head again, harder this time. "No. That's not true."

"Then how come you never talked to me again after I got back?"

"It's not true that it wasn't a big deal. It's not true that I started it."

"Then what *is* true?" My voice is rising, and it's probably carrying farther than it should, but I don't care. The rubber band snapped and all the built-up pressure in my chest is looking for a way out now, some kind of release valve. I'm breathing too fast, like I just ran a marathon.

Michael's eyes glitter. "You were upset then too. Just like now. Something was clearly wrong, and I asked you what was going on, and you just brushed me off." His voice wavers and he looks away, like it's too much to keep looking at me. "You told me *someone like me* could never understand. And I'd been . . . I'd been trying to tell you who I was for *weeks*. I wanted to tell you before you left, and every time I tried, I just *couldn't*. I was too scared to actually say it; I kept hoping you'd guess, so I wouldn't have to. And that week . . ." His voice cracks. He rubs a hand over his face. "The week before your birthday, I brought the latest issue of Pet Avengers to Prime Pie Pizza while I was waiting for you to finish work, and Brendan Mitchell walked in and told me that was the gayest shit he'd ever seen me read."

Cold settles deep into my core.

"And then Brendan was at your birthday party, and . . ." Michael looks at me desperately. "I was dropping hints for *weeks*, Darby. I thought you knew, and you knew that Brendan said weird shit around me, and then he was there, and you told me *someone like me* could never understand . . ."

Someone's splicing videotape together in my head. I can see my younger self in the bookstore, shoulders hunched forward to hide my chest. I see myself insisting I have to leave; I have to get out of Oak Falls. But now I'm at my party too—back in my own body, painfully aware of every way it feels wrong. Painfully aware that my mom invited all these people in my class to take up space, to fill up a birthday party, so it wouldn't just be me and Michael.

And surrounded by my classmates, it was just so obvious that I couldn't fit in with any of them. I felt like I was all angles, sharp corners of me bursting out where every other girl was soft edges. I wished that I could dress like they did, and I felt so angry that I couldn't make myself do it.

I'm not a girl. It was the first time I remember thinking that. Exactly that. *I am not a girl, and I don't know how to explain that to anyone.*

"I didn't invite Brendan," I murmur, but my voice comes out weak, and it sounds like an excuse. Which it is.

Michael just shakes his head again. "It doesn't matter," he says thickly.

No, it doesn't. Because what matters is Michael thought I knew. He thought I knew he was gay, and when I said *someone like you wouldn't understand . . .*

It hits me like a thunderclap. I remember those words slipping out of my mouth, bitterly. I can almost see Michael—not the Michael in front of me now but the one I knew back then—drawing back, like I'd slapped him.

He said something like, *Wow, thanks,* in the sharpest voice I had ever heard him use. So sharp that it jerked me out of the angry, miserable, self-involved fog I was lost in. I didn't get what he was so angry about. That made him angrier. And I still don't remember everything we said, yelling at each other in the middle of my living room while everyone else edged away and tried to ignore us.

But it doesn't matter. Because I told him *someone like you wouldn't understand,* and he thought *someone like you* meant I knew he was gay. He thought I was telling him he couldn't understand me anymore because he was gay, because I thought there was something wrong with him, and I never wanted to trust him with any piece of me again.

And when he started yelling at me, I exploded, because I'd been waiting to explode for weeks, probably for months, and all of this just meant *I was right,* nobody would understand me. And then we were hurting each other, tearing away at the most vulnerable, invisible pieces of each of us, too terrified to reveal those pieces to the other person.

No wonder he didn't say goodbye before I left.

No wonder he didn't call me at boarding school.

No wonder he searched for another friend to replace me with. And he found Liz—he found someone queer, someone he could trust with that fragile part of himself. No wonder he didn't look back.

No wonder he tried to move on.

Olivia's face flashes into my mind. The way she looked at me expectantly, eagerly, when I came out to her in that random lounge at NYU. The way she was so eager to come out to me.

The fierce way we hung on to each other that first semester. The way we hung on to Ian when we found him. The way all four of us still hang on, even in New York, where there are queer bars and drag shows and a giant LGBT center. Because sure, maybe it's easier in a place where there are more of us and where we don't feel quite so weird, but we are still making space. We are always making space for ourselves, and the only reason I ever learned how to do that—the only reason I was ever *okay*— was because I met Olivia. Because I met Ian and Joan.

Because I realized I wasn't alone.

All the air crushes out of my lungs.

"Michael," I whisper, "I'm so sorry."

From the direction of Main Street, the bell in First Church starts to chime.

8:00.

And I know, like someone flipped on a light in my brain, what I have to do.

No, more than that. What I *want* to do.

And I have to hurry, because I'm almost out of time.

I reach out and grasp Michael's limp hands tightly in my own. "I'm so sorry," I say again, my voice shaking. "I didn't know you were gay. And I didn't realize what was happening. And I want to talk to you more about this, but I have to go. I just . . . I have to go do something, and it can't wait. But I'll be back. I'll be right back."

He stares at me, and then opens his mouth, but he can't seem to find any words, and I can't wait for them anyway.

"I'll come back," I say again, even though I'm not entirely sure I will—or entirely sure I'll be able to—and then I let go of his hands and I dodge around the edge of the crowd toward the door that leads down from the roof deck.

CHAPTER TWENTY-SIX

AUGUST 31

I don't wait for the elevator. I slam into the stairwell, pounding down the stairs so fast that my shoes slip multiple times and I have to grab the railing before I go flying headfirst. I jump the last few steps at the bottom and then I run through the lobby, out the front door, and down the sidewalk. The warm night air sticks in my lungs and my footfalls vibrate my bones as I pelt toward the bookstore.

The bell tower's last chime rings into the air above me.

The streetlights are on all up and down Main Street. Most of the storefronts are dark; Ethel May's is still open, a few families sitting at tables outside. Someone is mopping the floor behind the window of Subway. The lights framing the window of Cannova's blink garishly into the night.

But all I really care about is In Between Books. And behind the frosted letters on the window, a few fluorescent lights are still on.

I don't slow down. Don't give myself time to think about what I'm doing, what I'm about to do, or even time to think about what will happen if I can't get in, because the sign on the door is turned to CLOSED . . .

I just run straight to the door and *pull*.

It opens so fast that I stumble backward, the bell overhead jangling. The comforting musty smell fills my nose as I cross the threshold, gasping for air, eyes adjusting to the half-light. The magazine stand is here. The handwritten signs. I'm in the past.

"Darby?" My voice comes out hoarse and cracked.

The floor creaks, and there's my younger self, just stepping out of the back room, holding a stack of books. Confusion crosses Young Darby's face. I'm sure it's partly because the store is closed and I just barged in anyway, but in the back of my mind, I realize I've never called this version of me by my name.

"Um." The books slip and Young Darby quickly slides them onto the counter. The spines glint in the glow from the streetlights outside the window, all of them a dull, muted red. "Hi. The store's closed."

"I know." I'm out of breath. My throat is dry and my head is pounding. "I'm sorry. But there's something . . . I need to tell you something."

"I'll be here tomorrow too," Young Darby says blankly. "Just for the morning, and then I have to pack—"

"It's important." *And I don't know if I'll be able to find you. And even if I could . . .* "It can't wait."

A frown crosses Young Darby's face. "Okay. But . . ." Young Darby turns, glancing up at the book clock over the storage room door. "I have to go in a minute. It's my birthday party tonight."

My younger self looks back at me, maybe trying for a smile, but it doesn't quite materialize. Because it's not a party I'm excited about. It's a party I'm having because I have a birthday party every year, and I couldn't figure out how to tell my mom I wasn't sure if I wanted one this year, and by the time I was sure I definitely didn't, she'd already invited people, and it was too late.

And anyway, I didn't know what I'd say if she asked me why.

The fluorescent light over the counter flickers. My eyes jerk toward it and I think I can see the shadowy shape of a person behind the counter. Just for a second. And then the shape is gone.

My heart hammers. *I'm running out of time.*

I have to do this now. I have to say all this now, before I fall into the present again.

I drag in a breath. "There's something you know about yourself. Something we've been talking around. It's something big and life-changing and so simple at the same time. You know who you are, even though you probably haven't said it out loud to yourself yet. And I know—believe me—how hard it is to look around at this place and feel like there's room for you to exist. How hard it is to see any kind of future for yourself."

The light overhead dims and then brightens. The table of new releases seems to shift a few inches, the stacks of books growing and shrinking, their spines shifting colors. Almost like I'm looking at everything through only my left eye and then switching quickly to my right.

No, no, no. I need to stay here. Just give me a few more minutes.

"I know you're about to leave and go to this new school," I say, and desperation is creeping into my voice. "I know you're hoping that will be an escape, but . . ." I focus as hard as I can on my younger self standing next to the counter, watching me with wide eyes. "Don't assume you'll lose people once they know who you are. Take care of yourself. Protect yourself. But don't hurt yourself more by shutting people out."

Young Darby glances away, shrinking inward. "I don't know what you're talking about."

Oh, kid. "Yeah, you do."

"You don't know anything about me." But it doesn't sound defiant this time. It sounds afraid, like a phrase held up as a shield.

The fluorescent light above us flickers again, and now I think I can hear music, distantly. Something jazz again, muffled and muted.

"We've been over this," I say. "You remind me of me, remember?" I almost laugh, but it gets stuck in my throat. "And I know enough about me."

Young Darby looks at me. A deep look. So deep that I feel exposed.

And then I see it—a slow hint of recognition. Not that I'm *me*, not that we're the same person.

A recognition much deeper than that.

Very quietly, Young Darby says, "If you knew, why didn't you tell me?"

Because you'd ask how I knew. Because I didn't know if you'd believe me. "Because nobody else can tell you who you are."

Young Darby draws a breath, and the music is fading in my ears now, and I hear the breath shudder. "So now what? You're here to tell me everything's going to be okay?"

"No." I swallow. "I'm here to tell you to trust your friends."

Something flashes through Young Darby's eyes. Doubt, or maybe fear. "What's that mean?"

"It means you don't need to start over." Now Young Darby fades in front of me. For a disconcerting second, I can see straight through my younger self to a row of books—like Young Darby has turned into a ghost. I squeeze my eyes shut. "You don't need to start over, because if you want to be yourself—all of yourself—your friends can come with you." I open my eyes. Young Darby is solid again. "Don't assume you're too much or too weird or too new. I know not everybody is safe, and you need to be safe, but . . . but sometimes it's worth taking the risk. You'll know when it's worth taking the risk, and then . . ." I swallow again, because my throat is closing up. "And then you have to, because the only alternative is to be alone, and that's so much worse."

Young Darby looks down at the stack of books on the counter. I catch a glimpse of a bird on the cover of the book on top of the stack. *Catching Fire.* The bookstore is going to be so crowded tomorrow. Or . . . as crowded as In Between Books ever got when I worked there.

"I don't even understand me." It's a whisper. Young Darby rubs a thumb over the corner of one of the books. "I don't know how anyone else is supposed to."

"Welcome to the world." I let my breath out and shrug. "I don't understand me, either. But honestly, that's just how it is for everyone. I mean, some of us have to try harder, but . . . we can still choose who's with us while we fumble around."

Young Darby blinks, but I see a tear slide down one cheek. "How can you be so sure? I mean, maybe that's how it works for you, but . . ."

"I'm not," I say. Which is the truth, after all. "But I have a feeling."

Young Darby looks up at me, almost accusing. "A feeling?"

I nod.

My younger self wavers. Looks down at the books again. And then says, "The only friend I have is . . . I mean . . . it's Michael."

I nod again.

"He's going to be at my birthday party tonight." Young Darby swipes quickly at one cheek. Maybe hoping I won't notice. "What if you're wrong?"

I open my mouth and hesitate. Because even though I want to say I'm not wrong, even though I want to promise that I know the outcome of this and everything will be fine . . .

The truth is, I don't know. I only have a feeling. The Michael I know is the one I just left on the roof deck—and he's not the same as he was thirteen years ago, just like I'm not the same. I can't pretend I know someone who no longer exists.

Which means that finally, Young Darby and I are in exactly the same position—neither of us have a fucking clue what's coming.

"You keep going anyway," I say. "And you find people who understand. They're out there." And that, at least, I know to be true.

I see my younger self's shoulders rise and fall, and rise again. Young Darby hesitates, and then . . . "Okay. Maybe I'll tell Michael."

Whatever's holding me together shatters. My knees go weak and my breath rushes out of my lungs.

The muffled music is back in my ears—closer this time. Behind Young Darby, I see the storage room door close by itself. The table of new releases is shifting again. A shadowy shape moves behind the counter. I could almost swear it's Ann, Hank's daughter.

"You'll be okay," I say to Young Darby, but I'm starting to feel like my younger self is very far away. I look up at the book clock over the storage room door. The burgundy cover of Sherlock Holmes saturates and then fades.

8:15.

I look back at Young Darby. The whole store around me seems to be shifting now, shadows flitting across the floor, darkness creeping in and out of the corners, books flickering on the shelves, the music growing louder. Only Young Darby stays the same in front of me, the light never changing on my younger self's face.

I take a step forward, and before I can second-guess myself, before I can think better of it, I reach out and pull my younger self into a hug.

The music cuts out, like someone's switched off the stereo. The light above us flicks on and off, sharply, like someone's playing with the switch. The stack of red books on the counter vanishes. A faint flowery smell fills the air.

Young Darby's arms wrap around me tightly.

I'm out of time.

I'm falling. I can feel it.

I let go of my younger self, stepping back, breaking Young Darby's grasp.

"Good luck," I say.

"Wait," Young Darby says.

But I don't wait. I can't wait. "You'll be okay," I say again, and then I turn and head for the door.

It occurs to me, in the few seconds before I reach it, that I should have texted Olivia before barging in here and killing my phone's battery. Olivia—or the group chat. At least say, *Nice to have known you.*

Because I have no idea what's going to happen now. Whether I fall out of the past or whether I make it through this door . . .

If Young Darby trusts Michael—if my younger self goes to that birthday party and things go differently—maybe that'll change my past. And if that happens, maybe I'll just cease to exist. Maybe I'll disappear.

If Young Darby changes everything about his future, what happens to me?

I reach out and grasp the doorknob. Push the door open. The bell jingles. And I step outside.

CHAPTER TWENTY-SEVEN

AUGUST 31

"Oh, sorry!"

Someone bumps into me. I stumble. Turn around.

It's Ann, just coming out of the bookstore. She has a bag over her shoulder. Keys in her hand. "Sorry," she says again. "I didn't see you."

I'm on the sidewalk. I'm on the sidewalk in front of In Between, and she's closing the door behind her, locking it. Behind the frosted window, the store is dark.

"No problem," I say automatically.

I'm here. *I'm here.*

What's that mean?

"I heard it's your birthday tomorrow?" Ann says, tucking her keys in her bag.

"Yeah." I don't know how she knows this, but it's Oak Falls. Everyone knows everything.

"Happy birthday," she says, and then she turns and walks up the sidewalk.

I stare after her and then look back at the bookstore. I go up to the window and lean close to it, cupping my hands around my face.

It's dark. I can't see anything except the faint outline of shelves.

"Darby?"

I turn.

It's Michael. He's standing farther down the sidewalk, the steeple of First Church rising into the sky behind him. And he's looking at me, anxiously.

What's going on?

I'm in the present. In *my* present. Everything looks just the same as it did before I went into the bookstore. I still remember fighting with Michael at my birthday party—my 2009 birthday party. Does that mean nothing changed? Does that mean Young Darby didn't trust Michael after all? Didn't tell him the truth, or they got in a fight anyway?

"What are you doing here?" I ask.

Michael walks toward me. "I followed you. Or . . . I tried to." He glances away and rubs the back of his neck. "I mean, I actually kind of lost you . . . You're fast. But I had a feeling you might be heading here."

I glance up at the clock on the side of First Church. Just past eight fifteen.

Am I still here because back in 2009 Young Darby hasn't gotten to that birthday party yet? Does that make any sense?

Time has been moving in parallel ever since I first walked into the bookstore. Every time I went back, it was the same date, the same time, as it was outside. So maybe it's still working like that. Maybe the minute my younger self talks to Michael—if that happens—will be the moment everything changes here in my present.

Or maybe the change will happen at midnight, once it ceases to be August 31 anymore.

Who knows? All of this is supposed to be impossible anyway.

"And you didn't pick up your phone," Michael says.

I jerk out of my thoughts, focusing on his face. "I . . . my phone died. The battery ran out."

He stops a few feet away. "What's going on?" he asks.

Selfishly, a small part of me wants to ignore him. Because I don't know how much time I have left. Because it still seems like I could stop existing, and I have no idea when it might happen.

But then again, if I'm going to stop existing, I don't want to leave things like this, do I? I gave Young Darby a chance to fix things. I should fix things too.

I think, for a second, about just saying fuck it and telling Michael the whole truth, as wild as it sounds. Tell him I'm a time-traveling existential crisis with gender feels and just see what he does. I might disappear in a few minutes anyway, so what does it matter?

But I can't do it. Maybe I don't want him to think I've lost it. Maybe I don't want him to ask a million questions. Maybe it's just that there's some truth I *do* want to tell him, and I don't want to waste time trying to explain everything that's happened in the bookstore first.

"I had to catch Ann," I lie. "I know it sounds ridiculous, but there was a book I really wanted to get for my mom, and I had to order it today for it to get here in time, and . . ." I do my best to look rueful. "I forgot to go earlier and my phone died, so . . . I wanted to try to catch her."

A frown passes across Michael's face. He doesn't look like he totally believes me. "It couldn't wait until tomorrow?"

"No." I let my breath out. "But I . . . I really did mean it. I'm really sorry."

He shoves his hands in his pockets. "It's kind of a weird reason to run out in the middle of—"

"No, I mean, I'm sorry for everything that happened back then. I really didn't know you were gay, and I had no idea anybody was giving you a hard time . . ." I stop. This isn't what I want to say—not what I want to focus on when I don't know how much time I have. "I was really wrapped up in my own shit. I think . . . I think I knew I was trans, but I couldn't even really admit it to myself. I got convinced nobody else would understand. That the only way to be myself—all of myself—was to leave. And somehow being at my birthday party . . . it just made it all so obvious. I said you wouldn't understand because . . . because I thought nobody would." I take a breath, and it hurts, like it's slicing right through me. "I thought it would be easier if I just started over. If I never gave anybody the chance to see the real me and decide to run." I swallow. My throat is closing up again. "I guess I started with you."

Michael has gone very still. "I didn't . . ." His voice cracks. "I thought you were rejecting me."

"Yeah, well . . ." I tip my head back, because my eyes are prickling, and maybe if I look up, gravity will keep the tears in. "When you didn't talk to me after I got back . . . I guess I kind of thought the same thing."

He looks down at his shoes. "I'm sorry," he says. "I think some part of me knew you weren't okay, even before you left. I mean, I could tell you weren't comfortable in . . . well . . . the way you were." He looks up. Takes a breath. "I think I hoped you were gay. That's . . . that's why I thought you might guess about me. Sorry." He flushes. "I didn't know what trans identity was back then . . ."

A smile tugs at my mouth. "That makes two of us."

The corner of his mouth turns up. Just for a moment. And then the smile fades. "You didn't call me," he says. "Or email. That whole semester you were gone."

His voice is so full of leftover hurt that I desperately wish the sidewalk would open up and swallow me, just so I don't have to face it. "I know. I . . . I'm bad at that. I let distances get too big, and then I tell myself it's better that way. I didn't know how to fix it. So I just . . . didn't."

He shrugs one shoulder, but it looks . . . sad. "I wish you'd told me."

Some version of me is trying to. "I know. Me too."

"Do you think if you had . . ." He hesitates, rocking back on his heels. "Do you think if you had, you would have stayed?"

I almost ask what he means. If he means, would I have stayed and not gone to boarding school? Or would I have chosen a college closer to home? Or would I have come back to Oak Falls after college the way he did?

I guess it doesn't really matter—ultimately, they're all sort of the same question.

If I had told Michael who I was, would I be living in Oak Falls now?

"I don't know," I say, because I don't. Did I run away from Oak Falls because I was trans and I thought there wasn't space for me? Or was I always going to leave?

Does the piece of me that doesn't know how to belong here now, that doesn't know how to sit through high school football games, that can't quite be alone with myself in the nighttime stillness . . .

Was that piece always there, or is it part of who I became after I left?

I don't have the answer. It's such a tangled knot, I'm not sure I ever will.

I let my breath out, looking up at the clocktower again. It's almost eight thirty.

"Should we go back?" I ask. "I guess we kind of deserted my mom."

"Yeah," he says. "Let's go back."

There's some distance opening back up between us. I can feel it. We poured everything we'd been ignoring into this space, and even though I finally figured out what drove us apart, and I finally figured out how to fix it . . . it's still pushed Michael farther away. And there's no quick way to get him back. There are too many scars still there that we've uncovered. And scars take time to heal.

And time is one thing I'm not sure I have.

But even across the distance, Michael still holds out his hand. I look down at it and then around at Main Street. "You sure? I mean, there are people around . . ."

"For now," he says.

So I take his hand.

We don't say anything as we walk up the street. But I keep repeating in my thoughts, *We're here we're here we're here.*

NOBODY ASKS WHERE I disappeared to when we get back to the roof deck. A few of Mom's older friends are already saying goodbye, and Liz and Amanda are talking to John and Lucas, and they all seem perfectly happy to let me stand next to them with Michael, neither of us adding much to the conversation. My brain is turning foggy. I try to stay present, try to burn every detail of what's happening around me into my mind. I keep asking Michael what time it is; finally, after the fifth time, he asks what I'm worried about.

"Just . . . condo regulations," I say, which isn't entirely a lie. "Quiet hours."

I didn't need to worry about that. People drift away one by one or in small groups. John says he has to get up early to be at the farm, and he and Lucas wish me another happy birthday and head out. Jeannie Young assures my mother she can come visit the yard penguins any time and my mom manages to (fairly genuinely) thank her for the penguin throw blanket.

Eventually, it's just me and Mom and Michael and Liz and Amanda. And Mr. Grumpy, who seems to think it's way past his bedtime and has flopped on the deck under the folding table. We clean up the empty cake pan and the scattered cups and plates. Michael hauls the trash bag down to the dumpster while Liz and Amanda wrangle the cooler and my mom gathers her presents. I nudge Mr. Grumpy to his feet. He lets out an annoyed grunt, but he trots after me to the door.

Amanda and Liz manage to get the cooler into Amanda's car, and they each give me and my mom a hug, and then they drive off into the dark and the quiet. Mom takes Mr. Grumpy's leash from me and goes to unlock the Jeep, leaving me with Michael, who's standing, waiting, next to his truck.

"Happy almost birthday," he says.

I smile. "Thanks."

He holds out a hand, and I reach out and grasp it tightly. But he doesn't come closer to me, and I don't move, either. There's still too much between us, filling up this space. And for now, we both need to leave it be.

"See you tomorrow," he says.

A knot rises in my throat, but I nod. I don't know what else to do. "Yeah. See you tomorrow."

He lets go and climbs into his truck, and I turn and walk back to the Jeep. I hear the truck's engine start behind me, but I don't look back as Michael rumbles away out of the parking lot.

I climb into the passenger seat of the Jeep and let my breath out, long and slow. "Mom."

She turns the key and the Jeep sputters to life. "Yeah, honey."

"You know I love you, right?"

She looks at me, eyebrows raised. "I love you too, Darby."

I manage a smile, and she smiles back, the crow's-feet around her eyes deepening. She reaches out and squeezes my arm. "Let's get home," she says. "I'm wiped."

I DON'T KNOW what time it is when I finally fall into bed, but outside, it's starting to rain—a pitter-patter that turns into a steady drumming on the roof as I plug in my phone. I manage to take off my pants and then I face-plant in my pillow. I am more tired than I have ever been.

I consider, for half a second, lifting my head up to wait for the moment when my phone turns itself back on, so I can check the time. So I can try to guess what my younger self is up to. Whether anything might have changed by now.

How much time I might have left.

But I don't do it. Partly because I'm actually too tired.

Partly because what's the point?

I have no idea what's coming. I have no idea whether I'm running out

of time in my own present. Whether I'll wake up tomorrow morning. If
I wake up, whether I'll remember any of this or if I'll somehow be a different person.

Whether, if I don't remember any of this, I'll even really be *me*.

Knowing what time it is won't change any of that.

The door of my room creaks open and Mr. Grumpy wheezes his way
in. He sits up and puts his front paws on the bed.

I lean down, hauling him up on the sheets next to me. He flops by my
feet with a contented sigh.

And I close my eyes, listening to Mr. Grumpy snoring and the thrum
of the rain, and imagine that tomorrow, I'll somehow find myself in a
random bar in New York, where Ian will be hangry, and Joan will scroll
her phone, and Olivia will wrap me in a hug.

CHAPTER TWENTY-EIGHT

I wake up.

It takes me a minute, blinking at my bedroom ceiling, to recognize it. My eyelids are heavy. I feel groggy and far away, like I was really deeply asleep. Maybe I was. For the first time in days, I can't remember dreaming . . .

My stomach clenches and my heart hammers so hard I feel sick. I sit up—too fast. My head spins.

Mr. Grumpy grunts awake, picking his head up off my feet. He gives me a sleepy look and yawns.

I gasp for breath, hands sinking into the mattress behind me. Warm sunlight filters through my open bedroom window, along with a faint earthy smell of wet pavement and muddy ground. Leftover hints of last night's rain.

I scramble for my glasses on the nightstand. Pick up my phone. *Thursday, September 1. 9:43 a.m.*

The screen is a jumble of text messages.

JOAN CHU
Welcome to your thirties, loser

IAN ROBB
Sending you virtual beers and fries, Darb

OLIVIA HENRY
Happy birthday, babe. Love you and miss you

IAN ROBB
Sexier fries. In case that wasn't
clear. The gay ones.

I pull my feet away from Mr. Grumpy and swing myself out of bed. I feel practically loopy. I stagger over to the window and stare through the screen. The sidewalk and the street are still dark from the rain. Drops of water sparkle on the grass. Steam rises off the rental car where the sunlight hits its roof.

It definitely rained last night. Just like I remember.

I remember everything. The party. Deserting Michael. The bookstore. Michael waiting for me outside . . .

I glance around my room. It looks just like it did last night. Empty and bare, except for my open suitcase and the clothes scattered around it.

I take a deep breath, trying to slow down my heart. And then another one, because I realize I'm breathing.

I'm breathing.

I'm here.

I exist.

Outside the window, a cicada starts to buzz. Which makes me realize that aside from that cicada, it's quiet. No radio vibrating the walls from the kitchen. No NPR.

Panic knots my insides. I yank open my door and race down the hallway.

And there's my mom, turning around from her spot at the kitchen table. "Good morning! You slept late!"

She's here.

The panic evaporates so fast, I have to lean against the wall to keep from folding up right on the kitchen floor.

Mom frowns at me. "What's wrong with you?"

I open my mouth, but I have no idea what to say. I can't exactly tell her that I messed with my own future, and a part of me was terrified that I now existed alone in some weird purgatory. Even though that doesn't really make any sense.

All I say is "You're not listening to NPR."

She gives me a very patient look. "Of course not. I packed the radio yesterday."

I look at the counter. It's empty—no radio, no dishes, no toaster or coffee maker.

Right. Moving. *Duh.*

"Are you okay?" Mom asks.

"Yeah." My voice sounds hoarse. My throat feels dry and gritty. I look around at the stacks of boxes in the living room and next to the dining table. The bare walls. The bare windows, devoid of their dated country curtains. And the date I read on my phone finally catches up with me. "It's September first."

"Yes, it is!" Mom pushes herself up from the table and wraps her arms around me so tightly that I cough. "Happy birthday, sweetheart."

I'm thirty.

I wait for it to hit me. For the realization to really sink in. For Saturn to return or whatever is supposed to happen according to the Astrology Queers.

But all I feel is a desperate urge to get to the bookstore as fast as I can.

"I have to go," I say over my mom's shoulder.

She lets me go and steps back. "What? Now?"

"Yeah. Just a quick errand." I'm already retreating back down the hallway. My heart thuds again, almost painfully. "I just need to run to Main Street."

"Okay." Mom sounds doubtful. "Well, pick me up a pretentious coffee while you're there, would you?" She sighs and puts her hands on her hips, looking around the bare kitchen. "I clearly packed the coffee maker too early . . ."

Back in my bedroom, I throw on clothes, grab my wallet and keys, and leave the house without even brushing my teeth. I'm definitely pushing well over the speed limit as I drive toward Main Street, swinging around the bends in the road fast enough that the Jeep pulls to the side and leans rather alarmingly.

I slow down when I get to Main Street. It's two minutes after ten and Main Street is barely awake. The only signs of life are the stroller moms, back at their café table in front of Magic Beans.

I park the Jeep right in front of In Between Books. The sign in the window is flipped to OPEN. My heart pounds so hard that I feel lightheaded as I reach out and grasp the doorknob. The bell jingles as I cross the threshold.

I stop. The doorknob slips out of my hand. The door creaks closed behind me.

Everything inside me sinks.

The mustiness of books and paper is gone. The store smells flowery. The handwritten signs have been replaced by typed ones, and where the magazine stand should be there's just the table of journals and mugs. The new releases are all covers I don't recognize and none of them are the shiny red of *Catching Fire*.

This is the bookstore of the present. I know it is, but I still can't stop myself from pulling out my phone, just to be sure.

My battery is at 95 percent.

No. No no no . . .

I swallow the panic rising in my chest and turn around. I walk back out of the bookstore to the sidewalk. Maybe if I just give it a minute, the portal or whatever it is will be there again.

But when I walk back in, everything looks the same. Everything *is* the same. Solidly in the present.

94 percent.

"Can I help you?" someone asks.

For a split second, my throat tightens and my heart leaps, because there's a teenager behind the counter. One with short brown hair.

But my heart drops in the next moment because this kid is a stranger. She's wearing long earrings and eyeliner. And glasses—slim wire-frame glasses.

"Sorry." My voice comes out thick. "I was just looking for someone."

"Oh." The girl looks around. "I don't think anyone else has come in yet. We just opened."

"Right. Thanks." I turn and wander into one of the aisles. I can't just leave. I can't help hoping that perhaps, if I just wait a little longer, I'll suddenly round the corner of a bookshelf and find myself back in 2009, even though I know it's never worked like that before. I've only ever fallen *out* of the past. I've never fallen *into* it.

I walk up and down the aisles, but every time I turn a corner, the neat printed labels are still on the next row of shelves. Every time I get a glimpse of the counter, the girl is still sitting behind it, scrolling on her phone. I'm running out of aisles to walk through, and a lump is rising in my throat that I can't seem to swallow, and my eyes are filling up . . .

I'm here, but my younger self is gone. I can't ask that Darby what happened with Michael. I can't ask if they fought, or if they shared truths instead.

And I don't remember anything different. I remember everything I remembered yesterday. Nothing has changed for me.

What does that mean?

I reach the last row of shelves, but the bookstore stays the same. Quiet and flowery and solidly part of this new Oak Falls. I reach out and touch the spine of a book on the shelf. The thick paper of the hardcover's dust jacket is smooth and weirdly grounding under my fingertips. The books might be different, but they feel just like I remember them. Just like they always have.

"You sure you don't need any help?"

I glance at the girl behind the counter, watching me with raised eyebrows. "No, thanks." I manage a smile, even though it feels wobbly. "I used to work here, actually. Just . . . stopping in for old time's sake."

"Oh. That's cool."

"Yeah."

She's clearly expecting me to say something else, but I can't come up with anything. I don't want to make shallow conversation about working in the store. I don't want to tell her about *back then* or *when I was a kid.*

For one thing, that would make me feel super old. But also . . . it feels too private. It's something I want to keep just for myself.

My eyes wander up to the Sherlock Holmes book clock above the storage room. More faded in the here and now but still ticking away. The fountain pen hands point to 10:15.

I take a deep breath and slowly let it out. "Have a nice day," I say, and walk to the door. Push it open. The bell jingles. I step back out onto the sidewalk.

And hesitate, chewing my lip. I can't quite leave it there.

I turn back on an impulse, opening the door again and stepping back inside because *what if what if what if* . . .

But the store is the same as it was a second ago. Solidly in the present. *That's it.*

I don't know how I know, but I *know.* However I traveled—it's gone. Finally, really gone. Singularity collapse. Or whatever the technical term would be for something that shouldn't have been possible in the first place.

I leave the store and go back out to the sidewalk. Main Street looks exactly the same as it has every day that I've been here, but I feel like I'm staring at it through a window, or a screen. Looking in on something that's not mine. Like the pull, the tug, all of the *what ifs* around me are collapsing too.

I pull my phone out of my pocket. Scroll again through the group chat, past the birthday messages. And then I open my contacts, and—finally—I call Olivia.

She answers after the second ring. "Darby. Happy birthday. I'm so, so sorry."

The lump is back in my throat. For a second, I can't talk.

"Darby?"

"I'm here." My voice cracks. "Thanks for the texts and everything. And . . . I'm sorry I was such an ass."

"No, no, *I* was the ass," Olivia says. "I was in fine ass form and you don't need to apologize. I feel like the worst friend. I shouldn't have said any of that stuff about Oak Falls."

"It's okay." It's not, but she knows it, and I know it, and we both know that what I'm really saying is *We'll be okay.* "I mean, it basically *is* in the middle of a cornfield. So."

She gives a tiny anxious laugh. "Well . . . I'm still sorry, and I really . . . um . . . I mean, how is everything?"

Everything?

I open my mouth, but it takes me a moment to find words. *Everything* is too much for me to even wrap my brain around. I have no idea where to start or even what I'd want to say. "It's . . . been a lot."

She's quiet. And then—"Are you okay?"

Am I?

I'm here. That's something.

And also, I feel like a wrung-out sponge. Like I've been running for days, or weeks, or, hell, maybe even years, and someone finally told me I could stop. Like I've been searching for something for decades only to find out it never existed in the first place.

And at the same time, I feel free. Because if there's nothing to run from and nothing to run to, then there's just . . . me.

Which is kind of a relief.

"I think," I say slowly, "I will be. And . . . can we call a truce? Because I really fucking miss you guys."

I hear the rush of Olivia letting her breath out. "Oh my god, yes. Please. I miss you so much. I mean, we all do, but . . . but, yeah. I really miss you."

"Maybe that Saturn return thing hit both of us hard, huh?"

She laughs, and it sounds a little teary. "I've been telling you!"

"Yeah, okay, in this particular instance, you were right."

"I'm always right," she says. And then quickly adds, "Except when I'm super, super wrong, like when I called the place you grew up a redneck shithole."

A smile pulls at my mouth. "I honestly don't think you'd hate it if you came to visit sometime. I mean . . ." I glance up and down Main Street. "You'd probably mostly hate it—but it's not all bad."

Another silence. "When's the move?" Olivia asks.

"Tomorrow. Movers are coming first thing in the morning."

"How's the new place?"

"It's nice. Brand-new, so . . . nice. And big for a condo. I mean, bigger than a lot of stuff in New York."

"Probably cheaper too," Olivia says, and now her voice sounds pained.

"Yeah."

"So . . . are you staying?"

That's the million-dollar question. Or it *was* the million-dollar question. At some point. It was the whole reason I came here, wasn't it? Not just to help my mom move. But because I was flailing and I said, *What if I moved back to Oak Falls,* and then I decided to do it, because why not . . .

But now, after *everything* . . .

I still don't know what I'm doing with my life—because I don't know what career I want, and that's what everyone really means when they ask what you're doing with your life. I don't know if I want to revive my old dreams—publishing job, academia—or if they belong to a previous version of Darby and I need to find something new.

But I know where I belong, and who I want to be with, and I feel like my heart is splintering and mending at the same time.

"No," I say to Olivia. "I don't want to stay."

"Do you think you might come back?" She sounds hopeful. "Because, the thing is . . . I didn't want to tell you right away because I didn't want to make it sound like I was putting pressure on you—I *don't* want to sound like I'm putting pressure on you—but Dan's moving out."

My mind draws a blank. "Dan?"

"Uh . . . our roommate? Ian's ex? Darby, you've *met* him."

Oh. *Dan.* Right. Of course. "I haven't seen that guy for months. He's never around."

"Yeah, because he was basically living with his boyfriend. I guess they've decided to make it official now, so he's moving out. He kind of told us last minute, but whatever. Anyway, I know it's me and Joan, and we're a couple, but we've got this extra room, and Joan doesn't want to use it for an office, and we kind of want a roommate, so . . ."

A flutter goes through my stomach. "So?"

"So there's a room for you, if you wanted to come back. I mean, it's not like the rent is cheap, but it's not too bad, and I don't think our landlord's going to raise it, and all of us could help you cover until you find a job or something . . ."

Every last piece of tension in me evaporates. "I want to come back."

"You do?" She sounds more anxious than I've ever heard her.

"Yeah. Can I move in with you guys?"

"God. Yes. Darby, of course. Please. It's not a huge room, but it's nice, and we usually split on groceries and stuff and take turns doing chores . . ."

She goes on, telling me the rent—which isn't cheap, because nothing in New York is, but it's less than what I was paying for my studio—and when Dan is moving out, and how they split the chores and the groceries . . .

But I'm only half listening. In my mind, I'm picturing coming home from whatever job I end up with and not being alone. I'm picturing waking up in the morning and cramming into that tiny kitchen with Olivia and Joan, and probably Ian at some point, all of us trying to make coffee and get breakfast and spell out dirty limericks with the fridge magnets. I'm picturing bringing home bagels and getting annoyed when they disappear a lot faster because it's not just me eating them anymore. I'm picturing existing in a big city full of people trying to find themselves, and letting myself be one of them, and letting that be more than enough—letting that be wonderful.

I mean, I'll wish that it all felt more stable and the subway didn't run slower at night and there weren't trucks idling at two in the morning when I'm trying to sleep, but . . .

"So . . . can I tell Joan?" Olivia asks.

I jerk out of my thoughts. "Yeah. And Ian. I'll text when I have more figured out, like when I'm actually leaving and everything . . ."

"Okay." Her voice is full of relief.

I hesitate, and then I say, "Oak Falls still means something to me."

A beat of silence. "I know," she says in a small voice.

"I need to come back here sometimes, and I need room to get annoyed at New York sometimes."

"I know. And . . . I mean, I get annoyed at New York too. I just got so scared about you leaving. You're . . . all of you guys . . . you're my family."

I swallow. My eyes are hot. "Yeah." And that's all I can manage to say.

"Keep me posted?" she asks.

"I will." And I end the call and cross the street toward Magic Beans.

CHAPTER TWENTY-NINE

I text Michael as I'm waiting for the barista to make two lattes. I ask him if we can talk.

He texts back immediately.

MICHAEL WEAVER
Yes. Where?

I hesitate, chewing my lip, thumbs hovering above my phone. I can't go to his house. I know, somehow, that this will be much harder if I go to that house. And even though I know what I want, even though I know what I need—maybe for the first time ever—the act of choosing, *actively* choosing, hurts more than I ever thought it would.

ME
Meet at the falls in an hour?

Three little dots pop up on my phone screen. Michael typing. They bounce and then disappear. Bounce and then disappear. Finally, after the third time:

MICHAEL WEAVER
ok

A twinge goes through me, because I know he's wondering what's going on. I know he wants to ask—that he probably started to ask before deleting what he wrote.

But I don't want to try to explain any of this over text.

I drive back to Mom's house with the lattes in the cup holders. She's on the phone when I walk in the door, pacing back and forth in the kitchen, in shorts and a blousy tank top, while Mr. Grumpy watches from his spot on top of a pile of papers that we still need to recycle.

She jabs her finger at her cell phone. *Movers,* she mouths at me.

I nod and hold out the cup of coffee. Her eyes light up. I mouth back at her that I have to go out again, and she seems to get the message. Or she doesn't care. She waves at me and then says into the phone, "No, no, *two* bedrooms, not three . . ."

I don't really need to turn right around and leave the house again. I told Michael an hour—and apparently forgot that nothing in Oak Falls is that far away, and I could have easily gotten back with the coffee and then out to the Falls in under half an hour. But I can't just sit around here. I'm too jumbled up for that.

So I take the most winding route I can to the far edge of Krape Park. I even drive all the way around the golf course just to make it take longer. And I still pull off the side of the road next to the overgrown merry-go-round sign twenty minutes early.

But I'm not the only car. Michael's pickup is already parked, leaning off the road onto the grass. The cab is empty. I can't help smiling a little, even though it kind of hurts. Both of us still anxious and early to everything.

Michael's already sitting on the Lookout when I reach the bottom of the Falls. I can see him up there through the leafy curtain, knees pulled up, idly scrolling on his phone. At least he's not looking at me, which makes the slow climb up the overgrown steps, pulling myself along on the exposed pipes, a little less awkward.

My heart hammers when I reach the top, and it's only partly because of the climb. "Hey."

He looks up, but he doesn't look surprised or startled. I have a feeling he heard me coming. He doesn't have earbuds in this time, and it's not that easy to stealth-climb the Falls steps. He nudges his glasses up on his nose with one knuckle. "Hey."

"How long have you been here?" I shuffle carefully over and sit down next to him, letting my feet dangle over the edge of the bluff.

"Not that long." He looks down at his phone and then sets it down on the rock.

We're quiet, both of us watching the mist rising up from the Falls, evaporating into the air in front of us, occasionally with a bit of rainbow catching the light. The roar of the waterfall covers up the sound of my pounding heart and the five times I have to swallow, trying to figure out how to speak.

In the end, he's the one who breaks the silence. "You're leaving."

It's not a question—just a simple statement. I look at him, and he looks back at me. The sunlight filtering through the canopy of leaves overhead catches in his gray eyes and shines on his rumpled auburn hair. He's wearing his beat-up jeans and a faded U of I T-shirt, and something about his glasses, and this old college T-shirt, and his sinewy arms—it makes me feel like I can finally see how my best friend from thirteen years ago turned into the man next to me. I can see high school Michael, and college Michael, and this Michael all at once.

And I feel sad, all over again, that I missed so much. "Yeah, I am."

He nods slowly, like he's processing this, and looks back out at the mist rising in front of us.

I shrink, small and guilty. "How'd you know?"

He shrugs one shoulder, resting his elbows on his knees. "I don't know. I think part of me always knew you weren't going to stay." He glances at me. "I mean, there was a reason you left in the first place."

"Yeah, but that was because I didn't know there could be space for me here." I don't know why I'm arguing, because it doesn't change what I came here to say. "If I'd understood that . . ." I swallow, my mind flashing back to the bookstore last night. For a second, I think, again, about telling him everything. To hell with whether he'd think I'd lost it. I want to tell him every impossible thing that happened and believe that he'd believe me.

But I can't. Maybe there are some risks I can't make myself take. Or maybe I just don't quite want to share all of that, not even with Michael.

"If I'd understood that," I say, "I'm not sure I would have been so eager to leave."

Michael slowly lets his breath out. "Maybe not. But you did leave. And it changed you."

My throat tightens. He's saying everything I was going to—but it hurts so much more hearing it from him. "I'm still me," I say, even though it feels weak.

"Never said you weren't." It's not accusing. Not angry. Just soft and even. "People change. You changed. I changed, even without leaving. It's just life."

The shapes of the leaves around us blur. There's a weight on my lungs, like a heavy block of iron. "You ever wish things had gone differently?" I ask. "Or wonder what would have happened if they had?"

He's quiet, for so long that I start to think he's just going to ignore me. And then he shifts, leaning back on his hands, and he says, "I wondered that pretty much every day after we both went to college. Every time I came home for a break and you weren't around. I'd get mad at myself for not trying to fix things that last year of high school, when it would have been so much easier because we saw each other every day. And after I found out that you'd come out, I felt . . . madder." He ducks his head and glances at me self-consciously. "I guess the longer I let it go on, the harder it felt to . . ." But his voice runs out.

Go back.

Rip up all the scar tissue.

Sit in that place of hurt all over again.

"Yeah," I say. "I know what you mean." I feel horribly sad for a moment that I didn't think about him every day. That, as more time went by, it got easier to bury it all.

But I guess that was my way of building scar tissue. Clean break. And as much as I wish I could go back and change that, it's still made me, well, *me.*

It's the reason I have Olivia and Ian and Joan.

And I don't really want to change that, either.

I take a slow, shuddering breath and say the thing I've been bracing myself to say ever since I texted Michael to meet me here. "You could come with me."

His eyebrows jump. "Come with you?"

"To New York." My heart is pounding wildly again. "There are tons of schools there; there must be teaching jobs. You could come with me and—"

"Darby—"

"—be someplace with a Pride March, with so much queerness like it's no big deal, and you wouldn't have to worry about holding my hand or kissing me—"

"What happened to needing a break from New York?"

I look down at the rock, stubbing a finger over the pocked surface. "I just . . ." But I don't know what to say. I don't know how to explain that I'll always get annoyed by how loud it is, I'll be frustrated every time I have to haul something home on the subway because owning a car would be worse, and I still have no idea what kind of job to look for or if I'll ever be able to quit renting and buy a place.

And I care about all that and simultaneously don't care at all because it's worth it. Because maybe I don't need to love everything about a place to belong there. Maybe I can choose to belong, even if occasionally pieces of me don't quite fit, because I belong with the people I found. The people I chose.

Because I did choose them, even if I didn't realize that's what I was doing.

"It's the best fit for me." I look up at him. "And I . . . I need to go back."

He nods and looks back out at the Falls, chewing his lip. And then he looks at me, eyes pained, and says, "I fit here."

"You could just come and try it out," I say, even though I know what the answer's going to be.

"You and I have been . . ." He shakes his head. "It's been less than two weeks, Darby. I've lived here for . . . well, forever. I know you don't understand it, but I love this place. I love the people I have here. I don't need to be someplace with a Pride March or a ton of gay bars. And I know you think I'm going to high school football games and sitting with Natalie and Brendan to fit in or something, but . . . I like going to the football games. Natalie and Brendan aren't as bad as they used to be, and yeah, they still are really fucking straight and sometimes annoy the shit out of me, but this is a small town. Everybody annoys everybody else sometimes. And maybe sometimes I get anxious at the thought of holding hands in public, or what might happen if someone sees me kissing another guy, but . . ." He shrugs. "People aren't big here. People don't do PDA, even if they're straight. And I . . . I'm still trying to find some happy medium. I'm still figuring out how to be me here, but even with all of that, I still fit. Here. I need . . ." He looks around at the Falls, and the shady seclusion of Krape Park. "I need this."

I feel like he's drilled a hole straight through me. Even though I knew it was coming, a tiny resentful piece of me feels like he's telling me that this small town in the middle of nowhere matters more to him than I do.

But the bigger, calmer piece of me knows that this is exactly what he's telling me, and of course he is. Because leaving changed me, and staying changed him, and his people are here, just like mine are in New York.

Maybe Oak Falls isn't a place that always made space for either of us, but he stayed anyway. He made space. He dug in and held on and decided that it was enough. It was worth the work.

"So, we're saying . . ." I swallow, but I can't seem to get rid of the lump in my throat now. "That whatever this is . . ."

Michael leans forward, taking his weight off his hands. "It doesn't need a name."

"But it's ending, right?" I know the answer to this already too, but I have to say it anyway. I have to hear him say it.

"Yeah," he says.

I have a wild urge to suggest long distance. To suggest some kind of compromise. Who cares if it's only been two weeks.

But I swallow it. I know, deep down, that we both need more freedom than that. That we both need to let this exist and end in a way we can choose, rather than risk it disintegrating slowly as we both get pulled away.

I reach out, and his hand comes up, and I grasp it tightly, like if I squeeze hard enough, I can make up for every year I was somewhere else. He squeezes back.

The question escapes me before I can stop myself. "Do you ever think maybe there's some other version of everything? Some version of reality where things went differently?"

Michael looks down at our interlaced fingers. "Like a parallel universe?" he asks.

"Yeah. Like that."

He's quiet for a while. I watch him—counting his eyelashes, watching the dappled reflections glint off his glasses.

"You remember Mrs. Siriani?" he says finally.

I blink. "Our physics teacher? Yeah, sure."

He swallows. "I read this paper she left in the teachers' lounge once. It was mostly weird quantum stuff I didn't totally understand, but . . . it was saying that there's this theory of the universe. It says that every time we make a decision, reality splits, like a tree branching."

I shift closer to him until our arms are touching. Until I can lean my head against his shoulder.

"So in this version of life," he says, "we follow one branch, the branch that leads us on from the decision we made. But maybe there's another life where we follow the other branch. The branch that leads us on as though we made the opposite choice. Who knows—maybe there are infinite realities, and some different version of us lives in each of them."

The Falls are swimming in front of my eyes again. "That's some weird quantum shit."

A laugh jerks out of him—I feel it in my bones. "Yeah. So . . . maybe in some other reality, I left. Maybe in some other life, you stayed."

My mind goes back to Young Darby staring at me in the half-light of the bookstore, full of fear and hope and vulnerability.

Maybe so.

Maybe it's not that nothing changed. Maybe everything did. On another path. For that version of me.

Michael's fingers loosen until he's just letting our hands rest together comfortably.

But it still feels like a stage of letting go.

"You know," he says, "I had sort of a weird dream last night."

"What kind of dream?"

"We were back in high school, at your seventeenth birthday party."

My breath hitches.

"But we didn't fight. I think I knew we were supposed to, in the dream. But it was sort of like I was watching us, and we didn't. You told me who you were instead. And I told you who I was." He takes a breath. Holds it. "Kind of like instead of falling apart, we fell together."

I feel like my heart has stopped. I'm completely still. "We did?"

"Yeah. I don't know exactly; it's kind of fuzzy now, trying to remember it."

I lift my head off his shoulder and look up at him, but he's squinting into the mist of the Falls.

"I think . . ." He hesitates. "I think I fell in love with you. And you fell in love with me."

"Then what?" I'm afraid to breathe. Like I'll break something if I do. "What happened?"

He shakes his head. "I don't know. I woke up." He looks at me and a small crooked smile tugs on his mouth. "Kind of weird."

"Yeah." A bubble expands in my chest. The lump in my throat is slowly dissolving. I can breathe again. "Yeah, kind of weird."

"When are you leaving?" Michael asks quietly.

"Soon, I think." It's easier to say now. "Maybe tomorrow. I want to make sure everything goes okay with the movers before I go."

He nods. "Have you told your mom?"

A small jolt of anxiety goes through me. "Not yet. But . . . I think she'll be okay."

Michael glances at me and smiles. "Oh, she's always okay. She'll be even more okay now that she won't have to look at Jeannie's penguins."

A laugh bursts out of me, but I sort of want to cry at the same time. "I'm going to come visit more. Maybe I'll even get my New York friends out here sometime. You'd like them."

"I'll come visit New York," he says. "Over a break."

I don't know if he really means it. I think he does. I don't know if it will actually happen, but I think he means he wants it to.

"Can I call you sometimes?" My throat is closing up again. I squeeze his hand. "Can we still talk?"

He leans over and very gently kisses my forehead. And that's answer enough.

CHAPTER THIRTY

The house is quiet when I get back. It looks so strange now. Each piece of furniture is an island in a sea of boxes, and the walls are somehow so much more *obvious* without any of the framed pieces of art I'm used to.

"Mom?" Even with the carpet and the boxes, my voice still echoes, bouncing off the empty walls and bookshelf.

No answer. I go into the kitchen. The paper coffee cup from Magic Beans is sitting on the counter. I lean over and look through the window over the sink. Mom's sitting on the grass in the backyard, staring at the tire swing, Mr. Grumpy beside her.

I go out the back door. "Hey."

She jerks, wiping at her eyes. "Hi, sweetheart." She turns and looks up at me, and her face looks a little red. The saw from the basement is sitting on the grass in front of her.

Wait a minute. Has she been crying?

I don't remember the last time I saw my mom cry. She's too stoic. Or too sunny. Or too . . . something.

"What's going on?" I ask.

"Oh." She waves a hand dismissively. "I'm fine. I just thought I'd try to finally cut down this tire swing, but it seems I can't actually do it by myself."

I glance at the saw. And then back at the tire swing. Guilt twists inside me, because I told her I'd do it, and here we are, the day before she's supposed to move, and it's still hanging from that tree branch. "Sorry, Mom, we can . . . I can help. I'm sure we can get it down."

"I know." She pushes herself up, brushing off her shorts. "I just thought I could do it myself and save you the trouble, but then it was too hard to hold the swing and saw the rope at the same time."

"It's not a big deal." I have no idea why she's so upset over this. "I'm here. We can do it now."

"Oh, this isn't about the swing." She wipes at her eyes again. "I just started thinking about all the memories I have of you and this swing, and your uncle Darby and this swing, and I got a little sad for a minute."

I blink in surprise. "What's Uncle Darby got to do with the swing?"

"It used to be his swing. When he was younger. Your grandpa put it up here after you were born."

She never told me any of this. Which I guess isn't that surprising. She never talked about my uncle all that much. I always assumed it made her too sad. He mostly existed as that picture on her dresser—Uncle Darby in his air force uniform, permanently in his twenties. The only things I know about him are that he was five years younger than my mom and he died in some kind of helicopter accident. And then she named me after him, because I was born shortly after he died.

I look back at the tire swing. No wonder it looks old. "I'm sorry."

She sighs. "It's okay. I'm ready to move on, and I have been for a while, it's just . . . still sad."

"Yeah," I say, because I get it. Finally. The way you can love a place and be certain you're ready to leave it. "Mom, I'm going to go back to New York."

She sniffs and looks up at me. "That's what you want?"

It's not challenging. She's not trying to guilt-trip me. She's just asking. Just making sure.

I nod. "Yeah. But . . . but I won't, if you need me here."

She lets her breath out with a huff. "Darby, I'm just fine. I'm moving into a condo! I won't have to clean gutters or cut down tire swings. And I have people. I'm not lonely or alone if that's what you're worried about."

It is. But I guess she's right. My mind goes back to the party on the roof deck and all the people who showed up for my mom. She might have beef with Jeannie's yard penguins, but I have a feeling if I hadn't been here and she really couldn't cut this swing down by herself, she probably would have gotten Jeannie's help. Or called one of her teacher friends. Or, hell, maybe she would have called Michael. Which is still a little weird to think about, but I should probably get used to it.

"I think my people are in New York," I say, which feels a little cheesy, but it's true. And I mean it.

She smiles and reaches out, wrapping her fingers around mine. "Well, I've got that second bedroom in the condo. It's always for you, anytime you want it."

My throat tightens. "I'm going to come back and visit more."

"Good. You should. I'm fine here by myself, but I still miss you. So does Grumpy."

We both look down at the basset hound, who's currently snoozing in the sun, long ears fanned out across the grass. He does not look like he's going to miss me at all.

"You have a place to go in New York?" Mom asks.

That makes me smile. I might be thirty now, but Mom will always mom. "Yeah. You know Olivia and Joan?"

She purses her lips, thinking. "Yes. Your gay friends."

"All my friends are gay, Mom."

She frowns. "That's not true. You had that friend—the video game guy—he was straight."

"I'm moving into the room that used to belong to his ex-boyfriend."

She raises her eyebrows. "You need to call me more often, Darby. I can't keep track of which of your friends are gay now and who they're dating."

I open my mouth to tell her my friends have all been queer for a long time and none of their relationships are that new, and change my mind. Because she has a point. I do need to call her more often. "Okay, well . . . Olivia and Joan need a roommate, so I'm going to move in with them."

"Good." She nods approvingly. "When do you think you'll leave?"

I let my breath out slowly. "After the movers come. Tomorrow."

"Well, I've still got the TV plugged in," she says. "After you pack up, we could watch some *Marble Arch Murders*."

"Definitely." I gently untangle my fingers from hers, lean down, and pick up the saw. "But I think we better cut this down first."

She takes a breath—I see her shoulders rise. And then she nods. "It's time."

It only takes a few minutes to cut down the tire swing with my mom holding the tire steady and me sawing through the rope. The rope is so dry and old that it sends dust and tiny rope bits flying everywhere before it finally parts, slithering off the branch so fast that we both jump backward. The tire hits the ground with a thump and the rope lands in a pile on top of it.

It takes both of us to heave the tire upright and roll it out of the backyard and down the driveway to the street.

"I'll call and schedule a bulky item pickup," Mom says. "It's fine to leave it there until then." She hesitates. "Who knows, maybe someone will come by and pick it up and use it for their kids."

I look down at the dried and cracked rubber, slowly wearing away around the indent made by the rope. "Maybe."

* * *

JOAN CHU
Heard you're coming back

OLIVIA HENRY
Can't wait to be roommates!!!

IAN ROBB
Great. I'm gonna have so much FOMO

OLIVIA HENRY
You could quit being a hipster
and move to Queens, Ian
I'm just saying

JOAN CHU
Do you need job leads, Darby?
I can ask around

IAN ROBB
Yeah same! Let me know, Darb

ME
Thanks, guys. I'll figure something out.
I mean I have no idea what I want to do.
But also, it'll be fine. If I'm with you guys.

JOAN CHU
Oh yeah we're not going anywhere. This
is family. You're stuck with us, bro.

CHAPTER THIRTY-ONE

I can't decide if it's impressive or just maddening how fast the movers get everything loaded into their truck. Sure, almost everything is already in boxes, but even so. They haul out the mattresses and the beds as though they weigh nothing. Cart out the furniture like it's practically an afterthought. It takes me as long to pack up the rental car as it does for the movers to pack up their whole truck. Mom helps me carry the boxes and my bags, and we wedge everything back into the hatchback until it's so full again that there's only room for me in the driver's seat.

"Stop if you get tired," Mom says, as I close the hatchback's trunk.

"I will."

"And call me when you get there."

I smile. "I will, Mom."

The movers are closing up the truck. Mom drifts away to talk logistics with them, about where she'll meet them, about where they should park at the condo.

Mr. Grumpy waddles over to me, tongue lolling out of his mouth. I crouch down and hold out my hand. He runs his forehead into it.

"Thanks for hanging out with me, old bud," I say.

He gives me a very morose look. Or maybe that's all the forehead wrinkles.

Eventually, the movers climb into their truck and start up the engine and pull away, rumbling off to the condo. Mom wraps me in one more hug and then tries to coax Mr. Grumpy toward the porch, away from the rental car. He looks between us. Finally, she bends down and picks him up with a groan, staggering up the driveway to the garage, where the Jeep is waiting—packed up with artwork and the birthday mugs and a few other breakable things.

I climb into the rental car and stick the key in the ignition, but for a minute, I can't turn it. I just sit there looking at the house. It's just a building, and it hasn't felt like home for a long time, and still. A twinge goes through me, at the thought of some other family moving in. Some other family changing my mom's outdated kitchen. Some other kid filling my bedroom with their stuff.

It's going to be really weird next time I visit my mom. I wonder if I'll ever even go by this house again, or if it'll be easier to let it go if I don't and just avoid the whole street.

I let my breath out, slowly, until the knot in my stomach unties itself and my shoulders lower.

There's this theory of the universe. It says that every time we make a decision, reality splits, like a tree branching.

I turn the key. The rental car engine rumbles to life.

In this version of life, we follow one branch, the branch that leads us on from the decision we made.

I back down the driveway into the street. By the garage, Mom holds up Mr. Grumpy's paw and waves it at me. He does not look into it. It makes me smile.

But maybe there's another life where we follow the other branch. The branch that leads us on as though we made the opposite choice.

I turn the car down the street, watching my mom and Mr. Grumpy get smaller in the mirror. Watching Jeannie Young's penguin army fade behind me.

Maybe there are infinite realities, and some different version of us lives in each of them.

I roll down the windows, letting warm wind whistle in my ears and ruffle my hair. I breathe in, deeply—the smell of grass and dirt and maybe something colder and crisper. Fall, just around the corner. I decide not to take Main Street and turn instead toward the back roads.

Maybe in some other reality, I left. Maybe in some other life, you stayed.

I follow the loop of West Avenue, and Michael's white farmhouse comes into view under the wide blue sky. The lawn chairs are empty on the porch. Michael's pickup sits at the end of the driveway, parked behind Amanda's old Corolla.

For the briefest moment, something tugs inside me. I think about stopping.

And then the moment is gone. I drive past the house, picking up speed. I let it fade away in the mirror and I turn around the bend, headed for the county highway. A bubble slowly expands in my chest.

There's a theory of the universe.

I hit the highway and the wind roars, buffeting my eardrums. The bubble in my chest feels like it's lifting me—like I'm weightless, flying on the wind rushing through the car. The view outside my windows turns to farmland, endless green that's only interrupted by a few groves of trees and the occasional silo. Above it, the sky is flat and blue and wide, scattered with wisps of white clouds. I let my eyes wander across all of it, burning it all into my mind, to hold and come back to sometimes when New York gets too big and busy.

Every time we make a decision, reality splits, like a tree branching.

I roll up the windows and pick up my phone, finding Olivia's number and switching to speaker phone.

While it rings, I wonder what the universe would look like if I'd stopped at Michael's house in that moment when I considered it. I wonder what it would look like if I pulled over to the side of the road right now and just took a break, sitting outside and staring at this field for an hour. I wonder what my life will look like when I unpack everything at Olivia and Joan's apartment. When I return the rental car. When I fall asleep to the noise of a city.

For the first time in a long time, I feel like I'm moving toward possibility. Toward something I chose.

Toward so many choices still left to make.

The phone stops ringing. "Darby?"

There's a theory of the universe . . .

"Hey, Olivia," I say. "I'm coming home."

ACKNOWLEDGMENTS

To Patricia Nelson, who continues to be simply the best agent: your unwavering enthusiasm for this book and your tireless championing of it gave me the courage to take risks and keep going, and I am eternally grateful.

Thank you to Sylvan Creekmore for believing in this story and my ability to tell it.

To my editor, Peter: Darby and I were so lucky to land with you; your thoughtful notes and boundless excitement made this book a thousand times better, and me at least 50 percent calmer.

Thank you to everyone at Avon and William Morrow: editorial directors Tessa Woodward and May Chen, publisher Liate Stehlik, and deputy publisher Jennifer Hart for believing in this book; the design team and artist Jessica Cruickshank for a stunning cover; my copyeditor, David Hough; Laura Brady and the whole production team; the incredible marketing and publicity crew, especially DJ, Deanna, and Jes; and everyone on the sales and library teams.

Special shout-out to Deanna Day for the singular service of thinking through time-travel logistics with me, and for hunting down what is truly the most niche Marvel reference imaginable.

Many thanks to Emma Alban and Jen Ferguson for reading and listening.

And finally, thank you to Harry W. Schwartz Bookshop, the independent bookstore that once existed in my hometown, for giving me my very first queer book, before I even knew I needed it.

ABOUT THE AUTHOR

Edward Underhill grew up in the suburbs of Wisconsin, where he could not walk to anything, so he had to make up his own adventures. He studied music in college, spent several years living in very small apartments in New York, and currently resides in California with his partner and a talkative black cat. He is the author of the young adult novels *Always the Almost* and *This Day Changes Everything*. *The In-Between Bookstore* is his first book for adults.